FRANCIS RAY is Arabesque's best-selling-romance writer. She has appeared on the *Blackboard* national bestseller list in the top five with her titles FOREVER YOURS, SPIRIT OF THE SEASON, UNDENIABLE, and ONLY HERS.

Praise for:

FOREVER YOURS:

"Francis Ray writes warm, sensual romance that is sure to please readers . . . and touch your heart."

—Jayne Anne Krentz

"Fastmoving, sensual and with dashes of h~~umor, Francis Ray~~ . . . nicely launch[es] the A~~rabesque line~~"

—~~Jour~~*nal*

U~~NDENIABLE:~~

"Francis Ray's fresh inimitable style of storytelling has assured her the success she deserves and the acclaim she's earned. Readers run, don't walk, to your nearest bookseller and buy this book."

—*Romantic Times*

ONLY HERS:

"Her inimitable style, irresistible humor and extraordinary talent grace the pages of her . . . latest book . . . She is one of the few authors who never disappoints her readers."

—*Romantic Times*

INCOGNITO:

"This author knows how to mend a broken heart and breathe life back into it."

—*Gothic Journal*

ENJOY THESE ARABESQUE FAVORITES!

FOREVER AFTER   (0-7860-0211-5, $4.99)
by Bette Ford

BODY AND SOUL   (0-7860-0160-7, $4.99)
by Felicia Mason

BETWEEN THE LINES   (0-7860-0267-0, $4.99)
by Angela Benson

SILKEN BETRAYAL

Francis Ray

Pinnacle Books
Kensington Publishing Corp.

http://www.pinnaclebooks.com

PINNACLE BOOKS are published by

Kensington Publishing Corp.
850 Third Avenue
New York, NY 10022

First Printing: August, 1997
10 9 8 7 6 5 4 3 2 1

Printed in the United States of America

Chapter One

Lauren Bennett had a mean right swing.

On the sixteenth floor of Crescent Communications cooperate headquarters in Santa Clara, California, CEO and founder Jordan Hamilton sat behind his desk and studied the black and white photo that unerringly captured the mixture of wonder and excitement on Lauren Bennett's face as she sent a softball deep into left field.

Instead of running, she had grinned and glanced over her shoulder. The camera had followed the motion.

The next photo was that of a little boy, arms raised over his head in excitement, his mouth wide open. It didn't take a genius to guess what he was yelling to her.

Jordan leaned back in his chair and smiled. "Yeah. Once you hit the ball there is the small matter of making it to first base."

She had made it to first base, and eventually home plate. The moment she was off the field she was met by the little boy, who launched himself into her arms. The impact toppled her backward-facing baseball cap from her head.

Tendrils of curly black hair that had escaped from her ponytail framed her beaming, heart-shaped face. Her head thrown back in triumph, she held the child securely against her slim body and twirled him around.

Another smile tugged the usually implacable line of Jordan's well-shaped mouth. He could almost feel their happiness.

There were more photographs, dozens of them with the two together. Her biting her lip as he slid into home plate, her sitting on the front porch of their small home with a forgotten book or magazine as she watched the little boy ride his bicycle, her running to the school bus with an open umbrella on a rainy day.

The same thought always struck Jordan as he viewed the moments in time. There was a deep bond of love between the two. But that was as God and nature had intended. Mothers loved their sons. At times, they also protected them. Just as Lauren Bennett sought to protect her son, Joshua.

Jordan studied the beautiful woman, her five-year-old son nearly coming to her waist, and dipped his dark head in silent tribute to her courage and fortitude. She had done well—but not well enough.

If he had found her, their common enemy could, too. Before that happened, he had to make sure Lauren Bennett was firmly on his side and ready to cooperate fully with his plan.

She held the key that he had been searching for for six long years. That he had invaded her privacy to obtain the information bothered him little. He had learned early in the cutthroat world of business and life that the old adage "The end justifies the means" was often true.

Looking at the determined tilt of Lauren's chin, Jordan realized she wouldn't come easily to his side, but he had no intention of giving her a choice. He could fight clean. Or dirty.

Even as his brain formed the thought, something within him rebelled against the idea as he turned his gaze again to the happy little boy. Jordan, of all people, knew what it was like when your world turned upside down and the wonder left. He didn't want to take from Joshua what had been ruthlessly torn from *him.*

What if there was no other way? Then, he would do what needed to be done, and worry about his conscience later.

Leaning back in his chair, he studied the other pictures of Lauren as a working mother. In each she appeared efficient, cool, poised. The ponytail and jeans were replaced in picture after picture by conservative suits with hemlines never rising higher than just below her knees.

Deep in thought, Jordan scratched his full beard with blunt-tipped fingers. To all appearances, Lauren Bennett was a conscientious employee, a good mother, and a loyal friend to the few people who had managed to get close to her. She should be commended. At another time, he would have.

Now, that was impossible. Instead, he was about to shake up her world and hope that when things settled she and her son could still smile.

The intercom blinked. An efficient female voice said, "Mr. Hamilton, your car is waiting downstairs, and the jet is ready for takeoff."

Jordan lowered the photo of the laughing mother and child, then pushed to his imposing height of six-foot-three.

"Promises are hell, but then, so is life sometimes." Powerful strides carried him from his office without a backward glance or a moment's regret for what he was about to do.

Lauren Bennett stood on the tarmac of Shreveport Airport and watched the white jet taxi down the runway. On the tail were two bold red crescent shapes. Anyone remotely connected to multimedia would recognize the logo of Crescent Communications, the largest black-owned electronic and telecommunication business in the country.

"He's almost here, Lauren."

"Lauren, do I look all right?"

Lauren heard the reverent tone in her boss's voice and the preening one of the office manager of Scott Resources. Of the two, she was more inclined to comfort her boss. In the five years she had worked for Benjamin Scott as his executive assistant, she had never seen him so nervous. He had faced down angry stockholders with less agitation.

In those same five years she had watched Cynthia Douglas work herself up from sales to a corner office. In her early forties and twice-divorced, Cynthia was elegant, determined and self-assured or so Lauren had thought until it was confirmed that

Jordan Hamilton was looking for a new public relations firm to represent his company in the southern region of the states. If Cynthia checked her makeup one more time in the tiny gold compact, the spring was likely to snap.

"Lauren, did you hear me?" asked Cynthia, her perfectly manicured red nails lightly touching her dyed, strawberry blond curls.

"You look spectacular as usual, Ms. Douglas," Lauren answered truthfully. Along with her considerable brain power, Cynthia had a pretty face and a voluptuous figure. To those who whispered behind her back that she loved to show off that figure in formfitting clothes, Lauren kept her opinion to herself.

"You're sure his suite is ready?" Benjamin asked, his white handkerchief making another nervous swipe across the bald spot on his head. His hairline had long since receded to the middle of his head.

"Yes, Mr. Scott," Lauren patiently assured him for the umpteenth time. He had never questioned her in the past, but then they had never had a potential client with the clout of the man they were about to meet. "The limousine will take Mr. Hamilton directly to the Four Seasons Hotel. There he'll be given VIP status in registering and shown directly to his room."

"I'll go with him to make sure," Cynthia said, a small smile hovering over her magenta-colored lips.

Lauren glanced at the older woman in surprise and met her stern stare. If Cynthia wanted to alter the plans, Lauren didn't mind. Cynthia was too smart to jeopardize a deal by coming on to a client, but she was egocentric enough to want to be the one who gained the glory if they landed Crescent Communications.

"Excellent," her boss said. "We'll show Jordan Hamilton that Scott Resources is the company for him."

"That we will," Cynthia agreed.

Although Lauren didn't voice her opinion, she was just as confident of the company's ability until a broad-shouldered man stepped into the plane's doorway and looked straight at them. Riveting black eyes moved from one person to the other in their small group until they stopped on her.

As if from a distance, Lauren heard Cynthia mutter one

explicit word. Only a foot away, Lauren should have been able to understand, but all her attention was on the imposing figure watching her.

Suddenly, Lauren knew how Alice felt when she fell down the rabbit hole. Spiraling out of control with no chance to find purchase. Frightened, yet oddly fascinated at the same time.

"It's him," Mr. Scott whispered. "It's Jordan Hamilton."

Lauren had already guessed that. What she hadn't figured out was why she had reacted so strongly to his presence.

The back of her hand touched her forehead. Perhaps she had picked up her five-year-old son's virus. Her skin was warm, moist. Considering it was mid-May and the temperature was in the high eighties at eleven-thirty in the morning, she was fine.

"I've heard he's a force to be reckoned with," murmured Benjamin.

And heaven help those who stand in his way. The thought came out of nowhere, leaping into Lauren's mind and refusing to leave. She had no idea why it had come, but over the years she had learned to trust her instincts. As much as possible, she would steer clear of the man watching her so intently.

"No pain, no glory," Cynthia said. An anticipatory smile on her caramel-colored face, she took a step forward.

Lauren remained where she was and wished Mr. Scott hadn't insisted she come. He had been so worried that something might go wrong, that he had been adamant about her accompanying them. It had taken weeks of telephone calls and faxes to get Jordan Hamilton's hectic schedule to coincide with Mr. Scott's. He wouldn't take a chance on something else going wrong at the last minute.

Finally, Jordan came down the gangway and started toward them, his long strides bringing him to them much too quickly. Lauren pressed her lips together to keep from biting them. Jordan Hamilton was a man who should be taken in small doses.

Tall and muscular, he moved with the innate grace of a dancer, the assurance of a man secure in himself. He wore his power as effortlessly as he wore his wheat-colored Armani suit.

He stopped inches away, towering over them with his imposing height. For the first time in years, Lauren was acutely aware of her five-foot-four inches.

"Mr. Hamilton. Good morning and welcome to Shreveport. I'm Benjamin Scott, and this is my office manager, Cynthia Douglas."

"Good morning, Mr. Scott," Jordan greeted, then turned to Cynthia. "Ms. Douglas."

Cynthia extended her hand without hesitation. "May I add my welcome to that of Benjamin's? It's a pleasure and an honor to meet you."

White teeth flashed in a bronze, bearded face. "The pleasure is all mine," Jordan said, but his gaze had already moved on to Lauren.

Benjamin quickly made the introduction. "Lauren Bennett, my executive assistant."

"Ah yes, the unflappable Ms. Bennett." He smiled again and extended his hand. "I hope my schedule changes didn't inconvenience you too much?"

At that moment Lauren understood the reason for the awed tone in Benjamin's voice earlier. If the sheer magnetism of the man didn't get to you, the smoky voice and direct gaze would. The closely cropped, coal black beard and mustache only added to the mystique.

Jordan Hamilton would have probably been right at home with the pirates who roamed the waters off the coast of Louisiana hundreds of years ago. He could probably have pillaged and plundered with the best of them.

At her continued silence a black brow arched. "Ms. Bennett?"

Heat rose in her cheeks as she realized that his hand remained extended. Hastily, she lifted hers. Immediately it was enveloped in his larger one. She expected the firm grip, but not the calluses or the surge of awareness that zipped through her.

Startled, she jerked her hand free. The tingling sensation remained. Without conscious thought, she rubbed her hand against her navy blue skirt. His dark gaze followed.

Embarrassed, she tried to cover her *faux pas.* "Good morning, Mr. Hamilton. I hope the heat and humidity don't bother you while you're here."

"Very few things bother me, Ms. Bennett," he said.

Feeling chastised and oddly out of her element, Lauren barely kept the smile on her face.

Benjamin stepped closer. "We have a limo waiting to take you to your hotel. The car and driver will be at your disposal the entire time you're here." He motioned toward the long, black, stretch vehicle parked directly behind them. "Lauren has arranged everything."

Once again Jordan turned his penetrating gaze on her. "This works out perfectly. There may be some necessary changes to my schedule, I'm afraid. Ms. Bennett and I can discuss them on the way to the hotel." Long fingers gently closed around her forearm.

"No," Lauren squeaked, then strove to regain her composure and her voice. "I mean, I'm not going with you. Ms. Douglas is."

Jordan's handsome face lost none of its pleasantness, yet somehow Lauren was aware of his displeasure. "As much as I'd like Ms. Douglas's company, it would expedite matters more if Ms. Bennett accompanied me." His gaze settled on Benjamin. "However, if this presents a problem I'll make the necessary adjustments myself. I simply thought since Ms. Bennett knew my schedule and yours, she was the most logical person to help with the changes. Was I mistaken?"

"No," Benjamin and Cynthia cried in unison.

Benjamin continued, "Lauren can go with you to the hotel, and once you're settled, work out the schedule changes. I'm at your disposal."

"I have the Gaddis report to get out," Lauren reminded him, more than a little panic in her voice.

Her boss's worried gaze went from Lauren's to Jordan's. "I won't need that until next week. It can wait."

Once again she felt Jordan's penetrating gaze on her. "Ms. Bennett?"

It took only a second to make up her mind. She might be small, but she wasn't a wimp . . . at least in most things. "Your luggage is already in the car. Shall we go?"

"After you," Jordan said. This time he didn't touch her.

He might forgive, but he didn't forget. She turned to her boss and tried to convey her apology for upsetting him. "You can depend on me to take care of everything. I'll be back at the office as soon as I can."

"Take your time," Benjamin said, his shoulders only slightly less taut than they were a minute earlier.

"Yes, I agree," Cynthia added.

Giving them both an encouraging smile, Lauren started toward the limo, very much aware of the silent man close behind her. Nodding to the driver holding open the door, she climbed inside and took a seat with her back to the driver.

Jordan got in behind her and took the seat across from her as she expected. Most people didn't like riding backwards. The door closed, shutting them inside the luxurious surroundings, for better or worse.

She swallowed. Not a comforting thought. Neither was the way his gaze silently ran over her. It wasn't sexual, just . . . probing.

"Haven't you forgotten something?" he asked.

Lauren gasped. Her hand and her gaze went to the front of her white blouse, expecting to see the buttons undone and it gaping open. Seeing neither, she lifted puzzled eyes to him.

The corner of his sensual mouth lifted, whether in amusement or exasperation she couldn't tell. "Your purse. It's occurred to me that since you didn't expect to come with me it must be someplace else."

Her gaze jerked to the tinted window of the limo to see Benjamin's late model blue Lincoln pulling away. He had grown up in Florida, and even after spending the last twenty-odd years in Shreveport had yet to acclimate to the heat and humidity. He had probably headed for the air-conditioned comfort of his car as soon as she and Jordan walked away.

Since Lauren had ridden in the back seat of the sedan, it wasn't likely he or Cynthia would notice her navy handbag in the back. She had left it there since, unlike Cynthia, she had no reason to take it with her while she waited for Jordan's plane.

"The driver can catch him if you like."

Lauren shook her head. "That won't be necessary. It will be safe, and there's nothing I need in it."

"No comb? No makeup?"

"My hair has a mind of its own, and I've never worn much makeup," she said, and immediately regretted the words, because Jordan leaned back against the leather seat, his gaze taking a silent inventory of her.

She clamped her hands together to keep from touching her brownish-black hair to see if more strands than usual had worked their way loose from the clip at the base of her neck. Curly hair had been nice for her as a teenager because she liked to swim, but it was a trial to her as an adult who seldom got the chance anymore.

She moistened her lips before she had time to think about the telling nervous gesture. "How was your flight?"

"Fine."

"There's a bar if you wish something."

The corner of his mouth tilted. "Thank you. I'm fine."

Lauren groaned inwardly. Of course he knew there was a bar. A limousine was nothing new to him. She was acting like a fruitcake. She had entertained dozens of clients in the past without one mishap. Why was she letting this man make her lose her cool?

"Do I make you nervous, Ms. Bennett?"

Shock straightened her spine. "What?"

"Ah, I guess that answers my question." He favored her with another heart-melting smile. "Despite what you've probably heard, I don't bite."

Unable to help herself, she let her gaze move to his tempting mouth again. It was as wicked as the rest of him. Lauren flushed.

Eyes narrowing, Jordan opened the bar and poured her a glass of bottled water. "You look as if you could use this."

Lauren took the glass, glad for the promise of moisture and coolness to her dry mouth. *Get a grip, girl.* She was a mother, for goodness sake!

"How long were you waiting for me?"

Unashamedly Lauren took the out he offered her. "Longer than I thought, apparently."

"Do you want to put your feet up?"

"Oh no," she hastened to assure him. "I'll be fine." When he didn't looked convinced, Lauren took another sip of water.

She had barely taken the glass from her lips when the back of his hand lightly touched her cheek. She jumped an inch off the seat.

"At least I know your reflexes are working properly," he mused, and sat back. "I was only seeing if you were hot. Benjamin would never forgive me if I didn't take care of you."

Lauren took another sip of the water. Jordan Hamilton probably thought she was a nut case, and she couldn't blame him. Enough was enough. Holding the glass firmly in her hands, she squared her shoulders and looked straight into the depths of those killer eyes.

"Please don't hesitate to let us know how to make your stay pleasant," she said.

"I assure you. you'll be the first to know."

Lauren blinked. She wasn't sure she heard the sensual promise in his words as much as read it in his eyes. Then, it was gone. He sat relaxed with his arms crossed lightly in front of him, as if nothing had happened.

Perhaps nothing *had* happened. Perhaps she was the only one fighting hormones, or whatever the heck was wrong with her.

Glancing out the window, she breathed a sigh of relief on seeing the towering white structure of the Four Seasons Hotel. "What type of changes would you like to make in your schedule?"

"I'd rather wait until after lunch."

"Lunch?" she squeaked.

"You know the meal between breakfast and dinner."

"But you didn't say anything about eating."

Dark brows bunched over ebony eyes. "I wasn't aware that I had to."

Lauren's face heated at the reprimand, but she wasn't backing down. "That's not what I meant. I just need to get back to the office."

"I understand completely, Ms. Bennett. I'm equally busy. Therefore, the sooner we finish lunch the sooner you can leave." He glanced out the window. "I believe we're here."

Chapter Two

Jordan got out of the car and extended his hand to assist Lauren. He wasn't surprised by her reluctance to touch him again or to follow him. Of all the things he had taken into consideration in finding Lauren Bennett, intense sexual awareness wasn't one of them.

In the past he had liked his women to be tall, a bit on the voluptuous side, and uncomplicated. Lauren was none of those things. She probably didn't weigh a hundred pounds dripping wet. Her head barely reached his shoulder. If he was any judge of women, and he was, her body was nicely curved. Sleek rather than lush. A definite departure from his usual taste.

"Ms. Bennett?" he coaxed.

Tentative fingertips touched the palm of his hand. Her golden brown eyes widened as if she expected lightning to strike her. The jolt that transmitted itself to him was just as powerful, and as dangerous in its own way.

She wasted no time in standing on her own. She didn't wipe her hands this time, just kept them clenched.

Giving the attendant his name for his luggage to be tagged, Jordan tipped the man, asked the limo driver to return in an hour, then turned to Lauren. "After you, Ms. Bennett."

Lauren spun from him and walked toward the revolving door. He had half expected her to be halfway across the lobby by the time he got inside, but she stood a few feet inside the door, her back to him.

He saw the reason. The crowd was so thick that the lobby looked like a bargain basement sale at Macy's.

"No wonder Benjamin had to get me a hotel room. Is it always like this?"

"S—Since the casinos have been added to horse racing as a legalized form of gambling, the tourist business has been very good. That's why we keep a room for clients," she explained, her voice oddly breathless.

He glanced down at her, saw her lips clamped tightly together. "Are you all right?"

"Y—Yes," she answered, her face averted.

He didn't believe her. He also didn't like the idea of her being sick. Benjamin should take better care of his employees.

Gently taking her arm, he maneuvered them through the crowd to the concierge's desk. "I'm Jordan Hamilton. I have reservations. My associate isn't feeling well. I'd like to shown directly to my room."

"Yes, Si."

"No," Lauren said, cutting off the man. "I . . . I just felt a little closed in. Must be the heat from earlier."

Jordan studied the pinched quality around her mouth, then asked the watchful hotel employee, "Is there a quiet restaurant in an open area?

"Yes. I'll get someone to show you." The young man flicked his wrist and a bellhop appeared. "Please show Mr. Hamilton and his guest to Fontaine's. And don't worry about checking in, Sir. I'll take care of everything. Will you be needing one or two keys?"

"One," Lauren answered quickly and tried to free her arm. Jordan held on. "One."

The man nodded. "I'll have the registration form and the key delivered to your table."

"Thank you," Jordan said.

"This way, Sir," said the bellman.

Lauren tried to protest again. "All this isn't necessary. I'm fine."

"Humor me. I'm a potential client, remember?"

Lauren gave him a look as if to say she wasn't likely to forget, then followed without any further resistance.

Jordan could feel her relax almost the moment they stepped inside the elegantly appointed room with its silk wall coverings and glittering chandeliers. Fresh flowers, gleaming silverware, and pristine, white linen tablecloths were on every table.

The highlight was the immense atrium that allowed the sunlight in the daytime and a view of the stars at night. A place for lovers. Too bad it was going to be wasted on them.

"A table for two?" asked a waiter who greeted them almost immediately.

"Yes, please," Jordan said, and they followed the rotund man to a secluded table tucked away by a trickling fountain. After seating them, he presented them with menus bound in soft leather. "Gustaf, your waiter, will be with you momentarily."

As soon as the man left Lauren said, "I'm fine, Mr. Hamilton. You didn't have to go to all this trouble. We could have eaten anywhere."

"Then this is as good a place as any." He opened his menu. Feeling her gaze on him, he lowered the menu. "Yes?"

"You're very good at getting your way, aren't you?" she asked, a hint of accusation in her voice.

"It seems to beat the alternative. Now, please order, and once we finish we can go over the schedule." He paused. "If that's agreeable with you."

She pushed the menu aside. "I'll just have a salad."

His gaze swept over her again, noting her slimness. He couldn't decide if she was being stubborn or telling the truth. Then another possibility occurred to him. "You aren't on some crazy diet, are you?"

Her head came up, her chest poked out. Jordan thought he might have to reassess one thing about her body. She wasn't as small in *that* area as he had thought. The word 'handful' came to mind.

"I'm not very hungry," she told him.

"Well, I am." He went back to studying the menu. "I haven't eaten since I had lunch yesterday at Nikko's in Seattle."

When Gustaf arrived, Jordan ordered a thick porterhouse, two appetizers, and a salad. With gentle cajoling, he managed to get Lauren to at least eat enough of the grilled mushrooms to satisfy him.

However, as soon as the meal was finished, she was back on the schedule. "What changes did you wish to make?"

He could certainly see how she had managed to make a new life for herself, probably with little help from anyone. He had met few people who were as focused and determined.

"I need to change today's one pm appointment with Benjamin to tomorrow at ten. I have a conference call from overseas scheduled for that time. Depending on the outcome of that call there may be other calls. They might run late, so the five P.M. cocktails I was to have tonight will have to be pushed to seven. I know it switches everything around, but it can't be helped. I have to be in New Orleans by tomorrow at two," he finished, and noted with satisfaction that she hadn't even blinked.

"Of course I'll have to check with Mr. Scott, but I don't see any immediate problems. You may have a problem with the hotel caterers," she said.

"I don't. My secretary has already called them while I was airborne from Seattle, then alerted my other people, who are flying in this afternoon about the changes," Jordan said.

Lauren smiled. "Poor woman."

Jordan was dazzled by the smile. Lauren Bennett could easily become a problem. "It might interest you to know that she made the same remark about you each time I've had to change my schedule."

Lauren shook her head. "I don't know how she keeps up with you."

"Sometimes I think she wonders herself."

For a moment they simply smiled across the table at each other.

"Excuse me, Mr. Jordan. Your key, Sir. Just sign here."

Jordan pulled himself away from gazing at Lauren's delectable looking mouth and signed the registration slip. Key in hand, he stood, placed some money on top of their bill, then reached for her chair.

"The limo is probably waiting outside to take you back," Jordan said as they made their way from the restaurant.

"No, the car is for you," Lauren protested. "I'll get a cab."

He stopped in the wide hallway lined with lush, tropical plants leading to Fontaine's and stared down at her. "Ms. Bennett, if the car is at my disposal, I plan to use it. I know you don't think I'm going to let you call a cab when the limo is available. Why do you think I asked the driver to return?"

Lauren tucked her head. "Thank you."

She certainly liked being independent. He briefly wondered if she had always been that way, or if her self-reliance had been learned as one of life's hard lessons. "You're welcome."

He started toward the entrance, his hand on her arm. He felt her slight shiver and wondered if she felt his. This was not going the way he planned.

Outside, he ushered her toward the waiting limo. Waving the driver away, he opened the door. "I'll see you tonight, then."

"I'm not coming."

He frowned. "I asked for all the key personnel at Scott's to attend. That definitely includes you."

"I have a prior engagement."

He looked at her for a long time. "Any chance of changing the date?"

"My son's kindergarten class is singing for the final PTA program," she said, pushing aside any unease at letting her boss down. Joshua always came first and, Benjamin always understood.

Jordan didn't have to look at her hand again to know she wasn't wearing a wedding ring. "I don't blame you. You should be there. He's a lucky little boy."

Her face lit up. She hadn't expected Jordan Hamilton to be so understanding. The tension eased around her mouth. "I'm the lucky one. Joshua has been practicing his solo part for weeks. Unlike me, he can carry a tune."

"You sound like a doting mother."

"Guilty." The wattage of her smile increased.

"Is his father the same way?"

The smile shattered. "His father died before he was born."

"That must have been very difficult for you," he said, watching pain tightening her features, hating the fact that he had put it there. Knowing that before their association was over he might have to put more there.

"Yes it was." Turning, she got inside the car.

"The party will probably last until ten. Any chance of you stopping by?" he asked, holding the door.

Lauren stared straight ahead. "I don't think so. Joshua will be tired, and it's a school night. Good-bye, Mr. Hamilton."

Jordan closed the door and watched the limo pull away. "Not good-bye, Lauren. Not by a long shot."

It wasn't until the limo stopped in front of Scott Resources and Lauren reached for her purse to tip the driver, that she realized she didn't have her purse. There was no doubt in her mind that Jordan hadn't forgotten. He was too sharp. Apparently, he had a noble streak to go along with his pirate instincts.

Thanking the driver, she went inside, glanced toward the elevator, then headed for the stairwell. She was too keyed up to stand the small enclosure. She took the stairs at a fast clip to the second floor, her legs long since having gotten used to the strenuous task.

As soon as she opened the stairwell door, she saw the receptionist pick up the phone. No doubt to call Cynthia. Lauren didn't stop until she stood in front of her boss's door.

"Come in."

The door was barely open before she heard someone behind her. Cynthia must have sprinted all the way. Standing to one side, she let the other woman in ahead of her.

"Well, how did it go?" Benjamin asked as he came around his desk.

"He needs to reschedule the appointment with you today for ten tomorrow, and push back the cocktail party tonight until seven. He had an overseas conference call," she told them.

"Did he say anything about business?"

"No. We just had lunch and discussed the schedule," Lauren told them.

"Lunch," Cynthia echoed, her eyes narrowed. "He took you to lunch. Where?"

"It doesn't make any difference where he took her," Benjamin said.

The alertness in Cynthia's gaze said it did. "So you were with him for over an hour and you didn't learn anything?"

Lauren looked at their two expectant faces and felt as if she had let them down. She had been concerned with maintaining her equilibrium about Jordan, then with fighting the panic of being closed in. She hadn't really thought of business. "I'm sorry."

"Don't worry, Lauren," Benjamin consoled. "It's probably for the best. Jordan is not a man to be pushed into anything. That's the reason for the party tonight, for him to get a feel for us, and us a feel for him. Three of his top people are flying in, I understand."

"I have a PTA meeting; I won't be there," Lauren reminded them.

"That's right. Well, go call Jordan and tell him the changes are fine, and the rest of us will see him at seven," Benjamin told her.

Throwing a glance at Cynthia, who was watching her closely, Lauren left the office and called Jordan. He answered the phone on the second ring.

"Jordan Hamilton."

The deep timbre of his voice chased down her spine. Her breath trembled over her lower lip. "Mr. Hamilton, this is Ms. Bennett."

"I recognized your voice."

The admission oddly pleased her. She had spoken to his secretary several times on the phone, but never to him. "The changes are agreeable to Mr. Scott, and he and the staff are looking forward to seeing you tonight."

"I don't suppose you've changed your mind about stopping by later. I could send the limo for you."

She twirled the cord on her finger, noticed the action, then stopped. "I'm sorry."

"So am I. Good-bye."

"Good-bye." Softly, Lauren hung up the phone. Jordan Hamilton could be a problem if she let him.

"You've got a problem."

Lauren looked into the worried face of her best friend and neighbor, Sonja Adams, who kept Joshua after school. Lauren's heart raced. She glanced around the room wildly. "Where's Joshua?"

"Calm down. He's fine." The full-figured woman caught Lauren's hand as she started past her.

"Then what's the matter?" Lauren asked anxiously.

The other woman sighed. "He says he's sick. That he doesn't want to sing tonight."

"Sick? Why didn't you ca—"

"Lauren, you know I would have called you or taken him to the doctor myself if I thought there was a problem." Sonja studied Lauren a long time. "His temperature is normal. He ate his snack. I've even heard him laugh a couple of times at the cartoons he's watching. It's not his stomach that's bothering him."

Lauren's trembling hand touched her temple. She had prayed, had hoped, that things would get better. But she should have learned her lesson—six years ago—that prayers and hopes sometimes aren't enough. "Where is he?"

"On the couch in the den watching TV."

Slowly, Lauren went into the other room. Joshua was on the floral couch, a light blue blanket over him. He looked so small. There was so much that she wanted for her son, so much she had to deprive him of to keep him safe.

"Hello, Honey. How's Mama's big boy?"

He straightened, a smile forming on his brown face, then it was gone. He slumped back against the couch. Both arms circled his stomach. "My tummy hurts."

She sat beside him. "Where?"

"There." He pointed to his belly button.

Gently her hand pressed the area. Although he watched her with wide eyes, his expression didn't change. "How was school today?"

He jerked his head toward the TV set. "Okay."

Her foreboding increased. "I bet there was a lot of excitement about the PTA meeting. I'm looking forward to you singing."

"My tummy hurts too bad." He rolled onto his side.

Lauren knew her son. She had seen him scared and in pain before, and each time he had wanted to be held as much as she had wanted to hold him. Sonja was right.

Something else was bothering him. Lauren was afraid she knew what it was. "Is there a notice about the meeting in your backpack?"

Silence.

Her hand stroked his solemn face. "Joshua?"

"I guess," he admitted quietly.

Lauren lifted the backpack from the end of the couch. Inside she opened his folder and found the announcement. Halfway down the page she found her answer.

There will be a special prize for the student who brings the most relatives, and a pizza party for the class that has the most relatives.

Her chest hurt, and her eyes stung. She could give him love, but it wasn't enough. She couldn't give him the extended family that his friends had. It would always be just the two of them.

Picking Jordan up, she drew him into her arms. After a moment's resistance, his arms went around her neck. "I know you wish things were different and I wish that for you, too, but it's not."

"Why?" he asked, his voice teary.

Because your only living relatives hate the air I breathe. "Your father would have loved you, and so would my mother. They didn't want to leave you anymore than you wanted them to." She gently pushed him away. Relieved to see he wasn't crying. "They'd want you to sing tonight."

"You think so?"

She smiled tremulously. "I'm positive. Love never dies."

"You won't die and leave me too, will you, Mama?"

The knot in her throat thickened. "No, Honey. I'll be with you and love you always."

His arms went around her neck again. "I love you too, Mama. I just wish I could be like the other kids sometimes."

Pain ripped though Lauren and she held him closer. *Nathan Strickland, may you rot in hell for what you've done to my son.*

Chapter Three

Jordan Hamilton stepped off the elevator on the floor of Scott Resources with a determined glint in his black eyes. Lauren Bennett was proving more elusive than he had anticipated. While he understood her motives for not being at the cocktail party last night, her absence had delayed his plans.

He freely admitted to himself that if he had met Lauren under different circumstances his reasons for seeking her out would have been more conducive to satin sheets and long hot nights. He had a hunch that the mysterious lady had enough fire beneath those prim little suits she wore to burn a man to ashes.

Too bad he'd never find out. Despite the temptation, he wasn't looking for an affair, but something far more important. To accomplish his goal, he had to gain her trust. That was going to be impossible if she kept evading him. All of his instincts told him that was exactly what she was doing.

She hadn't liked the strong sexual attraction between them anymore than he had. She was going to do her best to stay out of his way. He couldn't allow that to happen.

"Good morning," he said to the pretty receptionist. "I'm Jordan Hamilton. I have an appointment to see Mr. Scott."

"Yes, Sir," the young woman said, beaming. "Down this hall, last door on the right."

"Thank you," Jordan murmured and moved in the direction she had indicated. Too bad Lauren wasn't that easily swayed, but she would be before he was through.

With the thought firmly in his mind, he opened the door marked 'Benjamin Scott' and came to an abrupt halt on seeing the woman who had been uppermost in his mind for the past four weeks. Lauren sat behind her desk, her gaze on the documents she was entering into her terminal. Even without her noticing him, there was something about her body language that said *off limits*.

Most men wouldn't heed that message. She was simply too beautiful. However, it was those golden brown eyes of hers that drew Jordan like a lodestone.

Deep. Mysterious. Sad one moment, weary the next. He had gone to sleep last night thinking of those eyes. The door closed with more force than necessary.

"Good morning, Ms. Bennett."

Slowly, she lifted her head and met his gaze. Jordan felt the temperature in the room drop thirty degrees. "Good morning, Mr. Hamilton," Lauren greeted. "You can go in. Mr. Scott is expecting you."

Jordan didn't move. "How did Joshua do last night?"

Her graceful hands on the computer keys trembled. "Fine. Mr. Scott is waiting."

"Are you sure you're all right?"

Cool eyes lifted to him. "Yes."

The temperature in the room dropped another ten degrees. He wiggled his toes to make sure they were still there. The lady obviously didn't want anything to do with him this morning or any other time, but something was bothering her.

Out of nowhere came the the unexpected urge to pull her into his arms and take the sadness away from her eyes.

If he did she'd probably hit him over the head with the glass paperweight on her desk.

She was having none of him. But from the tenseness of her body, her refusal to meet his gaze for more than a few seconds, she needed someone. He hated the idea that there was no one she could turn to for help.

He placed his business card on the tray of her keyboard. Her delicate hands paused, then continued typing. "My secretary will always know where I am if you ever want to talk."

"Thank you, but that's not necessary."

"Keep it, anyway." Opening Benjamin's door, he disappeared inside.

Lauren slumped back in her chair. She didn't need this in her life. Jordan Hamilton was a distraction she didn't need or want. Her son had to be her top priority, not trying to sidestep Jordan's unexpected and unwanted interest.

She didn't need a man in her life. All she needed was Joshua.

Her eyes closed. A picture of Joshua's expression last night—of anger mixed with envy—flashed before her. He had been sitting with his class when his best friend and his twenty-six happy relatives took the stage of the school auditorium. Sisters, cousins, aunts, uncles, and grandparents had all crowded around Henry, smiling.

She had desperately wanted to go to him, but that would have drawn too much attention to them. So she had sat there staring at him, trying to convey her love with her eyes.

He never looked at her again. Not even the announcement that his class had won the pizza party cheered him up.

Neither had the special breakfast she prepared for him this morning. He had picked at the homemade waffles. She had already called his teacher and left a message for her to call if he didn't eat his lunch.

Joshua had to be her main priority, her only priority. Tossing Jordan's card in the wastebasket, she went back to the keyboard.

Jordan listened to Benjamin Scott tout the success and qualifications of Scott Resources with only part of his attention. The other part was on the woman on the other side of the door. She was hurting.

He didn't know how he knew, he just did. From his sketchy report on Lauren, he knew of only two reasons for her to look as if the troubles of the world were upon her small shoulders—her son, or Nathan Strickland.

From the way she reacted when he mentioned the PTA meeting, he'd bet her problems had something to do with her son. But what could have happened between her proud announcement yesterday at the hotel and this morning?

"Jordan, we're ready to launch a multi-media blitz of the southern states from Louisiana to Maryland. Your corporate headquarters may be in Santa Clara, California, but you have deep roots in the south," Benjamin said, hands atop his desk. "We don't forget our own. You're from Baton Rogue, graduated from Grambling, and have several branches scattered across the South, including a research facility in New Orleans, where you grew up."

"You've done your homework," Jordan commented, but that was to be expected. "You're smaller than I would have liked."

"That's to our advantage. Surely you remember the days when you were small and hungry," Benjamin said.

Jordan's grin was wicked. "Each day was a trial and a triumph."

"Exactly. The journey is often as great as the final destination."

Jordan looked at the man across from him in a new light. Few people understood the drive behind success. "So you begin a new journey."

The older man leaned forward on his desk. "That's what I'm proposing. A new journey between Crescent and Scott. Cynthia Douglas has already worked up some unique ideas for your research division in New Orleans that involve the schools you attended and literacy. She has things set up in the conference room, if you have time."

"I have time."

"Good." Benjamin picked up the phone and dialed Cynthia's number. "We're on our way." He stood. "If you'll follow me."

Benjamin paused briefly to tell Lauren where they were going. She barely acknowledged Jordan when she glanced up.

That didn't bother him as much as seeing the tenseness around her mouth.

In the hallway Jordan could no longer keep quiet. "Ms. Bennett doesn't seem herself today. Is anything wrong?"

"If there was, I'm sure she'd tell me if she wanted me to know," Benjamin said.

Jordan stopped in front of the door Benjamin opened. He knew when he was being told nicely to mind his own business. Considering the potential monetary gain to Scott Resources if Jordan signed, Benjamin's character went up another notch in Jordan's estimation. "Did she?"

"No." The answer was clipped, final.

Realizing he wouldn't get any further information from Benjamin, Jordan entered the room. His plane didn't leave until three. A lot could happen in four hours.

"Ms. Bennett, will you have dinner with me?"

Lauren couldn't believe her ears or her eyes. Jordan should already have left hours ago. "What are you doing here?"

He smiled and perched his hip on the corner of her desk. "Asking you to dinner, and hoping you'll accept."

"It's almost two, and your plane leaves at three," she reminded him.

"I'm returning next week for another meeting with Benjamin. Surely he told you?"

He had, and just the mention of Jordan returning had her heart beating faster. "You don't have to have dinner with me to discuss your schedule. I'm sure your secretary and I can work things out just fine."

"I'm sure you could, if that was the reason. It's not."

His voice tingled along her nerve endings. Too dangerous. Too close. She swallowed. "Company policy prohibits employees dating clients."

"I'm not a client yet."

"The same policy applies."

"In that case, I'll have to find another PR firm."

He was halfway across the room before she realized he

wasn't handing her a line. Surging to her feet, she blurted, "I don't date."

Ebony eyes stared into hers. "You must have a good reason. Since I want to get to know you better, I'm open to suggestions."

The door opened before she could say anything. Benjamin's bushy eyebrows arched over dark eyes. "Jordan, did you need to see me again?"

Jordan cast a look at Lauren, then turned to her boss. "It appears I do."

Lauren clamped her hands together. Benjamin knew more about her than anyone. She had been six months pregnant, lonely beyond belief, and out of a job when he had run his shopping cart into hers. He had insisted on seeing her home. He had come back the next day, then two days later.

He had been easy to talk to. Before long she had told him her life story. His concern had grown with each word. He became her friend first, her boss second.

She soon learned it wasn't just her that Benjamin cared about, it was everyone he came into contact with. His heart was as generous as his wide girth.

He'd keep her secrets, but if he thought Jordan would be good for her Benjamin wasn't above turning a blind eye to the policy he had created and giving things a helping hand. She could only hope he'd realize that any type of relationship between her and Jordan was impossible.

"Something tells me you didn't come back to see me," Benjamin said.

Jordan noted that the older man didn't take a seat nor offer him one. "I was concerned about Lauren."

Benjamin shrewdly studied Jordan. Obviously, he hadn't missed the use of her first name. "I take it this 'concern' is more than professional."

"Yes."

"Company policy prohibits clients from dating employees."

"I have the same policy."

"Have you ever broken it?"

"I've never had a reason,"

Benjamin studied the younger man for a long moment. "Lauren didn't appear too happy just now."

"I plan to change that."

Benjamin folded his arms across his broad chest. "What if you can't?"

"I'm going to try, with or without your approval."

"Dammit, Jordan. Lauren isn't used to men like you." He took a step closer. "I won't have Lauren hurt."

"She's hurting now. You and I both know that."

"Some pain you get over, and some you have to endure a lifetime," Benjamin said.

"I know," Jordan said solemnly. "Have you ever heard of me using anyone for personal gain?"

"No, but you're hell on your enemies."

His face harshened. "I believe in retribution."

"You're not the only one. I hope you'll remember that. Deal or not—if you give Lauren any more reason to hurt you'll have to answer to me."

"Fair enough. I'll see you in a week." Opening the door, he was not surprised to see Lauren standing in almost the same spot where he had left her.

"It appears we'll have to postpone our discussion," Jordan said. "Good afternoon, Ms. Bennett." Then he was gone.

The word "postpone" had her swinging back to her boss for an explanation. "What did he mean?"

Bushy eyebrows lifted in his mocha-hued face. "To answer that, I'd have to know what you were discussing, wouldn't I? Care to give me a hint?"

Lauren bit her lip. Mr. Scott's shrewd eyes narrowed perceptively, but all he said was, "I'll be in Cynthia's office if you need me."

Lauren stared at the closed door. Mr. Scott hadn't canceled the appointment with Jordan for next week, so Jordan must have changed his mind. She breathed a sigh of relief and went back to her desk.

The arrival an hour later of pink azalea bushes in a large

white wicker basket made her breath catch. Puzzled, she read the card, after questioning the delivery person to make sure the flowers were indeed hers. She had never received flowers before.

I hope these can do what I couldn't, make you smile. Call if you ever need a friend.

J.H.

Her eyes closed. A wisp of longing worked its way through her. Friends were in short supply. But she had willingly accepted the alternative to protect Joshua. She wasn't about to change her mind now. With trembling hands she tore up the card.

The Gulfstream was ready for takeoff when Jordan rushed up the gangway and quickly took his seat in the jet's wood-paneled cabin. Minutes later the plane swept down the runway, then rose and banked east heading to New Orleans. From the window he stared down at buildings growing smaller and smaller, a frown on his face.

Lauren had been hurting and there hadn't been a thing he could do about it. The unknown reason still made him uneasy. Her refusal to accept even casual friendship bothered him. It was as if she were afraid. The possible reason made him more determined than ever to see his plan through.

Lauren was made to smile. Those moments in the restaurant when she had dropped her guard and laughed or smiled had been to him like catching sight of a rainbow—rare and all the more precious because of its rarity.

Somehow he'd get her to laugh and smile again. And he'd be there to see it.

He thought of the flowers. Sending them had been an impulse. His secretary wouldn't believe he had actually sent flowers himself. That's what had made him late. Decisive Jordan Hamilton, who made million dollar deals, couldn't decide on a floral arrangement.

He grimaced and unbuckled his seatbelt. Enough of thinking about Lauren. He had a company to run.

Getting up, he took a seat at the small conference table already occupied by his vice-president and the president of his research facility in New Orleans.

"All right, gentleman, make me happy. How close are we to being the first to get the video phone on the market?"

If Jordan wasn't happy at the end of the meeting that had to be concluded in the president's office of Crescent Communications Research building, he wasn't unhappy, either. Although his researchers weren't making as much progress as he had hoped for in developing the technology for the phones, his satellite-based Internet hookup however, was ahead of schedule.

In four years the satellite system would link phones, computers, and TV's in a seamless global network. The potential profits were staggering. Wealth was power. If he couldn't get justice in one way, he'd find it in another.

It was after nine when Jordan pulled his Bronco into the detatched garage of his nineteenth century French Colonial home. He had fallen in love with the house as a young boy, when he and his sister had come to New Orleans to live with their paternal grandfather.

Rumor had it that Jean Lafitte once lived there. The thought that a real pirate had slept, eaten, walked, in the three-story structure always filled Jordan with awe. He had never forgotten the house. Four years ago, when it had come on the market, he had made sure his offer couldn't be refused.

He opened the back door and was met almost immediately by his grandfather, Hollis Hamilton, his gleaming, black cypress cane thumping loudly on the shiny, hardwood floor with each halting step he made. As always, the initial sight of his once robust grandfather tore at Jordan's heart.

This was the man who had reared him and his sister when other relatives wanted to split them up, saying a sixty-year-old widower couldn't handle two teenagers. He had proved them wrong and never looked back.

None of the relatives had seemed to understand that all three of them needed someone who had been close to and loved Randolph Hamilton, his father. Their shared grief sustained them when nothing else had.

The live-in housekeeper, Mattie Johnson, was a few steps behind Hollis. Jordan wouldn't call her a hoverer, but she was never far way from his grandfather. At one time Jordan and his sister, Angelica, had speculated on a possible romance. His grandfather's stroke two years ago had brought that talk to an end.

Mattie was too practical to mind what couldn't be changed. His grandfather was too proud to accept what couldn't be changed.

" 'Bout time you showed up," Hollis said, his grin wide, his right hand gripping the round head of his cane.

"Welcome home, Jordan," Mattie greeted. "Can I get you some coffee, or something to eat?"

"Both, please." Jordan grinned.

"I'll bring it into the dining room." A smile on her round, coffee-colored face, she started toward the kitchen.

"Don't keep me waiting. Out with it. Did you see her? Did you see Lauren Bennett?"

The words were repeated, not in confusion as was the case initially after the stroke, but in excitement and expectation. Expectation Jordan had only recently seen in his grandfather— since they learned of the existence of Lauren Bennett six weeks ago.

"Yes, Grandaddy, I saw her," Jordan said, gently taking his grandfather's left arm and steering him toward a straightbacked, tapestry chair at the dining room table.

The gray-haired man eased down into the chair, his gaze still on his only grandson. "Did she have the ledgers?"

"I don't know." He rushed on. "Grandad, I can't very well go up to her and ask for something that will undeniably bring her into contact with Strickland again."

"But you have to," Hollis said. "It's the only way to clear your daddy's name."

"I know that. But I have to move slow on this. She disappeared once. She can do it again."

Hollis leaned back in the chair. "If she does, Eleanor's boy will find her again."

The corner of Jordan's mouth lifted at the incongruity of calling his cousin, Drake Lansing, a boy. Standing six-foot-six, weighing two sixty, the thirty-two year-old Drake was hardly a boy. However, in Jordan's grandfather's eyes they were still boys shooting marbles in the hard-packed red dirt.

Drake wasn't offended by the name, any more than Jordan was. They knew the love behind the words, and knew they were their own men.

Drake had made the opposition cringe on the football teams they played in high school and college. With his computer genius, he had made the competition of Crescent Communications do the same thing.

"When are you going back?

"Anxious to get rid of me?" Jordan teased. "You must have Mattie fixing all those foods the doctor took you off of."

He snorted, but his voice was warm. "She's as bad as Angelica."

"You know you love every minute of it," Jordan said. The housekeeper spoiled his grandfather unmercifully. He glanced around. It was quiet. Too quiet. "Where are my baby sister and The Wild Bunch?"

"Scouting jamboree for the weekend." Hollis smiled. "She packed enough supplies to last a month."

"Can you blame her? You never know what Monte and the twins are going to get into. None of them have any fear. The girls are as bad as Monte."

"Keeps this house alive. It would be better if you came home and settled down."

Jordan, who had heard the request with increasing regularity, sidestepped the issue. "My schedule is too hectic for me to think of anything except work."

"You work too hard. You're rich enough. Richer than that thieving coward Nathan Strickland." Hollis's frail hand clamped around the cane.

Jordan placed his hand over his grandfather's. "Don't get yourself upset. I'll take care of Strickland."

Hollis relaxed back in his chair. Sweat beaded on his forehead. Jordan started to get up to get his grandfather some water, but Mattie was already there, setting a glass of chilled lemonade in front of him, then serving Jordan.

"Thanks, Mattie," Jordan said. She nodded and quietly left the room. Both knew he was thanking her for more than the food. As long as Mattie was there, neither he nor his sister need worry. Their grandfather was being cared for.

Jordan didn't touch his food until his grandfather took one, then another, sip of his drink. "I could always count on you, Jordan. That's why I called you after Strickland's boy called me. I didn't know what to think of it at first. I'd always heard Strickland and his son were close, yet he was on the phone telling me he had proof his father had kept a separate set of books, and embezzled funds from the newspapers he and Randolph owned together.

Jordan already knew the story, but still listened with patience. His grandfather had waited a long time for the revenge and so had Jordan.

"David," Hollis continued, "said his name was David Strickland. Said he wanted to meet me in person to hand over the books, but he was getting married the next day. I tried to get him to let me come to Charlotte, but he refused. He said the books were in a safe place. That not even his future wife knew about them."

Ice cubes clinked together as Hollis's hand shook. "But he never called again. He died in an automobile accident, and that thieving Strickland denied his son had ever been married." Hollis looked thoughtful. "You think he and his father's break up had something to do with his marriage to that girl?"

"It's possible. From what Drake has been able to find out, she didn't come from the type of family Strickland liked to associate with," Jordan said, continuing the conversation for his grandfather's sake.

"Meaning she didn't live in some fancy house and have some highfalutin' job," Hollis sneered.

"Strickland's a snob."

"He's also a thief. He stole money from your dad's company. He never got over that failure." Hollis's pale face tightened. "Strickland made your daddy's last days hell, and he's got to pay. You'll keep after the girl in Shreveport until she helps us, won't you? You won't give up?"

"No, Grandaddy, I won't give up, but Lauren Bennett is running from me as fast as she probably ran away from Strickland," Jordan admitted, shoving his coffee cup away in disgust.

Hollis snorted again. "Can't believe that. Women fall all over themselves for you."

Jordan chuckled. "Believe me, it's true."

"Turn on the charm, Boy. Get her to stop running and notice you. You have to get your hands on those ledgers if she has them."

"Grandad, there could be complications if I do," Jordan said, his meaning all too clear.

"I know that. I haven't lived seventy-odd years for nothing. But the way I see it, you don't have much choice," Hollis said. "No matter what, you've got to see this through. Your father can't rest as long as that bastard goes unpunished."

Jordan nodded. He remembered too well the pain and misery on his father's face after *The Carolina* filed bankruptcy. He had sunk his life savings, his heart, his soul, into the biweekly newspaper. He hadn't been able to accept its failure. Never once did he suspect he had been cheated by his new business partner. Strickland was a respected, if pride-filled man in the community.

Randolph Hamilton was a broken man who never recovered. Nathan Strickland had to pay.

Jordan turned flint-hard eyes on his grandfather. "I'll see it through. I'll find a way for her not to run. You have my promise."

Chapter Four

I don't need this in my life. Not now. Why did he have to come back to Shreveport?

Hands clamped around the steering wheel of her late model sedan, Lauren watched in mounting tension as the cars in front of her inched closer to the valet parking of the Four Seasons Hotel. The high temperatures and the busy tourist season had the white-shirted attendants hustling to keep up with demand.

She wished they weren't so efficient. She didn't want anything to put her face-to-face with her company's newest and most important client any sooner than necessary.

Mr. Scott had been elated when he had received the call from Jordan giving him the go-ahead to do the PR for his research facility in New Orleans. Of course, Cynthia had said it was her concepts that clinched the deal.

Lauren hadn't cared what had clinched the deal, only that it meant Jordan Hamilton would have more reasons than ever to contact her boss. Lately, she hadn't been able to get Jordan out of her mind, and last night he had invaded her dream.

A very erotic dream.

She had never seen the inside of a ship's cabin, yet she had no difficulty conjuring up the wide bed latched with chains to the bulkhead, the tumble of sheets. Nor Jordan, his white shirt open to the waist of his tightly-fitting, black leather pants, laughing down at her, his white teeth flashing in his darkly handsome, bearded face.

Suddenly his clothes were gone, and he had joined her on the immense bed. His—

She started at the impatient blast of a car horn behind her. With firmness, she banished the remnants of the dream. Her breathing erratic, she stepped on the gas and moved up two car lengths. Three more, and she would be in front of the revolving doors.

Her slim fingers flexed on the steering wheel. She moved up another space. Her heart rate increased. Now, thanks to Benjamin Scott's belief in all of his clients receiving the personal touch, she might have to find out for herself what 'postpone' meant.

She glanced at the basket sitting in the seat next to her. The iridescent polyethylene paper caught the reflection of the late afternoon light and radiated a prism of rainbow-hued colors.

The basket, filled with a bottle of vintage wine, lush strawberries, and imported chocolates, had been especially created for clients of Scott Resources. The occasion was Crescent Communications' acquisition of a lucrative military contract.

The thick vellum card inside was embossed with the company letterhead and Jordan's name. As Benjamin's assistant, she had often delivered similar gifts, but none had disturbed her more. She wished Cynthia wasn't out sick with a summer cold.

The way Cynthia's big brown eyes lit up when she talked about Jordan, she'd probably have a relapse when she learned she had missed an opportunity to be alone with him. Although Lauren had been truthful about company policy against dating clients, if Jordan took an interest in the vivacious and personable Cynthia, Benjamin would give them his blessings. He respected Jordan, and believed in his integrity too much not to.

Her car door opened. Warm air rushed in, carrying with it the faint scent of the rain the weatherman had predicted. She glanced at her watch. Seven forty-eight. Plenty of time to get home before nine P.M. as she'd promised. She grabbed the basket.

An engaging smile on his boyish face, the valet welcomed her to the hotel, took the basket with one hand, and helped her out with the other. Before she had learned she had to see Jordan, she might have returned the young man's cordial greeting.

Now, with tension coiling tighter and tighter through her, all she could manage was a wan smile as she placed her hand in his. The basket in her arms, she entered the opulent lobby of the hotel.

As a week earlier, the immense room was a sea of chattering, moving people. Hectic on weekdays became chaotic on weekends. It was just her bad luck that today was Friday. Add a convention or two, and you couldn't walk two feet without passing another person. The crowd might be good for tourism, but it still made her uneasy, hemmed in.

It was too much of a reminder of almost six years ago when she had been trapped in the mangled wreckage of a car and unable to move. Maybe in ten years she'd stop hearing the screams. Maybe, in her lifetime, she'd stop hearing her own. Her short, oval nails bit into the cellophane paper.

She fought to push the memory away and superimpose it with the one person who had sustained her since—her son, Joshua. He was the joy and light of her life. She thought she had raised him without any of her fears or insecurities. Until recently.

Anxiety whipped though her, but she refused to believe that whatever was bothering her five-year-old couldn't be solved with love and understanding. He just needed to know she would always be there for him. That meant getting back to him as quickly as possible.

Squaring her shoulders beneath her conservative, teal suit jacket, she crossed the lobby. Going up the three steps, she turned the corner—and froze.

In front of each of the ten elevators was a cluster of people. Even at the best of times, she didn't like the pressing confinement of elevators. Usually she could manage if she concentrated hard enough, but the combination of all the people, disquieting thoughts of Jordan, and worry about Joshua made that impossible.

One of the reasons she had taken her job at Scott Resources was its location on the second floor of a downtown office building. Her co-workers had a running joke about Lauren being into fitness because she used the stairs so much. Her sturdy pumps were classified as "old folks shoes."

Someone brushed against her to get to the closing elevator, bringing her back to the present. The jovial passengers cheered when the young man made it just in time. Moistening her dry lips, she switched the basket to the other arm and walked closer. She had to get through this before she could go home.

Conquer one thing at a time. That's how she had learned to survive the past six years. First the elevator, then Jordan Hamilton—then home to Joshua.

From less than twenty feet away Jordan Hamilton watched Lauren Bennett with an odd mixture of curiosity and longing that would have sent her running from the hotel if she had seen him. He had taken careful measures to ensure that she did not.

A great deal of planning and a lot of promises had been made to bring Lauren within reach again. He was not going to move too fast and frighten her.

His eyes narrowed as he saw more than one man do a double take on seeing her. He couldn't blame them. Jordan had known and bedded his share of beautiful women, but he had almost been struck speechless when he first saw Lauren at the airport.

The lady was wary, though. She didn't give her friendship or her trust easily.

Jordan could have told the man trying to pick her up not to bother. Even from where he was standing, Jordan could see the coldness in her gaze. The man finally realized he was wasting his time and moved on toward the jazz club tucked on the other side of the elevators. Apparently the man liked an easy conquest.

Jordan enjoyed a challenge. The easiest way to get his back up was to tell him he couldn't do something because of the color of his skin, or because it hadn't been done before. He wouldn't give up until he had proved to the skeptics how wrong they were. Those victories were the sweetest, and carried the fondest memories.

Trying to get a woman to notice him would be something new, however. The corner of Jordan's mouth tilted upward with amusement. His grandfather had been right about women usually falling over themselves for him.

Even before he started making money, women came easily and freely to him. He was a sensual man. He liked the softness of women, and all the things which made them different.

Only Lauren tried to keep her distance. Her continued resistance intrigued him far more than he liked to admit.

He had known Lauren would be uniquely different from other women the moment he looked into her dark, troubled eyes. She was a puzzle that he was determined to solve.

The first question was why she could look straight through a man. That kind of total indifference from a woman could cut a man's pride to the core. Lauren was a master. The man she had turned down was probably in the bar downing his second straight whiskey.

Jordan didn't think she intended to hurt as much as she was trying not to be hurt. He had nothing to base his theory on except the flash of fear he had seen in her eyes the afternoon he told her he had to 'postpone' their talk. He didn't know why she was afraid, but he intended to find out.

Just as he intended to find out why she hadn't gotten on the elevator. She had had at least six opportunities since he began watching her. His brow furrowed. Perhaps she was thinking of leaving without seeing him. He took a step toward her, then stopped.

Benjamin Scott had assured Jordan that Lauren would deliver the basket to his suite, just as Jordan had promised that if he couldn't help her to smile at least he wouldn't add any new reason for her to be unhappy. That promise had kept him awake last night.

He had meant what he said, but he had a bad feeling that this whole thing could blow up in his face. He had to be careful.

Controlling his sexual desire had never been a problem until he met Lauren. A man who couldn't control his emotions couldn't control his destiny, yet he caught himself thinking more about Lauren than the promise he had made his grandfather.

The same way he was thinking he'd like to see her in something softer, more feminine, than the practical but dowdy little suits she wore. He grimaced. What he should be thinking about was a way to alter his plan. He had intended to 'accidentally' meet her in the lobby and invite her to have a drink.

He had been positive that if he had met her at his door she'd politely hand him the basket and walk away. He'd seen her dispatch the guy trying to pick her up. If he approached her now, she'd do the same thing. Somehow, he had to have some time alone with her if he expected to get her cooperation.

Just then, Lauren pushed the leather strap of her purse over her shoulder, clutched the basket more firmly, and merged with the crowd getting on the elevator. Even as Jordan smiled, he moved with the quick efficiency of a man who knew where he was going and how to get there.

He hadn't been a quarterback on the Grambling College football team for nothing. He still had some moves left in him. With a few 'Excuse mes' and smiles, he managed to be at Lauren's side as she stepped on the elevator.

People were jostling packages and bodies, attempting to squeeze aboard. Two men didn't make it. The elevator door slid halfway shut, then opened. Someone made a crack about hoping the elevator didn't get stuck they way it had that morning.

Mixed with a few good-natured laughs was a strangled sound from Lauren. The door slid completely shut and the elevator began its ascent.

Instinctively Jordan moved closer. "Ms. Bennett, are you all right?"

Her head jerked up. Large, sherry brown eyes stared up at him. Lips the color of a ripe plum trembled.

Fear. That wasn't the response he wanted from her. "Let me take that for you," he said, easily removing the basket from her hands.

"I—I want to get—" Her shaky words abruptly faltered as the elevator gave a thump and stopped.

For a full four seconds there was total silence, then a babble of frightened, annoyed voices shouted instructions to the elderly, well-dressed gentleman who had punched in most of the floors.

Jordan ignored everything except the increased pallor in Lauren's face, her tightly shut eyes, the way her nostrils flared as if she were having difficulty taking in air. His free arm slid around her shoulder and pulled her against his chest. She was as stiff and unyielding as the wall at his back.

"It will get going shortly," Jordan murmured, his hand making a relentless sweep up and down her back.

As if on cue, the elevator started upward again. Cheers broke out. Before the jubilant sounds faded, the elevator stopped. This time it shuddered. Lights winked. Screams splintered the air.

With a frightened whimper Lauren grabbed the lapels of Jordan's gray, double-breasted suit and tried to burrow into his chest.

With a savage curse, Jordan let the basket slide down between them, then wrapped both arms around Lauren. A couple of small children began to whimper. One woman was crying softly.

Over her head, he saw that the man everyone had shouted instructions to was fumbling to open the small metal door and get the phone. After less than thirty seconds of talking, he nodded, then said loudly, "They said they'll have the problem fixed in another minute or two. And get this, guests will receive free accommodations for the night and free room service. Other compensations will be given to non-guests. Who's going to order first?"

Amid comments about suing or upgrading their rooms and outlandish food orders, Jordan repeated reassurances to Lauren. The shivering of her body only increased, and so did his concern. The others were bouncing back, but Lauren acted as if she had been dropped into her worst nightmare.

Someone tapped him on the shoulder. He looked up and

found most of the people in the elevator watching him. He didn't mind for himself. He did for Lauren.

"Yes." His voice was clipped. It plainly stated he wished to be left alone.

"Y—Your room number and order?"

"Just tell them the Presidential Suite, and they'll take it from there." Turning from the speculative looks, Jordan once again centered his attention on Lauren. Only the curly, brownish-black hair on top of her head was visible. Warm, jerky breaths of air cut through his cotton shirt.

"Hold on, Ms. Bennett."

The elevator gave a jerk, then began to move. In a matter of seconds, it reached the next floor. Hotel representatives were there to keep the elevator door open, offer apologies, and keep the curious onlookers back. To no one's surprise, most of the people piled off rather than chance that particular elevator stopping again.

Jordan suspected that if he got off with Lauren, he'd have to blindfold and drag her back onto another. Then what would he do? The elevator was eight floors from his suite and ten floors from the lobby.

He had no choice. He pulled her closer.

"Hang on, Honey, we'll be off in a little while." If she heard him, she didn't give any indication.

Two men, one in a tailored suit and one in a dark brown uniform with *Maintenance* scrawled on his pocket, stepped into the elevator. The man in the suit took one look at Lauren and began offering effusive words of apology.

"Just make sure this thing doesn't stop or I'll have to answer to her, and then you're going to have to answer to me," Jordan told the man tightly.

Swallowing, the man in the suit punched in Jordan's floor, then asked the other two passengers their floors. Jordan wasn't surprised that the man knew who he was. Money was its own equalizer.

No one said anything as the elevator continued. The other two passengers got off on the sixteenth floor and were met by another hotel representative.

On his floor, the eighteenth and highest, Jordan merely lifted a dark brow as two more men in suits greeted him. They had pulled out all the stops for this one. But that was to be expected.

Customer service was everything if you wanted to succeed. It was the number one priority at Crescent Communications.

Jordan nodded toward the basket. "Grab that, will you?"

Picking up Lauren, he brushed past both men. By the time he reached his door, the older of the two men had his door open and was standing to one side.

Jordan paused at the threshold and turned to block the men's entrance. "Thank you, Gentlemen. I can take it from here."

The two men traded nervous glances. The one who had picked up the basket set it just inside the door. "Would you like a doctor sent up?"

"I'll let you know. Hold all calls." Stepping back, Jordan shut the door.

Chapter Five

Jordan crossed the room to the bar, with Lauren still in his arms. He managed to snag a bottle of whiskey and a glass, then headed for the couch and sat down. Placing them on the glass and iron coffee table, he gently turned her face toward his.

He cursed again.

Tears slowly glided down her brown cheeks. His blunt-tipped fingers felt the steady, strong heartbeat in her throat. Her skin was cool, not clammy. She was going to be all right.

"You're out of the elevator, Lauren. You're safe." Refusing to release her for a moment, he unscrewed the cap of the Jack Daniels and poured two fingers into the squat glass. "Drink this."

She jerked her head away from the strong smell and threw up her hands. "Don't," she cried. "I don't want to wake up. It hurts too much."

"What hurts, Lauren?"

She shook her head.

Jordan realized she was fighting him *and* memories. He easily captured her hands. "I'm sorry, Lauren, but you have to drink this. You have to come back and realize you're safe."

He put the glass to her lips and tilted. She spluttered, gasped, coughed, but most of it went down and stayed.

"That's it . . . just a little bit more," Jordan coaxed. Again he pressed the glass to her lips. He tilted the glass for a third time. Seeing the tinge of color in her cheeks, feeling the lessening of her trembling, he set the glass on the table in front of him.

"That's enough, or you'll have a headache in the morning and blame me." His knuckles stroked the smoothness of her cheek. "You're going to be all right. You're safe. No one is going to hurt you."

Settling back with Lauren in his lap, Jordan wished Benjamin had been more informative than merely saying Lauren hadn't had an easy life. Jordan thought the other man had meant her losing Joshua's father. Obviously it was more than that.

Jordan's confidential report on her certainly hadn't yielded any clues to her behavior. Taking the sorrow from her eyes and gaining her cooperation was suddenly turning into a more demanding and time-consuming job.

The question was, did he want to get involved with a woman who would require more from him than he usually gave in a relationship? In the past women had enjoyed his body, his wealth, his prestige. He liked to think he'd satisfied them, in and out of bed.

Instinctively he knew Lauren would require more from a man than a mind-blowing sexual encounter . . . if the man was lucky enough to get that far. She was obviously fighting demons from the past, and from all indications she preferred doing it on her own.

His company was experiencing the greatest growth in its eight year history. Every minute he spent away from business could translate into lost revenue. There wasn't going to be a quick resolution to gaining Lauren's cooperation and her trust.

He glanced down at the smallness of Lauren's body, remembered her mindless fear, felt the heat of her body burning into his—a heat he knew could set a man and the night on fire. But he'd never be that man.

The shrill ring of the telephone broke the hushed quiet of

the room. Lauren trembled. Jordan's arms tightened a brief second before he lifted the receiver. "This'd had better be good."

"How's Lauren?" came the agitated voice of Benjamin Scott. "The hotel manager called me, since you're in the company's suite."

"Better," Jordan told him. His hand swept up and down her arm. "An explanation would help."

A long sigh echoed though the receiver. "She has to be the one to tell you. I'm on my way over. I just thought I'd call first."

"I can take care of things by myself," Jordan said, finally coming to a decision. He wasn't walking away. He couldn't. Maybe if he helped Lauren slay her dragons, she'd help him slay his. "Don't worry, I'll keep the promise I made you."

"You'd better," came the curt reply. "This isn't going to help Lauren. She doesn't need any more problems." The line went dead.

Brow furrowed, Jordan dropped the receiver back into place. That was the second time Benjamin had mentioned 'problems' in connection with Lauren. What did that have to do with her fear of being trapped in an elevator?

He looked at Lauren as if to find the answer he sought. Her large brown eyes stared unblinkingly back at him. He sucked in his breath. He had never seen such naked pain before. He didn't want to see it now. Not in Lauren's eyes.

Without thought, he bent his dark head, and his lips traced the tracks of her tears. The taste of the salty moisture sent an unexpected jolt of protective tenderness and longing through him.

"I'd like to be your friend, Lauren." His strong hand cupped her face. "Will you trust me enough to let me help you?"

"No one can help me," she said, her voice as bleak as her expression.

"I'd like to try, Lauren," Jordan coaxed.

With a whimper, Lauren came out of his arms and stood. "No."

Jordan saw the wildness in Lauren's pinched face and reached out to comfort her. She flinched. "Lauren, what's the matter?"

"I—I want to go home."

"You're in no shape to go down eighteen flights of stairs, and I'm not about to let you get back on that damn elevator until I've a guarantee it won't stop," Jordan said. "If there's anything else you want and it's in my power to give it to you, it's yours."

The caring and sincerity in his voice reached through her anger and her pain. He had no way of knowing how being stuck in the elevator brought back all the anguish. She tried to think of Joshua, and succeeded only in thinking of the stormy night both of their lives were irrevocably changed.

Her throat ached. Tears pricked her eyes. She wasn't going to cry. She had cried and pleaded before, and she had been turned away with harsh, threatening words. This time she would not show her weakness. Even as the words formed in her mind, sobs erupted from her throat.

Strong arms pulled her against a wide chest. "I can't stand it if you start crying again. If you want to go home, you'll go. But you have to stop crying. We aren't going anywhere until you do. I won't have you stumbling and hurting yourself on the stairs."

His tender concern only increased her tears. He hadn't condemned her for her fears. He was trying his best to help her work through them.

"Honey, please, don't do this," Jordan pleaded. "I can't stand here helpless and see you hurting. Tell me how to help." His lips brushed across her tear-filled eyes, the curve of her delicate ear, the arch of her satiny brow. "Tell me what to do."

The curious unfurling of warmth in her body caught Lauren off guard. So did the desire to snuggle closer to Jordan's warmth, his strength. It had been so long. In an instant she realized why he had made her uneasy.

Deny it as she might, she wanted him. Somehow he had made her feel, and in doing so had opened her old fears and insecurities. His presence sharpened her pain and deepened her loss. Because no matter how she felt there could never be anything between them, not even friendship.

She turned her head from his searching lips, but she couldn't quite bring herself to leave the immeasurable comfort his body offered. "I—I want to go home."

"I know, and I'll take you as soon as possible," Jordan assured her. She looked so forlorn. He thought only of taking the unhappiness away. Slowly his mouth touched hers softly, once, twice, then settled with firm pressure.

A shudder went through Lauren. It had been too long since she had been kissed by a man. And never with the mind-drugging expertise she was now experiencing.

When Jordan's searching tongue slid over the roof of her mouth, she was just as powerless to hold back a soft moan of pleasure as she was to keep her tongue from darting out to meet his. Fueled by the heat of her building desires, she pressed her full length hungrily against him, her body trembling with need.

His questing mouth continued to take hers in a kiss which rocked her. Vaguely, she was aware of her jacket slipping from her. Helplessly, her arms glided up the hard wall of his chest and around his neck. She wanted, needed, to get closer to the heat, the delicious taste of him.

The honeyed taste and arousing touch of Lauren swept through Jordan's body like nothing he had ever experienced. The more he caressed and savored, the more he was consumed with an almost uncontrollable need to take Lauren to bed and show her how incredibly special she was.

And ruin all the plans it had taken weeks to set in motion.

With a fierce shudder, he tore his lips from hers. "Tell me what a bastard I am, but I'm not sorry."

Dazed, Lauren slowly opened her eyes. Trembling fingers pressed against her moist lips still tingling from Jordan's passionate kiss. God help her, she wasn't sorry, either, but to let herself care for Jordan would eventually mean as much pain as pleasure.

Blindly, she turned toward the door and freedom. A wave

of dizziness stopped her as effectively as if she had run into an invisible wall.

She swayed. Her heavy hand refused to lift further than her chin.

"Easy, Lauren." Jordan picked her up and sat her in a chair. "The whiskey I forced down your throat must be catching up with you."

Closing her eyes against another wave of dizziness, she leaned her head back on the couch. "How much did you give me?"

"Not enough to cause this, unless you have a low tolerance for alcohol or you skipped lunch."

Slowly her lids lifted. "I didn't eat lunch."

Assessing black eyes ran over Lauren's slim body. "When did you eat last?"

She wanted to tell him it was none of his business, but from his determined expression she saw that would be a waste of her time. She certainly wasn't going to tell him that she had been too nervous to eat since Mr. Scott had told her she had to deliver the basket because Cynthia was ill. "Yesterday at lunch."

"Yesterday!" he exploded. "You told me you weren't dieting."

Her chin lifted. "I'm not. I just wasn't hungry. Besides, if you hadn't given me the alcohol this wouldn't have happened."

"Humph," He pushed to his feet and walked over to the telephone. "You need to get some food into you. Fish, chicken, or beef—and please don't say you're a vegetarian."

"What's wrong with being a vegetarian?" she asked.

"Nothing. I just don't want you casting longing looks at my steak," Jordan explained. "What's it going to be?"

Her spine straightened. "Nothing. I'm going home."

"Of course, after you've eaten. Then, I'll check on the elevators and take you home."

She came out of the chair, swaying only for a moment before righting herself. "I'm not one of your employees, Mr. Hamilton. I don't have to take orders from you. I'm perfectly capable of taking care of myself, and that includes eating and seeing myself home.''

Jordan was fascinated by the flashing brown eyes of the angry young woman in front of him. So he was right. There was enough passion in her to burn up the night. However, he wasn't too thrilled by her continued defiance of him.

''All right, Ms. Bennett. I'll see you to the elevators.'' He caught the slight widening of her eyes as he bent to retrieve her jacket. She had expected an argument. She'd find out soon enough she wasn't up to leaving.

Helping her slip on her jacket and handing her her purse, he gestured toward the door. ''After you.''

Lauren turned away. Neither said anything as they left the hotel room and walked the short distance down the wide, plushly carpeted hallway to the elevator.

Stopping, Lauren stared at the control panel. Her hand lifted, wavered, fell.

She knew Jordan watched her. Seconds ago she had told him she could care for herself. Now, he knew she'd lied. Some fears she had yet to conquer.

Her hands clamped around her handbag. She couldn't stand in the hall all night. Joshua was waiting for her. What was she going to do?

A pinging noise sounded. The elevator doors glided open. Out stepped an elderly couple who nodded and continued to one of the six rooms on the floor.

A tall, well-built man wearing a hotel maintenance uniform stepped out, smiled and nodded. ''Going down?''

Lauren remained unmoved until she felt strong fingers curl around her upper arm. Jordan. Now he knew she had lied about her capabilities. Would there be pity or derision in his eyes? Without further thought she lifted her gaze and sought the answer to her unspoken question.

With concern he stared unblinkingly back at her. Then his attention centered on the man at the control panel. It was the same maintenance man they had met earlier.

''Is the elevator still having problems?''

''No, Sir, Mr. Hamilton,'' he answered, his gaze flicking

nervously to Lauren. "Management thought the guests would feel better if I was on board."

Jordan nodded his approval, then glanced down at Lauren. Obviously, the man's presence wasn't reassuring to her. She had a death grip on her handbag. He had thought of using the elevator to keep her with him until she felt stronger. He hadn't counted on the silent pleading in those big eyes of hers.

He hadn't lasted a millisecond. Not when he knew she looked through other men as if they didn't exist.

"The private elevator is working fine," the man offered.

Jordan thought of the small enclosure and dismissed the idea. It was going to be difficult enough to get her on this one. "Can you override the controls and take us straight down?"

Lauren's gaze lifted sharply. Hope vied with dread in her dark eyes. "Can you?"

The employee blinked. He looked as if he had been punched in the stomach. Jordan had seen that look of fascination on men's faces before. It was starting to annoy him.

"Well, can you?" he asked, more sharply than he'd intended.

The man jumped and turned his attention back to Jordan. "Not all of them. I'm sorry."

Lauren bit her lip and looked away.

Jordan stepped closer. He knew she was fighting memories again. He just wished he knew what they were. But this time she wouldn't be alone. "Just do the best you can."

"Yes, Sir."

Jordan's large hand circled Lauren's small waist. He felt her shudder. A reaction to him, or the coming elevator ride? He didn't know. Together they walked inside. The moment the door began to close, she stiffened, her eyes clamped shut.

Turning her slim body into his arms, he held her against his solid body, his back pressed against the enclosure. He would liked to have shielded her from curious passengers who would be getting on, but he wasn't sure how she'd react to being trapped between him and the wall.

The elevator stopped twice before it reached the lobby. Jordan waited until all the passengers got off before he followed with Lauren.

Near a secluded alcove with a settee, potted plants, and statues, he paused. "Do you want to sit down for a while?"

"I—I want to go home," she said, already trying to pull away from him.

Jordan was having none of that. "Where is your car?"

"Valet parking," she answered softly, her voice steadier.

"Let's go." He started toward the revolving glass doors.

He heard the crack of lightning twenty feet from the entrance. Outside, a black sheet of rain fell from the darkened sky. Only the arched concourse overhang kept the attendants and guests from getting drenched. The blowing rain was doing its best to change that. He cursed softly. There was no way he would let her drive home in these conditions.

"It might be better if you waited for the rain to let up."

"No." She shook her head. "I have to get home. I promised."

"Promised who?" Jordan questioned. He was surprised at the quick spurt of jealously.

Liquid brown eyes lifted. "My son, Joshua."

Relief he didn't want to feel swept through him. "Where's the ticket?" Her trembling hand lifted a thin strip from her jacket pocket.

The attendant was there to take it from her before Jordan could. "Thank you. You can pay over at the booth." Smiling, the perky woman in a yellow rain slicker ran toward the garage.

"I'll take care of it. You wait here." Jordan walked off before Lauren could protest. She would have followed, but she didn't know if her legs could support her.

First the elevator, now the storm. Thunder rumbled and lightning flashed, lightening up the darkened sky. Lauren shivered. It seemed everything was conspiring against her. She hated storms for the same reason she hated closed places. Both were connected to her deepest nightmare.

"You're okay?"

Lauren looked up at Jordan's sharply defined features and shivered for another reason. He was too handsome, and too adept at touching the loneliness in her. "Yes. Thank you for all your help. Good-night."

Jordan looked from Lauren's extended hand to the feeble smile on her pinched face, the sorrow in her eyes. "You don't really think I'm going to let you drive home alone, do you?"

The extended hand clamped around her purse. "I'm fine."

"Come on. Your car is here."

Lauren glanced around to see the same young woman waving her arm. Lauren made her legs move. To her surprise another attendant opened the passenger door. She opened her mouth to correct the error, but Jordan spoke first. "Thank you."

Stunned, she watched him hand the attendant some currency with one hand and urge her into the passenger seat of her car with the other. She balked. "What are you doing?"

"Making sure you reach home safely."

Another sort of panic widened her eyes. "I don't need you to take me home."

"You may not need me to, but I need to," he said.

Another stirring of warmth touched her. She pushed it away. "Thank you, but—"

"Ms. Bennett, unless you want to become the talk of the Four Seasons Hotel, I suggest you get in the car."

Lauren glanced around and saw they were indeed the center of attention. Jordan's good looks had probably drawn the women's gazes like a magnet—on the other hand, she made a habit of drawing as little attention to herself as possible.

Silently, she got into the car. He was right. She *was* too upset to drive, and the storm would make it worse.

Jordan went around the car and got in. After fastening her seatbelt, Lauren stared straight ahead, her hands clamped together. He wanted to reach over and touch her, but adjusted the seat to his long legs instead.

Although he knew, he asked, "Where do you live?"

She gave him the address, then glanced out the window.

Jordan put her boxy car into gear, and pulled off. Rain plummeted the car the moment they pulled out from beneath the protective covering. The windshield wipers barely kept up. The downpour was never more noticeable than when they went under the overpass to get onto the freeway. There was quiet. Then the relentless pounding against the car was ear-splitting.

"Is it safe?" came the hushed question.

He spoke without taking his eyes from the road. Traffic was a snarled nightmare. They had already passed one accident. "If not, I'd pull off no matter what you said."

"I know. Thank you."

He stole a quick look in her direction. In the dimness of the car he could tell nothing from her expression. He hadn't expected the thanks, nor the calm acceptance of what he had said. His gaze went back to the road.

Trying to get to know Lauren might take more time than he had anticipated, but he had a feeling the results were going to be greater, too. He just had to make sure that when this was over and he walked away, he wouldn't lose more than he had gained.

Chapter Six

"It's the fifth house on the left. The porch light is on," Lauren said, leaning forward eagerly in her seat.

Jordan slowed and squinted through the rain plummeting the windshield. All he could make out on the dark street were the vague shapes of moderate-sized houses. "You need a streetlight."

"I know. Calling downtown hasn't gotten one, though. It's the next house," she told him. Reaching up over the visor on the driver's side, she activated the garage door.

Jordan turned into the driveway, pulled into the garage, and cut the motor. He glanced over at Lauren to see how she was doing. She was already out of the car. By the time he stood, she had rounded the end of the car and was almost even with him.

"Slow down before you hurt yourself," he warned. "I'm sure your little boy is fine."

If she heard him, she didn't act like it, but simply opened the door with the key already in her hand and rushed inside. Jordan followed in her wake, trying to figure out if she was simply an overprotective mother or she had another reason for being anxious.

"Is he all right?" Lauren questioned in a rush.

An attractive, full-figured woman in her early thirties turned from washing dishes in the sink. Her assessing gaze went from Lauren to the man standing behind her.

"Sonja?" cried Lauren impatiently. This was no time for her best friend to go ga-ga over a man. "Is Joshua still complaining of a stomachache? I thought I'd be home before now."

Sonja's gaze finally settled on Lauren. Crossing her arms over her generous breasts, she rolled her eyes. "That little imp is fine. He hasn't complained once since you left, and he didn't start complaining until you told him you had an appointment."

Lauren shoulders relaxed. "I'd better go check on him." She was gone before the words were out of her mouth.

"I guess that leaves me and you to get acquainted all by ourselves," Sonja cooed, her voice dropping to a sultry whisper.

Jordan lifted a dark brow at the audacious woman dressed in black leggings and a red print blouse, then realized if Lauren trusted her enough to leave Joshua with her she was probably a harmless flirt. He smiled and stuck out his hand. "Jordan Hamilton. Why don't we spend the time getting acquainted while I prepare Lauren some hot tea?"

The grinning woman extended her right hand and placed her left over her heart. "A man at home in the kitchen. Good lord, if she doesn't want you, I do."

Jordan chuckled. "I should probably know your name first."

"Sonja Adams, and if you don't stop smiling at me like that, I may faint right here on this floor, and then where would you be, trying to pick me up?"

"Faint, and we'll find out."

Sonja hooted. "Whatever blew you into Lauren's life was a blessing. Come on, I'll show you where things are kept."

"Mama, I waited up for you!" cried the pajama-clad little boy from the bed as he tossed the book in his hands aside.

"I know, Sweetheart. Mama's sorry she's late." Sitting on the side of the bed, she pulled Joshua's warm, little body against hers. He felt good and smelled better. She loved him so much, this child that had been the salvation of her sanity, giving her a reason to go on living.

Leaning away, she studied his smiling face. His dark brown eyes with lashes as thick as hers were clear and bright. "Feeling better, I see?"

The smile disappeared from his cherubic face. "Yes, Ma'am, but it might come back."

Lauren smiled despite her worry. Her worry wasn't about the stomachache, but the reason behind it. "It might not, either. Now, which story should I read you?"

"The one about the boy's father taking him to get his hair cut," Joshua said, handing her the hardcover book. "Daddies do all sorts of things."

Lauren took the book with hands that were not quite steady. "Mommies can do all those things daddies do. I take you to the barber shop."

"But you can't sit in the chair like the daddy does in the story," Joshua said reasonably.

Lauren had to smile at his reasoning and logic. Leave it to her precocious son to think of something like that. "Not unless you want a baldheaded mother."

He giggled. "You're funny, Mama."

"I am, am I? Well, let's see how funny." She reached for him. He was already squealing and laughing. The lightest touches of her fingertips set him off. By the time she finished tickling him, the bedclothes were tangled and they were both breathing loudly.

Eye to eye, she smiled at her son. "I love you, Joshua, and I'll always be here for you."

The smile faded from his face. He scooted closer, but he didn't say anything. Her eyes stinging, Lauren hugged him to her. She wasn't enough. It hurt, Lord, how it hurt.

Listening to his small voice moments later saying his prayers as he once again asked for a daddy was almost more than she could bear. By the time he finished, her throat ached, her eyes stung.

Finding the book among the tangled covers, she opened to the first page. She was glad she knew his favorite story by heart, because her vision soon became so blurred with tears she didn't dare shed that she couldn't see a thing. What do you do when love isn't enough?

There was no answer, only the steady drone of her voice. Swallowing the lump in her throat, she continued until the last page. Slowly, she got out of bed and straightened the covers over her sleeping son. He looked so peaceful and beautiful.

Pride and love, and yes, worry, warred within her. Her little boy was growing up, but he was having a difficult time doing it.

She bit her lips. He was changing before her eyes, and there didn't seem to be anything she could do. Everything had been going perfectly until his elementary school started having so many family functions.

At first, he hadn't seemed to mind or notice. Later, when the classes began to receive ice-cream or pizza parties for the most family members in attendance, and the school posted each classes' sign in sheet, things began to change.

All she could do was keep on telling him how much she loved him, and hope that eventually it would be enough.

In the meantime, he wanted to be like the other kids in his class, like his friends on his T-ball team, but he couldn't. Because the family he wanted wasn't possible. A father. An extended family with cousins to play with, aunts and uncles to hug, grandparents to spoil him.

He didn't understand why it was just the two of them.

The cruel truth she could never tell him was that he did have other family members, but they had made it clear before his birth that they wanted nothing to do with her. She didn't mind for herself, but she did for her son. She'd never forgive her in-laws for their deliberate cruelty or the constant threat they imposed.

Lauren lived in constant fear that they would somehow find her and take Joshua away. Not out of love, but out of hatred and spite. So she lived a quiet life with few friends. Friends asked questions, shared lives. She couldn't. Joshua suffered because of a past he knew nothing about which threatened him nonetheless.

She touched his smooth cheek. She'd endure the tortures of Hell before she'd let her in-laws take him. Somehow she and Joshua would get through this difficult period.

She had been so proud when his academic achievements exceeded his age. Now she sometimes wished he hadn't tested two grade levels ahead. The older he became, the more serious he grew—and lately, the more manipulative.

Tonight it had been a stomachache, the night before it was a headache, the day before it was his leg. His pediatrician said he was physically fine. Emotionally, he just needed continued love and understanding until he realized that not having a father didn't make him any different from other children who did.

"I'll always love you, Sweetheart, and I'll always be here for you."

Laughter, one deep and obviously male, the other flirtatious and female, floated from the other end of the house.

She had left Jordan without a word, but from the sound of things, neither he nor Sonja missed Lauren very much. She grimaced again at her unfair thought. She was really feeling sorry for herself tonight.

Jordan had taken care of her when she fell apart at the hotel, then made sure she reached home safely. If she didn't have Sonja to watch over Joshua after school or when she had to work late, Lauren didn't know what she would do. Sonja was a notorious flirt who liked to pretend she could put any Southern belle to shame, but she was also her best friend.

Lauren needed a friend, but not the unnerving presence of her other guest.

Kissing Joshua, she rose and went back into the kitchen. Jordan and Sonja were sitting at the small kitchen table. She would have sworn she hadn't made a sound, but Jordan glanced around.

Once again she was struck by the intensity of his dark eyes. She shivered. This time she knew it wasn't from cold.

He stood. "How's Joshua?"

"He's fine. Sorry I rushed off like that." She wished he'd sit back down. He seemed to dominate her tiny kitchen. And her.

"I hate to leave good company, especially when it's so goodlooking, but I have to be going," Sonja said.

"Thanks, Sonja," Lauren said. "I don't know what I'd do without you."

"You know how much I enjoy keeping Joshua. Besides, it keeps me in practice for when I'm snapped up by some smart man."

"Don't forget lucky," Jordan said as he reached over and held the back of her chair.

Halfway out of her chair, Sonja shook her tinted auburn head in disbelief, her pretty, mocha-colored face animated. "If you have a brother or cousin, please send one of them my way."

"Just a cousin, and I don't think he's ready for a woman like you," Jordan told her with a smile.

Her long lashes fluttered. "I'll be gentle."

"I'll keep that in mind." Jordan thought of his serious cousin, Drake. "In the meantime, I didn't see a car outside. If Ms. Bennett doesn't mind, I can drive you home in her car."

"Of course I wouldn't," Lauren said, half-wishing she could be as self-assured talking and laughing with Jordan.

"No need." Sonja went to the hall closet and put on a stylish, red trenchcoat and matching hat. "I just live across the street. By the time you back the car out I'll be home."

Lauren followed the other woman to the back door. "Signal when you get home."

"I will," she said, then went down the steps. At the garage door she looked back over her shoulder and inclined her head toward Laura. "That one may be a ten-plus and a Keeper."

Jordan chuckled from close behind her, and Lauren wanted to stuff a sock in both of their mouths. Keeper, indeed. As soon as hospitably possible, she was sending Jordan on his way.

Lauren watched Sonja go into her house. The porch lights blinked twice moments later. Punching the button, Lauren watched the garage door go down. After it shut she closed and lock the door.

Almost immediately the phone rang. Picking up the receiver, she said, "All clear," then hung up.

"You two have quite a system worked out. I'm impressed."

Lauren folded her arms across her chest, not liking at all the way her heart fluttered every time he looked at her. "That we can take care of ourselves?"

"No. A woman has to be cautious in today's society. But to do it even when the likelihood of someone being out in a storm like this is commendable," he explained.

"I never take chances," she said, aware from the slight arch of his brow that they had gone beyond talking about safety measures.

"I hope you'll take one more." He walked over to the counter and picked up her teapot. "Sonja only showed me where things were. I steeped it myself."

She was tempted in spite of herself. How did the man know she liked to relax after a hectic day with a cup of tea? When she didn't move, he poured her a cup, added a half-teaspoon of sugar, and brought it to her.

"I'll try not to be offended if you don't like it."

"Mr. Ham—"

"It's Jordan, and drink your tea first. Then you can say whatever is on your mind."

She took the cup and headed toward the kitchen table. She wanted this formality over as quickly as possible.

Jordan had other ideas. Strong yet gentle fingers caught her free arm and steered her toward the sofa. Glaring up at him did little good.

He smiled. "I think you'll be more comfortable on the sofa."

"Next you'll be telling me to put my feet up," she said, and sat down.

"Actually, I was thinking of offering you a foot massage."

Lauren blinked, her gaze automatically going to his big, capable looking hands. Suddenly she realized she had been in her shoes for over twelve hours. It would feel so good to free them, to have his hands. . . .

She ducked her head. Thinking about his hands was exactly the sort of thing she was trying to avoid. She'd drink the tea and say good-night.

The first sip was delicious. The warmth curled through her

like a lazy sunrise. She sighed without knowing it, took another sip, leaned back in her chair, and closed her eyes.

Which was a mistake. The moment she became still again her body remembered her tired she was, how little sleep she had gotten the night before.

"Lauren, go lie down. I'll call a cab and let myself out through the garage door."

Her sliding body jerked back up again. "No, I'm fine. Really."

"You're falling asleep on the couch. The rain and the whiskey I gave you aren't helping." Taking the cup from her hand, he took it to the sink. "Go check on Joshua again and lie down. I can call a cab."

"I can't leave you alone in my house." she told him.

Dark eyes narrowed. "Are you saying you don't trust me?"

"Of course not." She came to her feet. "I let you drive my car, didn't I?"

The tilted corner of his mouth said he remembered her letting him do more than that. "You were very generous."

Lauren sucked in her breath at the thinly veiled innuendo. In the blink of an eye, he had gone from practical to seductive.

"If you want to continue your generosity and stay with me until the cab gets here, which could take a long time in this weather, I'm sure we can think of something to do to pass the time."

It was a threat. One blatant and boldly suggestive. Her traitorous mind fell into his trap by conjuring up a picture of her in his arms, his mouth as wicked as his hands on her body. Her breasts tingled. "Don't think I don't know what you're doing."

"I never thought for a minute you didn't," he said easily.

He wasn't backing down, but then a pirate wouldn't. Opening a door beneath the counter, she pulled out the yellow pages of the phone book. Retreat was definitely in order. "I'll check on Joshua."

"I'll call a cab."

Turning, she left the room, wondering if that twitch on his indecent lips was his attempt not to smile. The man had a sense of humor, a wicked smile, a sexy laugh, and a body to drool over. He might be a 'ten-plus and a keeper' as Sonja put it, but he was also definitely Trouble with a capital T.

"Are you the one who's gonna be my daddy?"

The sound more than the words roused Jordan from sleep. His eyes blinked open to find an inquisitive, small, brown face almost nose to nose with his.

"Mister, are you the one?"

The whispered urgency of the voice sapped all the drowsiness from Jordan. He hadn't stayed to make sure Lauren and Joshua were all right during the storm to be caught off guard. He uncoiled from his reclining position on the sofa, both hands wrapped around Joshua's slim upper arms to keep their heads from bumping. The boy's eyes widened.

"It's all right, Son. I won't hurt you. I'm a friend of your mother's," Jordan explained quickly. He seemed to have a knack for frightening members of the Bennett family. "Is something the matter with your mother?"

The burgeoning smile on the little boy's face died. "You came for my Mama?"

Jordan frowned at the strange phrasing, then attributed it to Joshua's young age. "Yes, I came home with your mother last night."

Shoulders slumped in his teddy bear print pajamas. He tucked his head. "Oh."

The boy's disappointment with Jordan's answer was obvious. What did a man have to do to make someone in this family smile? Jordan glanced down the narrow hallway leading to the bedrooms.

Empty. Lauren was too protective of her son not to be with him when he met a man she didn't quite trust for the first time. "Your mother's still asleep, huh?"

"Yes, Sir. I'd like to watch television, if it's all right?" he asked politely, staring at his feet.

"Sorry." Jordan released the boy, his puzzlement growing. He'd bet his portfolio that finding strange men asleep in the den wasn't a common occurrence for the somber little boy walking across the room, the ears of his pink bunny rabbit slippers flopping with each step. "Nice slippers."

"Thank you." Remote in hand, Joshua cut on the TV, clicked a couple of times until a cartoon appeared, then sat on the round, Oriental design area rug on the hardwood floor.

Swinging his feet to the floor, Jordan leaned back against the overstuffed cushions and studied the well-mannered yet distant little boy. Jordan's nephew and nieces were a noisy bunch. Sometimes it seemed as if there were thirteen instead of three of them. One was always talking or yelling. It was odd to see a child so self-contained.

A commercial came on and Jordan expected the boy to do what his nieces and nephew did—channel surf. Again he was surprised, when Joshua leaned forward instead, his fascination and interest obvious.

Smiling, Jordan reached into the inside pocket of his suit jacket. *Gotcha!*

Chapter Seven

Lauren woke from one minute to the next. Two things occurred to her simultaneously. She had fallen asleep in Joshua's bed last night, and she had left her company's foremost client alone in her den. The first wasn't unusual, the second had been rude and inhospitable. The trouble was, she wasn't sure if she had unconsciously fallen asleep or not.

Jordan Hamilton bothered her in the most elemental ways a man can bother a woman. And all her learned defenses weren't working.

Men had been trying to pick her up since she turned thirteen. She had developed early, and so had boys' interest. Even while she was pregnant with Joshua, men had still been after her. She'd had sense enough to know it wasn't her they wanted. They figured if she had done it once, she'd do it again. So she had developed 'The look'—total indifference with icicles dripping off the side.

It had worked. Until Jordan.

He was so sure of himself he probably thought the look was meant for everyone except him. The trouble was, she didn't know if he was far off target. The man shook her up, but he intrigued her, too. It had been a long time since a man had managed to do either.

Groaning, Lauren put her arm up over her head. The action wasn't so much to protect her eyes from the narrow band of sunlight that had managed to sneak in through the animal print curtains as it was a protest against her own foolishness. She had kept men at bay for six years. Then Jordan Hamilton showed up, and she went all gushy inside.

Throwing off her arm, she smiled. Gushy. Definitely a word from Joshua's vocabulary. Sighing, she sat up in the twin bed. She didn't have to worry about Joshua. She knew she'd find him overdosing on cartoons in front of the TV. He had purposely closed the bedroom door to insure more time.

On a school day, he'd still be snuggled under the covers— stubborn as a mule and as slippery as an eel. He, like most children, had a sixth sense when it came to Saturdays.

Getting out of bed, she opened the door and started down the hall. The sound of laughter knitted her brow. The tone wasn't high-pitched enough for cartoon characters. Then, she heard a distinct male voice. Her body identified the voice before the sound died. She didn't waste time trying to figure out why Jordan Hamilton was still in her home. She was going straight to the source.

As soon as she turned the corner of the short hallway she saw them, two dark heads almost touching. The trouble was, Jordan saw her, too. His dark gaze touched her, boldly running the length of her as if he had every right to do so.

Although she knew everything was hidden by the baggy jogging suit she had changed into after she left him last night, she had the irrational urge to check and see if everything was covered. Because Jordan was calmly peeling the layers away.

Even with her standing there in faded gray sweats and her hair a tangled mess, he was staring at her as if she was a banquet and he hadn't eaten for days. And even knowing it was all an act, she couldn't quite dismiss the answering awareness that curled its way through her.

She had been right in her first estimation of him. He was dangerous. A pirate in a suit. He didn't go by civilized rules.

He made up his own as he went along. A man like that wouldn't stop until he knew everything about a woman. She wanted him gone. Now.

"What happened to the taxi?" she demanded.

"Mama!" cried Joshua as soon he saw her. With a wild scramble, he climbed across Jordan's lap as if he had done it a hundred times and ran to her. "Look what I have."

Forgetting Jordan for the moment, she smiled at her son. "Good morning, Sweetheart." Bending down, she greeted him the way she did every morning—with a hug, a kiss, and a silent prayer of thanks.

Over his shoulder, she glanced toward Jordan. He remained in an indulgent pose, his back against the couch, his forearm propped on his updrawn knee. The other arm rested on the seat cushions.

He should have looked as rumpled as she felt after sleeping on the small couch.

He didn't.

The power in his long, muscled legs beneath the tailored slacks was clearly visible. The few wrinkles in his white shirt only added to his untamed appearance. The cuffs were rolled, the three top buttons were undone. His chest was almost as hairy as his face. Out of nowhere she remembered the unexpected softness of his beard against her skin, and how utterly arousing it had felt.

Heat pooled in her cheeks. She pulled her attention back to her son, to see him punching a series of buttons.

"See, I put my name in here, and it will stay forever."

A moment of unease swept through her. She forced herself to take a breath before she spoke. "What else did you put in there?"

His eyes never left the screen. "My phone number. See?"

Her unlisted number appeared on the screen. With a press of a button it disappeared.

"Mama," he wailed. "You pushed the wrong button. Now I'll have to put it back."

"Sorry," she said, and gently took the electronic organizer out of his hands. She stood, not even trying to hide her anger.

"You can wait outside for the taxi."

The quick flash of anger on Jordan's bearded face surprised her—it rose, sudden and fierce as a summer storm. "Joshua, what were we doing before your mother came in?"

The little boy looked from one to the other. "Playing a game."

"Who told you to put in your phone number?"

Joshua's head fell. "Nobody."

"These things aren't easy to work," Lauren said. "He couldn't have just picked it up." The implication was clear that he had somehow tricked Joshua into putting in the number.

"You have a bright son. I had to make a call and I showed him how to retrieve a number. He asked me how to put one in. The number I put in was a bogus one. If you'd like, I can show you." In one effortless motion, Jordan came to his imposing height of six-foot-three. "If you'll hand it back I will remove your number from the backup memory."

"I didn't mean to do anything wrong," Joshua said, his voice unhappy. He glanced up briefly at Jordan. "I just wanted you to be able to call me. If . . . if you wanted to."

"You didn't, Joshua. Your mother is upset with me, not you."

Lauren felt like a fool. She had insulted a guest in her house and made her son feel bad. She had stormed into this herself, and she had to get herself out.

On bended knees she faced her son. His continued refusal to look at her tore at her heart. Unsteady fingers lifted his chin. Gloomy eyes stared back at her. His lower lip was clamped between his teeth. He was near tears, and it was all her fault.

"Joshua, Mr. Hamilton is right. You did nothing wrong. This is Mama's fault, for saying things that I shouldn't have." The teeth remained firmly clamped. "You won't see Mr. Hamilton after today, so you see, there is no need for him to have your phone number."

"But I like him, Mama."

There was not going to be an easy way out of this. "I can see that you do, Sweetheart, but Mr. Hamilton is a client where

I work, and it's best if we don't see or talk to him if it's not connected to my job.''

"You mean Mr. Scott would get mad at you?"

"No, Honey, Mr. Scott wouldn't get mad."

"Then why?"

Lauren looked into her child's face and wondered if she had been wrong to teach him to ask questions until he got an answer he understood. She turned over several explanations, none of them suitable for a five-year-old or the big-eared adult behind her.

He makes me want things I can't have. He makes me remember how it feels to be desired.

"Why, Mama?" Joshua repeated.

"Sometimes we don't get along," she answered truthfully.

"But you always said I should try to get along with everyone," Joshua reminded her.

He had her there. There was no rational way out of this. But then, the way Jordan Hamilton made her feel wasn't rational. "I don't trust him."

"He's not a thief or anything, Mama," Joshua said loudly. "I checked when I found him on the couch sleeping. I thought he was the one, but he wasn't. But he's pretty neat, anyway."

Lauren's mind caught on the word "thief" and "checked." "You did what?"

"Joshua isn't any more trusting than his mother." Jordan walked over to them. "When he found me on the sofa, he thought I was a thief until he saw that I didn't have any loot and the front door was still locked."

All Lauren could think of was that if it had been a real burglar Joshua might have gotten hurt. "If there is ever a stranger in the house or in the yard, you come and tell me."

The smile faded from his little face. "Yes, Ma'am. That's what Jordan told me."

"Mr. Hamilton," she corrected automatically.

"If I call him Mr. Hamilton, and you know he won't take anything, can he stay for breakfast?"

That's the problem. He's already taken my peace of mind, Lauren thought. Leaning back on her heels she stared up at

Jordan. It was a long way to his glittering, black eyes. He wasn't giving an inch. She had to take him as he was, and no apologies.

"Mr. Hamilton is in town for business. I'm sure he has other plans once the taxi picks him up."

Jordan arched a dark brow. "You definitely have a one-track mind, Ms. Bennett."

"I'm not the only one," she shot back.

"Point taken."

Her brown eyes widened at his admission. The doorbell rang. "I believe that may be for me."

Jordan started for the front door, annoyed at the surprise, then relief, in Lauren's face. She'd be happy to see the last of him. He had no intention of granting her wish, just as last night he'd had no intention of leaving her alone with a small child during a severe thunderstorm. Especially after Lauren had been so upset at the hotel. She had a lot to learn about him, and one of the lessons was that he didn't take no for an answer.

Lauren thought all he wanted to do was get her into bed. He couldn't fault her on that, because the suspicious lady would be on target if the other problem didn't take precedence. He had to find out if Lauren Bennett could help them get Strickland.

Inches from the door, Lauren stepped around Jordan. "This is my house." Opening the door, she barely caught back a groan.

Both hands flew up as she tried to subdue her wild tangle of curly hair. There was no help for the way she was dressed, but at least her boss could only see her from waist up, due to the screened half door.

"Good morning, Mr. Scott. I wasn't expecting you."

Intent eyes studied her closely before speaking. "Good morning, Lauren. You're all right."

At his worried tone, her hands stopped trying to bring some order to her hair. "Of course. Why wouldn't . . ." Her voice trailed off as she watched his gaze travel beyond her. She wanted to sink into the floor in embarrassment. "I can explain."

"There's nothing to explain," Jordan said, coming up to stand beside Lauren. "Isn't that right, Benjamin?"

Lauren almost flinched at Jordan's cold voice. She looked back at her boss, and saw that he wasn't cowed a bit.

Through his thick trifocals he was glaring back at Jordan. His chest puffed out, stretching his mauve-colored polo shirt across his wide girth. "I trust Lauren implicitly."

"Good," Jordan said. "Now that that's settled, do we shake hands or go around to the back of the house?"

Benjamin grinned sheepishly. "I guess I deserved that."

"I guess I did, too." Jordan opened the screen door and stepped onto the porch to shake the older man's hand.

After a firm handshake, Benjamin handed Jordan a set of car keys. "You were right about the hotel, by the way. They didn't even want to let me into your room to get your keys until you reminded them of last night."

"They're lucky that's all I said." Jordan shoved the keys into his pocket. "Thanks for helping out. I think Ms. Bennett was beginning to feel stuck with me after finding me on her sofa this morning."

"I was the one who found you asleep on the couch," Joshua corrected, having squeezed his way out the door to stand by Jordan. "But he didn't take anything."

"What?" Benjamin looked at the other two adults for clarification.

Lauren wanted to melt into the floor again. Jordan smiled down at Joshua, then glanced at Benjamin. "An inside joke."

"I see," Benjamin mumbled. It was obvious he didn't.

"Thank you. Hope this doesn't make you late teeing off," Jordan commented.

"Nope. Clubs are in Ed's car. Luckily, the worst of the storm missed the golf course." He leaned closer. "Lauren, I've got a feeling I'm going to skunk him good today."

Benjamin's rivalry with his older brother was legendary. So were his losses. She gave him an encouraging smile. "Good luck, Mr. Scott."

"I'm sure we can find you a partner, Jordan, if you care to join us," Benjamin invited.

"Thanks. Maybe another time."

"I guess I'll be going. Good day." With a brief nod, Benja-

min went back down the steps and got into the passenger seat
of the Cadillac parked behind a huge, black, expensive-looking
European car. The man in the driver's seat waved and pulled
off.

Lauren watched the car until it disappeared. Jordan had a
car, and there was no reason for him to linger any longer.

As if reading her mind, he said, "I'll get my coat and be on
my way." Reentering the house, Jordan started for the den.

With a last look at his mother, Joshua followed. Jordan was
going to leave, but the happiness she expected didn't come. It
wasn't difficult to figure out why.

Jordan had been nothing but kind to her. True, he got to her
faster than the speed of sound, but he had never stepped out
of bounds. If things were different, she would feel flattered by
his attention instead of feeling like she was teetering on the
brink of disaster.

The two males came back into the living room together.
Jordan had his coat thrown over his arm. "May I have my
organizer back, please?"

She pulled the electronic device out of her pocket, where
she had stuck it when she went to answer the door. "The call
you made earlier was to Benjamin."

"Yes."

"It seems I owe you an apology, too." She took a deep
breath and plunged ahead. "What would you like for breakfast?
Pancakes, waffles, or French toast?"

"Waffles. Waffles," Joshua cried.

"How about all three?" Jordan asked.

"What?" she cried.

Jordan smiled at the look of incredulity on her beautiful
brown face. "Let's eat out. It's the least I can do for disrupting
your Saturday."

"Can we, Mama, can we?" Joshua was jumping from foot
to foot in glee.

Joshua needed this day. Maybe she did, too. But Jordan
definitely needed to be taken in small doses. "I have a lot to
do today. Tomorrow after church would be better."

"I wanna go today," Joshua whined.

"Tomorrow, Joshua, and if we don't get everything done today, we might not go tomorrow," Lauren informed her son. "You know what you have to do. As soon as I say good-bye to Mr. Hamilton I'll start breakfast."

"Waffles?" he asked.

She smiled at his hopeful expression. She made them from scratch. Some things mommies did do better. "Depends on how fast you get going."

He took off in a flash, only to stop at the door leading to the hallway and turn around. "Bye, Mr. Hamilton."

"Good bye, Joshua."

"You won't forget, will you?"

"No. I always keep my word."

"Bye." Joshua disappeared around the corner.

"I take it he likes eating out." Jordan smiled indulgently, his eyes crinkling at the corner.

Lauren folded her arms over her chest. "I think he likes you more, and I don't want him hurt."

Jordan sobered. "I wouldn't do that."

"Not intentionally, but just don't make any promises you can't keep. You're in town for the weekend, then you'll be gone from his life permanently."

"Are you afraid for Joshua, or yourself?"

She didn't back away from the question. "Both."

"Then it looks like I've got my work cut out for me."

Lauren's arms came to her sides. "Why are you doing this?"

"I told you I'd like to get to know you better."

"Why?"

"Neither you or your son take things at face value, do you?"

"It saves being hurt in the long run," she answered. Her in-laws had taught her well.

Jordan's gaze sharpened. "It's not my intention to hurt you."

"Just what is your intention?" she questioned.

At another time it would have been to see her first thing in the morning with her curly hair more mussed than it was now, thanks to his fingers. Instead of the suspicion in her soulful brown eyes, there would be a lazy, sensual satisfaction from a long night of good loving.

"Jordan," she urged impatiently.

Satisfaction curled though his voice. "Saying my first name wasn't so difficult, was it?"

"It slipped out," she admitted.

His sensual gaze swept over her. "I can only hope you make other slips."

Her body heated before she had time to control the reaction. Her fingers clutched unnecessarily at the neck of her jogging suit. "Nothing else is slipping."

He chuckled, a deep sound that did as much damage to her nerve endings as his gaze had earlier. "You really know how to wound a guy."

"Mama, come on, or we won't get finished."

Lauren glanced around to see Joshua with his bedsheets dangling from his arms. "I'm coming."

"I'd better be going." Jordan opened the screen door. "What time shall I pick you up tomorrow?"

"Eleven, I guess." She bit her lower lip.

"Don't lose courage, now. I promise to be on my best behavior. Good bye, Lauren." He glanced over her shoulder. "See you tomorrow, Joshua."

"Bye, Mr. Hamilton."

Lauren watched his long legs carry him swiftly down her walk to the waiting car. It didn't escape her that he hadn't fully answered her question, or that she was already anticipating seeing him again.

Sighing, she closed the door.

Chapter Eight

After checking his rearview mirror, Jordan pulled away from the curb. Before the Infiniti had gone two full revolutions, he was punching out a number on the rental car's phone. He needed some answers, and fast. There was only one person he trusted to obtain both.

An out-of-breath masculine voice answered on the fifth ring. "Yeah."

"Drake, you left something out of your report," Jordan said without preamble. They had been together too long to stand on formalities.

"We both know we were lucky to get what we have. If you hadn't sent me to Fayetteville to check on rumors that your vice-president was spending twice as much as he was making, I might not have heard of Dillon, South Carolina, and its quickie marriages," Drake commented.

"So you captured a thief and found our missing lady at the same time," Jordan said, his voice tightening.

"Hey, man, you can't put her in the same category with that thief Forster, or Strickland, either. She's as much a victim in this as anyone else," Drake said, his voice worried.

Jordan bumped a stop sign, then took a right onto the main

thoroughfare. He could almost picture his brawny cousin with a towel wrapped around his twenty-inch neck while he straddled his exercise bench, the phone lost in his huge hand. But he was one of the gentlest people Jordan knew.

Most people were awed by Drake Lansing's size and build; Jordan was attracted to his analytical mind. Drake, like Jordan, had used his size and athletic abilities to get a college education.

Drake now used his size and his mind to ferret out information for Jordan. There weren't many people who didn't have second thoughts about lying to two hundred and sixty pounds of solid muscle on a six-foot-six frame, or many computers that could keep their secrets from Drake, either.

"I know," Jordan finally said. "Forster will be spending the next ten years behind prison walls. Strickland will be joining him soon. For Lauren, I plan a much different future."

The worry increased in Drake's deep, Southern drawl. "Man, you aren't going to do anything foolish like fall for the woman, are you? I've seen you get that intense expression on your face while looking at her pictures."

"You have an overactive imagination." Jordan passed a slow moving truck.

"And it's usually right. That's why you pay me such a high salary," Drake shot back.

"Earn it by digging deeper into Lauren's background. I want to know why she was scared out of her mind when the hotel elevator got stuck last night."

"That would scare most women."

"Not like she was." Jordan would never forget the fear in her eyes as long as he lived.

"It could have something to do with her childhood, and not connected at all with what you're after," Drake reasoned.

"I have a hunch it's not."

"I guess that settles it, then. Your hunches are almost as good as mine. Looks like I'm going to be busy for a while. Where can I reach you?"

"Four Seasons in Shreveport. And Drake—"

"Yeah, I know. You want this yesterday. I'll check in tomorrow and let you know my base."

"Thanks. I knew I could count on you."

"You just watch yourself. I've got one of my feelings about this one."

"I can handle things. Don't worry." Jordan disconnected the call, wishing he felt as confident as he sounded.

Lauren wasn't going to be too pleased to learn that he had begun his pursuit of her for ulterior motives. In fact, she would be spitting mad if she thought for one second Jordan was using her or her son.

Jordan twisted uneasily in the car's soft leather upholstery. What had seemed like a good idea six weeks ago was starting to leave a bad taste in his mouth. He had foolishly looked at the photos of her and thought he had everything figured out . . . until he actually saw her, saw the fear in her eyes that seemed to be hidden from everyone else.

Drake had been right about the pictures, too. Two of them Jordan had studied at length. The first one unerringly captured the mixture of wonder and excitement on Lauren's face at the exact moment she had sent a softball deep into left field.

The next photo was of her looking over her shoulder in a pose that he thought of as saucy and *provocative.* He had been more than a little surprised to learn from the report that Lauren had been looking at *her son* instead of a man.

He'd been even more surprised to learn that she had struck out the other two times at bat. When she came to the plate, her company's team had groaned, the other side applauded. She had two strikes against her when she hit the line drive.

Jordan had understood her smile, her feeling of triumph. Lauren Bennett wasn't a quitter. She hung in there. But six years ago she had run.

She was still running. It was as if the woman in the pictures was another person. That fear angered him more than anything.

Nathan Strickland, the man Jordan was after, was a ruthless, unprincipled bastard. As far as Jordan knew he had never resorted to physical violence, but he could make your life miserable with his considerable wealth.

Jordan's hands clenched the steering wheel. He and his family had experienced firsthand the underhanded, dirty tricks

Strickland used to get what he wanted. Proving it was another matter. Lauren Bennett was the key.

If she helped him, she'd never have to be afraid again. He'd take care of her and Joshua. It was obvious she didn't trust people. Knowing her connection to Strickland, he didn't blame her, but somehow he had to get through to her.

She had dropped her guard enough to go out with him. At least he now had a chance. All he had to do was move slowly and keep his mind off her delectable body. That was one line he couldn't step over. It was going to be difficult enough to explain things to her when the time was right without being sexually involved.

To a woman like Lauren Bennett that would be the ultimate betrayal. She'd never forgive him.

He wasn't sure he could forgive himself.

"Are you sure he's coming back?"

"Yes, Joshua"

"You don't think he forgot, do you?"

"No, Sweetheart."

"What time is it?"

"Ten fifty four."

"He wouldn't forget would he, Mama?"

"No, Honey. He'll be here."

"You think he forgot where we live?"

"No, Joshua." Sitting on the sofa in the living room on Sunday morning, Lauren patiently answered Joshua's question and waited for the next one. The answers were as much a reassurance to her as they were to her son. She didn't want to believe she had made a mistake in agreeing to go out with Jordan.

Jordan was a very important man. Crescent Communications had branches scattered across the United States. Something could have come up. Thanks to her overreacting about her phone number, he had no way to get in touch with her. Not a comforting thought.

"What time is it now, Mama?" His nose buried against the

glass, the sheer curtain billowing behind him, Joshua continued his vigil.

"Ten fifty six," she answered. *Jordan, please don't stand him up.*

Joshua had been so proud of this outing. He had told anyone who would listen about his new 'friend' the moment they arrived at Sunday School. For once he hadn't minded his little red bow tie or red suspenders. He still wore them, with a white shirt and navy blue slacks.

Lauren hated to admit it, but she had spent some moments trying to decide what to wear herself. While anything would be an improvement over the way she'd looked when he last saw her, she didn't want to overdo it. This wasn't a true date, more like an outing. She had settled on a buttery gold dress with short sleeves.

Unobtrusively, she glanced at her watch. Ten fifty-nine. There was the distinct possibility neither of them should have bothered.

"Can I go outside on the porch and wait?" Joshua asked, his face unhappy. "I can see to the end of the street from there."

Jordan, if you stand him up I'll—The blast of a car horn interrupted her thoughts of carving her initials in Jordan's hide.

"It's Mr. Hamilton, Mama! He's back!" Joshua tore out of the house at full speed, the screen door slamming behind him.

By the time Jordan opened his car door, Joshua was standing by the driveway. "I thought you'd never get back."

"Sorry. I won't cut it so close next time." Jordan handed the little boy a blue gift bag decorated with balloons and streamers. "Maybe this will make up for things."

"Wow!" Joshua tore into the bag, pulling out the paper and colorful, shredded ribbon. His brown eyes widened. "It's like yours."

"Not quite. I doubt you'll need as many functions or as much memory as I do. Yet." Hunkering down to eye level, Jordan said. "Press f-r-i-e-n-d and see what happens."

Joshua's fingers quickly did as directed. Jordan's name, address and phone number appeared.

"Now, you don't have to wait for me to call. You can call me."

"Wow!" the child repeated and turned back to his mother, who stood a few feet behind him. He held up the pocket organizer for her inspection. "Mama, look."

Her hand rested on her son's shoulder. "Mr. Hamilton, you should have asked me first."

"I thought we had progressed to 'Jordan.' And you would have said no."

She chose to ignore the first statement and respond to the second. "We don't know you well enough to accept gifts."

Jordan glanced down at Joshua. "Then I'm glad I didn't ask. I made Joshua happy. I'm just wondering if I can put the same satisfied smile on his mother's face."

Startled, she gasped. "What?"

He grinned like the pirate he was, with a flash of teeth in his bearded face and enough charm to make any woman surrender her good sense. "I hope you'll be satisfied with everything I've planned."

Lauren wasn't sure if she liked the sound of that any more than the smile. "I'll let you know."

"Somehow I thought that would be your answer."

Almost two hours later Lauren was more than satisfied with Jordan's plans. The family restaurant he had chosen was located near the riverfront. The quaint, rustic, wooden structure was far enough away from the popular downtown casino to miss the bustle of the crowd even on a Sunday morning, but close enough for enjoyment of the view of the Red River. Most of all, Joshua was happy, and Jordan had been on his best behavior.

Lauren sipped her coffee while the two leaned against the wooden railing watching the boats go by. Both poses were identical: arms propped over the top railing, right foot crossed over left ankle. Joshua had long since discarded his bow tie and suspenders. She hadn't bothered to argue with him. Jordan wasn't wearing either, and that settled that.

He did look very good in his wheat-colored, raw silk jacket, beige shirt, and brown slacks. He wore his clothes with a careless elegance she liked. His primary concern appeared to be comfort. Style came second. He had the body and the looks to achieve both in whatever he wore.

To the casual observer, the tall, bearded man and the attentive little boy could have been father and son, like many in the crowded restaurant. Their hair and skin color were similiar. Both had dark eyes.

Joshua had certainly acted as if they shared a close relationship. He had hung onto Jordan's every word, ordered pancakes instead of waffles, and sat next to Jordan instead of her. She had to give it to Jordan—he hadn't seemed to mind. In fact, when she asked Joshua about his favorites Jordan had added them to both their orders. Just as he had not minded being dragged to see the boats.

Seeing the two side by side brought a smile to her lips and a pang to her heart. The cup rattled slightly as she put it down and looked away.

Joshua was plainly substituting Jordan for the father he wanted. Out of necessity, there weren't many male figures in his young life. His schoolteacher was female, his school principal was female, his Sunday School teacher was female.

The only other adult male he was around with any regularity was his T-ball coach. Mr. Henri was middle-aged with a receding hairline and a thick waist caused by his wife's Cajun/Creole cooking. The kids and parents loved him. He was nice, comfortable.

However, Mr. Henri didn't have the intensity or the charisma that Jordan possessed in abundance. Few men did. Neither did the photograph she had of Joshua's father.

It was virtually impossible for a five-year-old to remember and connect to a single black and white photo, no matter how often it was seen, when a man as imposing as Jordan was there in vibrant living color. While she understood, she still felt sadness in her son's joy.

Joshua's father would have loved him, cherished him, spoiled him. He would have done all the daddy things that Joshua wanted so much. But his father had never known of his existence. And because her in-laws hated her, she could never take their son home to make his father more real to him.

"Lauren, are you all right?"

Lauren glanced up and around. Jordan stared down at her with that probing intensity of his. He was too observant. She forced a smile. "I'm fine. Breakfast was wonderful, but we should be going."

"Ah, Mama. Mr. Hamilton said we could rent a boat if you said it was okay," Joshua moaned.

"I'm sorry, Sweetheart. We have things to do."

"But I did all my chores yesterday. I want to go on a boat ride," wailed Joshua, and he plopped into the seat across from her. His arm hit the plate, sending it crashing into his milk glass.

Jordan caught the glass before it spilled the contents. "Your mother said no, Joshua."

Her son seemed as surprised by the reprimand as she was. A small part of her was annoyed with Jordan for not letting her take care of things, another was disappointed that her son had behaved so badly.

"Yes, Sir."

Jordan took his seat and faced the little boy. "It's hard not getting things you want, but that's the way life is sometimes. Now, what do say we let your mother get her errands done? I bet she helped you lots of times when she had something she needed to do. I bet when you're sick, she takes good care of you when she could be doing something else."

Joshua looked at his mother a long time before he spoke, "She stayed at home with me when I had the chicken pox. She didn't fuss at me for making her miss work like Troy said his mother did. She even gave me all the red soda I wanted."

Bemused black eyes turned to Lauren. "Red soda?"

Her chin lifted. "He had a mild case since he had his immunization, but the red soda was supposed to make all the blisters pop out quicker."

"A home remedy, I take it." A grin tugged the corners of Jordan's sensual mouth. "Did it work?"

"He missed only three days of school." She didn't add that he became ill on a Friday and the Monday was a holiday.

Jordan nodded. "I'll have to remember and mention that to my sister for her brood."

"You have a sister?" Joshua questioned, his eyes intent.

"Yes. She's four years younger, and has three children. I call them The Wild Bunch, because they're so noisy and active."

"Gee, they're lucky. It's just me and Mama."

Once again Lauren felt inadequate. She wanted to reach across and touch her son, reassure him, but the table separated them. Casually she stood, picked up her purse with one hand, and curved the other hand around Joshua's shoulders.

"I think we'd better be going."

Jordan, who had come to his feet when she did, studied her briefly, then laid enough money on the table to cover the bill and the tip. "Let's go."

The three silent people leaving the restaurant in no way resembled the smiling, chatting trio who had entered.

Something was wrong. An idiot could see that by the way Lauren and Joshua were acting, but Jordan didn't know what or why. He cast a furtive glance at Lauren. Her hands were clamped around her purse and she stared out the window. Once she had made sure Joshua was safely buckled in in the back seat, she had assumed that position and hadn't moved since they left the restaurant.

Joshua was just as quiet. He hadn't asked one question.

Jordan couldn't believe everything had changed because the little boy had almost spilled his milk. He had seen more than his share of spills when he was around The Wild Bunch. He didn't have much of a basis to go on, but didn't mothers usually take that kind of thing as a given?

Especially loving ones, like Lauren. He couldn't imagine her getting upset and remaining that way over something so trivial.

Besides, she had seemed upset when he and Joshua returned

to the table. No, not upset. Unbearably sad. But was that sadness connected to her past, or some problem now?

He turned onto her street, a sinking feeling in his gut that she was going to politely thank him and say good-bye. The thought angered him. Something was bothering her, and he wanted to know what it was. He pulled into her driveway and cut the motor. He sat there for a moment, dreading the inevitable.

"Thank you, we had a wonderful time." She glanced over her shoulder at Joshua.

"Thank you, Mr. Hamilton," he said dutifully.

"You're both welcome." For the first time in his memory Jordan was at a loss for words.

With a wan smile, Lauren opened her door and got out. Having little choice, Jordan followed her and Joshua to the front porch. She opened the door and turned back to him.

"Well, good-bye, and thank you again," she said.

"Maybe we could see—"

"I think it's best if that didn't happen," she interrupted smoothly, and then ushered Joshua inside. Head bowed, he didn't resist.

"Lauren, talk to me. What changed at the restaurant?"

She glanced over her shoulder to see her son only a few feet away. "Go to your room, Joshua, and change clothes, I'm coming in a minute." She didn't turn back to Jordan until Joshua was out of sight.

"All right, Jordan, I guess you deserve a straight answer. Joshua is trying to substitute you for the father he's never known. He's . . . he's having some problems, and your presence can only add to them."

So that was it. Her reply answered some questions and posed more. "I disagree. My being around him would be the best thing that could happen to him now."

Lauren ran her hand through her hair in exasperation. "And when were you planning to be around? You're head of a major cooperation. You aren't going to have time for a little boy you hardly know."

Jordan's black eyes narrowed. "How do you know that,

Lauren? You're making all the decisions and passing judgment on me without giving me a chance.''

"I'm sorry if I sound critical and unfeeling, but Joshua's wellbeing is the most important thing in the world to me.'' Her gaze bounced off his well-defined features. "Getting ideas about you being a part of his life is the worst thing for him right now.''

"Are you sending me away to protect Joshua, or yourself?'' he asked.

She gasped, and her head came up sharply. Her brown eyes widened, then narrowed to pinpoints of fury. "Good bye, Mr. Hamilton. Have a safe trip home.''

Opening the door behind her, she walked inside and closed it with a final snap.

Chapter Nine

The click of the door closing somehow obliterated her anger as quickly as it had come. Closing her eyes, she fought the sudden stinging in her eyes. Was he right? Was she using Joshua as an excuse to hide from her growing awareness of Jordan?

She honestly didn't know. She did know Jordan Hamilton was out of their league. He might stick around for a little while, but then he'd get bored and leave. Leaving them both wishing for something that could never be. She had simply beaten him to the punch.

Knuckling her eyes, she plastered a smile on her face and went to Joshua's bedroom. He was what was important. She found him sitting on the bed.

He glanced up. He looked as sad as she felt.

"Mr. Hamilton's gone?"

She walked further into the tiny room she had lovingly decorated with whimsical, animal wallpaper and bright colors to make it cheery and happy. If only it were as easy to brighten up the life of a child.

"Yes, he has."

"We won't see him again, will we?" Joshua asked.

"No, Honey, I'm afraid not." She eased down beside him, her arm circling his waist.

"I'm sorry about the milk." Joshua stared at his black leather shoes.

Her hand cupped his chin and gently lifted until she could see his face. "I know. Why don't you get changed and start on your homework?"

"You mad at me?" He continued to stare at her with large, sorrowful eyes.

"Oh, Joshua. Of course not." She hugged him tightly to her, pleased when she felt him trying to hold her just as close. "I may not be pleased with the way you acted, but nothing could ever make me stop loving you. Nothing."

"I won't do it again, Mama," he promised, his voice a tiny whisper filled with sadness.

She swallowed the lump in her throat. Why did growing up have to be so hard? "I'm counting on you not to. Mr. Hamilton was right. Sometimes we can't have things we want."

"You don't think he's mad at me, do you?"

"No. He knew it was an accident."

"He was nice."

Lauren's smile was tremulous. "Yes, he was."

"You're nice too, Mama." Joshua hugged her tighter. "I love you better than anyone in the whole world."

"I love *you* better than anyone in the whole world," she said, fighting the stinging moisture in her eyes, not quite sure if she was crying for Joshua or herself, or both of them.

The phone rang. With a last hug, she stood. "Change clothes." Watching her son jump off the bed and go to his dresser at top speed, she whipped the last traces of moisture from her eyes.

You could always tell when a child was feeling better about something. They didn't walk. They ran.

An impatient ring reminded her that she had to answer the phone. Her steps quickened going to the kitchen. She plucked the wall phone in mid-ring. "Hello?"

"If you don't want him, I'll take him off your hands."

"Wha—Sonja? What are you talking about?" Lauren questioned, a frown working its way across the smoothness of her forehead.

"You tell me."

Sighing, Lauren leaned back against the counter and tossed her purse beside the toaster. Sonja was in one of her cryptic moods. But the conversation was weird even for her best friend. "Would you care to give me a hint as to what you're talking about?"

"A man."

"What man?"

"The one who makes you want to throw caution to the wind and run headlong into his arms . . . among other places."

Lauren straightened. "Jordan."

"Always knew you were smart. At least, about some things. Girl, what's the matter with you? Why would you get rid of a man who looks like that?" Sonja asked, the exasperation clear in her voice.

"It's for the best." Sonja must have seen Jordan bring them home and leave. "Continuing to see him would only make things more difficult for Joshua."

There was a long pause before Sonja said, "You're not going to see him anymore?"

The thought brought an unexpected pang of regret. "No, I'm not."

Her friend laughed in that distinctive way of hers that sounded like crystal wind chimes. "Then I suggest you don't go out on your porch any time soon."

"What are you talking about?"

"Apparently Jordan Hamilton doesn't take no for an answer as easily as some men."

"You mean . . ." Lauren's eyes widened as she took the phone as far as the cord would reach, which was still a foot from the doorway leading to the living room. No matter how she stretched or maneuvered, it wasn't enough. She hadn't wanted a longer cord because she was afraid Joshua might knock something over on the stove or counter and hurt himself.

Twisting the cord in her trembling hand, she straightened and tucked her lower lip between her teeth. "Are you sure?"

"Thirty-one is too young to be senile. Besides, what woman in her right mind could forget a man who looked like Jordan?" Sonja sighed. "That man is sin walking."

"It must be Jordan," Lauren mumbled, her gaze fixed on the open doorway leading to the living room.

"In the flesh. Now, go get him before he gets away."

The line went dead. Lauren looked at the receiver, then toward the front of the house. *Jordan, why didn't you leave? Why am I glad you didn't?*

She took one step, then another, until she was in the living room. Through her sheer ivory curtains she could dimly make out the outline of his black car. Hesitantly, she opened the door and stepped out onto the porch.

He sat on her small, wooden porch with his back to her, his head slightly bowed, his wrists resting on his upraised knees.

Although she knew he must have heard her, heard the creaking of the screen door she kept promising herself she would oil, he didn't turn. His utter stillness unnerved her. Jordan possessed a vitality that was almost a tangible force. Now it seemed . . . dim.

Nervousness turned to fear. "Jordan, what's the matter? Are you sick?"

"I'm sorry about the crack I made. I know you love Joshua more than anything." His deep, tantalizing voice that had teased, seduced, cajoled, comforted, sounded flat.

"Is that why you're still here—you wanted to apologize?"

"Partly."

He kept his back toward her, his shoulders slumped. There was a nasty virus that was going around Shreveport. Maybe he was sick. Tentatively, her hand touched his shoulder before she could caution herself not to.

She was unprepared for the gentleness and the warmth of his large hand as it closed over hers. Or the rightness and the longing.

Before Friday night she had thought she would never feel any of those emotions again. Six years was a long time to be alone. Yet, somehow she knew it wasn't the time span that had her body almost humming, it was something intrinsic in Jordan that made her respond to him and only him—the same way she instinctively sought to soothe whatever was bothering him by stroking his shoulder through his jacket. "What's the matter?"

"Where's Joshua? Is he all right?"

Now, she understood. Relief almost made her lightheaded. "He's fine. He's in his room doing his homework. He was worried that you might be upset with him. I see you had the same thought about him. You can leave with a clear conscience."

His hand clenched, his muscles bunched beneath her hand. "You don't know how I wish that was possible."

Lauren frowned at the top of his dark head. He was almost as mysterious as Sonja. She glanced across the street to the house almost identical to hers—except it was trimmed in gray instead of blue and had a wrought iron railing instead of wood— and knew her friend was probably watching. With Jordan holding Lauren's hand, Sonja was getting an eyeful.

"You can." Laura shrugged although she knew he couldn't see her. "I admit I was a little miffed that you corrected him at the table, but you did a good job. He likes you."

"What about you, Lauren?" Jordan asked and turned, his ebony eyes fixed on her.

Lauren sucked in her breath. Those eyes she remembered, hot piercing, all knowing. This was the reason their last conversation had ended so badly. She tried to withdraw her hand and found his strength equaled his gentleness.

"I won't hurt you. Stop before you hurt yourself!" he told her.

Lauren reacted automatically to the command in his voice, then berated herself for doing so. When would she ever stand up for herself? With as much dignity as possible she requested, "Please release my hand."

"I don't think so."

"What?"

"If I let you go, you'll go into the house and close the door on my face just like you did earlier. I don't want that to happen again. Please don't shut me out," he asked. "If you're not ready to tell me what's bothering you, I'll wait until you are."

Lauren was so surprised by his declaration she couldn't speak.

He grinned. "I think I just won my first argument with you." His face grew serious. "I want to be a friend to you and Joshua, if you'll let me. Surely there's room for one more friend in your lives?"

If he had badgered, she could have hardened her heart against him. Instead he used reasoning. She felt a growing need to banish the loneliness that was almost overwhelming her and her son. Both of them missed what they'd never had—a strong, caring man in their lives.

As if aware of her weakening, Jordan tugged lightly on her hand. "Come on, please sit down with me."

She sat, her hand still in his.

"You have a nice neighborhood," he said.

The switch in conversation was so far afield that she stared at him. "What?"

"You know you do that a lot," he teased gently. "I said I like your neighborhood."

She continued to look at him, trying to see if he was being condescending or flip, and realized Jordan Hamilton was neither of those things. He meant what he said.

There was true appreciation in his gaze as he glanced around. It *was* a good, stable neighborhood. The lawns were well tended, with mature oaks and magnolia trees, the houses either had brick or metal siding, and cars were in one or two car garages and not on the street.

"Thanks, but it's not what you're used to." She and her neighborhood were both nowhere in his class.

He lifted a heavy brow. "Why, Lauren Bennett, I do believe I heard some reverse prejudice in your voice."

Because he was right, she couldn't think of a sufficient reply.

"I forgive you, since you don't know me better." The tone in his voice said that wouldn't be the case for long. "I'll have you know I grew up in a neighborhood much like this one. There were many Fridays that I came home from football practice and still had to cut the grass."

"You were a big man on campus, I bet."

"Until I got home, and my father gave me a touch of reality," Jordan reminisced. "Our mother died when my sister and I were small. He had to be both parents. He was a great dad in those days."

Something about the way Jordan said 'those days' had Lauren looking at him sharply. "Did something happen to him as you got older?"

Jordan's face hardened. "He trusted the wrong man and loved the wrong woman. Yeah, something happened to him."

She found she wanted to know more about his childhood, but couldn't ask. That sharing of information was exactly one of the reasons she had limited her friends. So she simply let her hand remain in Jordan's.

"Are you a native Louisianian?"

She tensed in spite of herself. "No."

"Where are you from?" he asked mildly.

"A little town you probably never heard of." She stood. "I really should be getting back inside. I have a lot to do."

He didn't release her hand. "Maybe I can help."

"Somehow I can't picture you doing the ironing for the week," she told him.

He stood. On the step below her, he was at eye level, lip level. Much too close, yet she didn't appear to be able to move away. "You'd be surprised at the things I can do once I set my mind to it."

His sensual voice enticed, his warm breath beckoned. It would be so easy and so foolish to lean closer. "I—I really have to go."

"On one condition. Have lunch with me tomorrow?"

"I—I can't."

He sat down without relinquishing her hand. "I can be just as stubborn as you."

"Jordan, this is ridiculous," she said, but she was having a difficult time trying not to smile or be flattered.

"My thoughts, exactly. I want to be your friend and Joshua's. I understand your concern about Joshua, but I think you're wrong."

"You have a right to your opinion, but I'm his mother."

He came to his feet. "I know that. I was worried about you two. Both of you looked as if you were about to face a firing squad when you got out of the car. I couldn't leave you."

Warmth flooded her. "Jordan, I'm thankful for your concern, but we're used to taking care of ourselves."

"I respect and admire you for what you've accomplished, but you seem to have forgotten something," he said.

"What?"

"To live, to have fun. See, you're trying to pull away, and run from what you don't want to hear." His free hand brushed curly tendrils of hair from her face. "You're running from life, and where you go, Joshua goes."

Anger and panic moved through her. "You know nothing about me, to make such an accusation."

Some indefinable emotion swept across his handsome features, then it was gone. "I know we were having a great time until Joshua and I came back from the railing. You didn't just look sad. You looked defeated, lost. I knew before you said anything that you were going to want to leave. Joshua wanting to substitute me for a father isn't the only reason you want me to leave."

Her breath quickened. "You have an inflated opinion of yourself."

"You don't think highly enough of yourself."

She tugged her hands. "I want to go inside."

"Why?"

"Why?" She sounded incredulous.

"Yes, why. Give me one honest, logical reason for letting you go, and I will."

She looked into his handsome face, fierce in his determination to win this battle of wills, and knew she had lost. She knew she had gone past trying to protect Joshua, to protecting herself. Admitting her vulnerability to a man like Jordan was unthinkable. "You're a client."

"You'll have to do better than that. Benjamin has no problem with us being friends."

"You have him mesmerized."

Jordan hooted. "That's why he was ready to take a chunk out of me Saturday morning."

Lauren flushed. "He's very protective of his employees."

"Exactly. Yet, he left me here with you. So what does that tell you?"

"That he had a lapse in judgment."

"Lauren, you certainly know how to wound a man."

"Apparently not enough for you to leave me alone."

His face harshened. For a long time he simply looked at her. Then he released her hands. "You win, Lauren. One thing, please make sure Joshua understands I wasn't the one who gave up on him. You made that decision for all of us. Good-bye, Lauren. Enjoy your solitude."

He walked swiftly to his car and got inside. The motor roared. In less than a minute he was out of sight. She had finally succeeded in getting rid of him.

Slowly, Lauren opened the door. It was for the best.

"Mama, I need you to check my homework and sign," yelled Joshua.

"Coming, Honey." She didn't need a man to unsettle her life. All she needed was Joshua.

Jordan was blazing mad. Realizing his anger, he was only a couple of blocks away from Lauren's house before he pulled over to the curb.

Lauren Bennett was the most stubborn, the most pigheaded, the most irritating woman he had ever met. And she called to him as no other woman ever had. He wanted to take the sadness from her eyes as much as he wanted to bury himself into her silken warmth. She was too suspicious to let him get close enough to do either.

What a mess he had gotten himself into. He had had the colossal ego to think all he had to do was show up and Lauren would immediately fall under his spell. She'd be so taken with him that she'd tell him anything he needed to know. Ha! Showed how much he needed a reality check.

Lauren was her own woman. She might be attracted to him,

but she was fighting it every step of the way. She wasn't going to let it interfere with her solitary life. He'd have to figure out another way to get the evidence against Strickland.

The prospects weren't good. Lauren had been their best bet. And the lady wasn't about to help. She had buried her life before she came to Shreveport, and she wasn't about to take a chance on someone getting too close.

Jordan rubbed the tension from the back of his neck. He needed a stiff drink. Then he would call his grandfather and give him the bad news. On second thought, maybe he'd fly home. There was no sense in remaining in Shreveport.

Lauren Bennett was as lost to them as she had been six years ago.

"Mama, it's not behind there."

"It won't hurt to look." Lauren blew tendrils of hair out of her face, and pulled the twin bed out from the wall. Her shoulders slumped.

All she saw was a need to include the area behind Joshua's bed when she did her housecleaning. She slid the bed back carefully, so as not to scratch the hardwood floor.

"I told you, Mama—I left it in Mr. Hamilton's car."

"Honey, are you sure?"

"It's in his car, Mama."

Lauren plopped on the bed and stared at her son. His lower lip tucked between his teeth, he wasn't a happy camper. He hadn't been since fifteen minutes ago, when he'd discovered he couldn't find the organizer Jordan had given him.

She'd stopped ironing and immediately helped him search. They had looked everywhere, but it was nowhere to be seen.

"I'm going back outside to go over the yard." The miserable look on Joshua's face said it was a waste of time, but he trailed behind his mother, anyway.

The search didn't take long. Lauren had cut the grass on Wednesday, leaving a lush, green, flat surface. The organizer wasn't there. All Lauren's wishing and hoping hadn't made the device appear this time anymore than it had the other times.

"Mama, call and ask him to bring it back."

"Joshua, Mr. Hamilton is a busy man."

"But he wouldn't mind. He gave it to me. He'd want me to have it."

Lauren gazed at her son. There went his logical mind again. She didn't want to see Jordan Hamilton again. "I'll buy you another one."

"I want that one."

She hadn't thought that would work. Joshua, like most children, wanted specifics. Substitutions weren't allowed. "Joshua, I don't know if he's still here. The car he drove may have been rented and returned. Like the time our car was in the shop."

"With my organizer in it?" he cried. His lower lip began to tremble.

"I'm sure Mr. Hamilton checked the car before he turned it over to the agency," she added hastily.

"Then Mr. Hamilton has it. Call him, Mama."

They were back to square one. No amount of talking was going to change her son's mind. He could be as stubborn as his father, when he put his mind to it. With his life in turmoil, at odds with his family, David had insisted they not let the problems interfere with their plans to get married.

His son had inherited more than his father's love of math. Like it or not, she had to see Jordan Hamilton again.

Chapter Ten

"I'm sorry, but Mr. Hamilton has checked out."

"Are you sure?" Lauren asked the desk clerk. Although she had mentioned the same thing to Joshua, she hadn't honestly thought Jordan would leave today. His asking her out tomorrow had indicated he had planned to stay.

But that was before our argument.

"Yes, Ma'am," replied the attractive, middle-aged black woman. "I took the call myself."

Lauren felt Joshua's hand tighten in hers. "Do you know which airline he planned to use?"

The clerk shook her short braids. "I'm sorry."

"Thank you," Lauren mumbled and moved away, Joshua's hand clutched in hers. She wasn't ready to see the disappointment in his face. If she hadn't been so afraid of seeing Jordan again, she might have caught him before he left.

"What do we do now, Mama?" Joshua asked softly.

She couldn't put it off any longer. She looked down. There weren't tears, only expectation for her to make things right. "I don't know, Honey, but I'll think of something."

What that something was, she didn't know. Scott Resources had made the hotel reservation, but his office had handled the travel arrangements. All she knew was that he had flown in on a commercial airline. Short of calling the major carriers at the airport and having him paged, she was out of ideas.

She was positive the car he drove had been a rental, which meant the electronic organizer might be lost to them forever. He'd have had no reason to check the backseat.

Moving through the seemingly endless crowd of people, she headed for the front door. The feeling of being closed in wasn't so bad with Joshua by her side, but she was ready to put more space between her and the next person.

The moment the revolving door propelled them outside, she started to breathe in deeply, then couldn't seem to make her lungs expand any further. Jordan stood twenty-feet away from her.

"Mr. Hamilton!" Joshua yelled, and started toward him.

If Lauren hadn't been holding her son's hand, he would have run across the busy driveway. "Wait, Joshua."

Jordan straightened from getting into his car and turned toward the sound of his name. His gaze raked over Lauren before dropping to her son, who was waving frantically with his free arm.

Leaving the car door open, Jordan crossed to them. For once, his face was an emotionless blank. "This is an unexpected surprise."

"I left my organizer in your car. Can I still have it?" Joshua asked.

"Of course." A car horn honked impatiently. Jordan glanced back toward the four cars behind him. "I'm holding up traffic. Come on. There's a little park on the other side of the street."

"We don't want to keep you," Lauren managed.

"You won't." His cool, impersonal fingers lightly touched her arm, and he led her to his car. On seeing the two people accompanying Jordan, an attendant rushed forward and opened the doors for Lauren and Joshua.

Joshua happily climbed into the backseat. "Here it is, Mama. I told you I left it in Mr. Hamilton's car."

Lauren's door shut, and she realized there was no way she

could graciously get back out again. "I'm glad you found it, Honey."

"Why does that surprise me?" Jordan said, not even trying to keep the sarcasm out of his voice as he pulled away.

Lauren had known this was going to be difficult, but wasn't prepared for Jordan's cutting tone. He had always been so patient with her in the past. "Maybe you'll understand one day when you have children of your own."

"Maybe." Jordan circled the block and parked in front of a small city park. "Come on."

Lauren got out of the car and grimaced. Jordan couldn't have chosen a worse place to stop. Sights and sounds of families having a good time were all around them—the laughter of children, the yelling of two volleyball teams, the smell of food cooking on the smoking grills, parents calling to children to be careful—blatant reminders of all the things Joshua wanted in his life and didn't have.

"We have what we came for. We can leave now," Lauren suggested.

"Come on, Joshua, there's a vacant spot over there under that tree." Jordan reached for Joshua's hand. Immediately Joshua lifted his. Hands clasped, the two walked away without a backward glance.

Shocked and a little miffed at being left standing there, Lauren gritted her teeth, then ran to catch up. "Don't you have a plane to catch?"

"There'll be other planes," he answered without turning.

She noticed he was careful to match his longer strides to those of her son. Beneath the tree, Jordan sat with elegant grace, Indian-style, on the thinning patch of grass, with a careless disregard for his expensive tan slacks. Joshua tried to imitate Jordan and plopped in front of him.

Not sure of what was going on, Lauren sat to the far left of her son, close enough to hear, but out of Jordan's direct gaze. Not that he was paying any attention to her, anyway.

"I'm glad I got a chance to see you again before I left," Jordan said, very much aware of Lauren's watchfulness and her irritation. The lady certainly didn't like being ignored. Too bad. He had finally decided to concede to her wishes. If she wanted to remain a prisoner of fear there was nothing he could do about it.

"Me, too," Joshua said, both hands clutching the organizer. "We almost missed you 'cause Mama waited so long. I told her I left it in your car."

"Women are hard to convince sometimes even when the truth is staring them in the face. Men are much more sensible." Lauren's hands clamped in her lap, her soft mouth puckered as if she had tasted an unripe persimmon.

"Mama says I won't be seeing you again."

"I know."

Nearby a child squealed in delight. A dog barked. Joshua kept his attention on the man in front of him. "Mama says I can't call you, but I wanted this to remember you by. You won't forget me, will you?" he asked, his little voice strained and wavering.

"No, Joshua, I promise I won't forget you." Jordan was surprised by the strange stinging sensation in his throat. He glanced at Lauren to see her sitting rigid, her hands clamped tightly in her lap, her head turned away.

Obviously, she was hurting for her son. She'd known this wasn't going to be easy for him, but she had come, anyway—from the looks of her, in a hurry.

Normally conservatively dressed, she wore a pink knit shirt that clung lovingly to her breasts and faded jeans that encased her slim legs. Her hair was pulled on top of her head in a ponytail. She looked more like a teenager than an adult. She wanted nothing to do with him, but he couldn't deny she loved her son.

"Your mother is only trying to do what's best because she loves you so much," Jordan finally told the little boy.

"I wish you didn't have to go."

"I do too, Joshua," Jordan said, and meant every word. He came to his knees. "Can I have a good bye hug?"

Joshua went into his arms without hesitation. Over the child's shoulder Jordan watched Lauren swallowing convulsively. He absently wondered what she would do if he gave her a hug.

She needed one just as much. Punch him in the nose probably, since there wasn't a paperweight handy.

The unexpected sound of Joshua's bubbling laughter broke in on his thoughts.

"What's so funny?" Jordan leaned the little boy away.

"It tickles," Joshua answered, his small hands patting the full, black beard.

"It's saved me time from shaving twice a day," Jordan confided. "If my hair looked presentable long, I'd stay out of the barbershop, too."

Joshua made a face. "I don't like going to the barbershop, either. Mama takes me, anyway."

"As I remember, when I was your age I felt the same way."

"But I bet your daddy was there to take you."

Lauren sucked in her breath. Even with all the noise around them, Jordan heard the sound. Suddenly Jordan knew how a person felt when he found himself in a live minefield with one foot off the ground.

"He was," Jordan finally answered.

"My father died before I was born."

Jordan's foot was getting heavier by the second. "I'm sorry to hear that, Joshua, but you still have your mother, who loves you very much. Do you know that Friday night she was so worried about keeping her promise to you, that she was going to drive in the rainstorm? I think she would have walked if I hadn't driven her. She had promised, and that was all she could think about."

"She doesn't like to drive in the rain," Joshua confided in a loud whisper that easily reached his mother.

"But she would have. Mothers, good mothers, are like that. They take care of you when you're sick and fuss over you when you're well."

The little boy brightened. "Like the red soda, and the waffles even though she gets the whole kitchen dirty."

"Exactly. You're lucky to have your mother. Mine died when I was just a little older than you, so I know a little bit of how you feel. I'm sure if your father were alive he'd want you to take care of your mother. He can't be here, but he left you in charge.''

Jordan's light brown Italian loafer lowered another inch. ''Your mother probably misses your father as much as you do. But you know who keeps her from being sad, who wakes her up with a smile on her face each morning?''

Joshua shook his head, his big brown eyes intent.

Jordan's foot settled firmly on safe, solid ground. ''You.''

Joshua ran to his mother and hugged her. ''I'm glad you're my mama.''

Tears clouded her vision. ''I love you, Joshua. Always remember that.''

''I'll take you back now.''

Lauren blinked the tears from her eyes to see Jordan standing. The sunlight was behind him, silhouetting his muscular body and preventing her from clearly seeing his face. His dispassionate tone told her he remained upset with her.

Unfolding her jean-clad legs, she began to stand. Lean fingers closed around her arm until she was upright, then dropped away. Jordan's detachment disturbed her in ways she hadn't thought possible, and it was all her own doing.

He had been right. She *was* running from life. In some ways she was still the frightened young woman who had been run out of town and ordered not to come back. She had gone to protect her child, but her cowardice haunted her, kept her a prisoner.

''Mama, are you all right?''

''Yes—at least I will be. There's a vacant swing over there. Why don't you go try it out? I need to talk to Mr. Hamilton,'' she said.

''Keep this for me.'' Handing her the organizer, her son took off for the swing. She waved to him when he was seated with both hands clamped firmly around the chain, then centered her gaze in the middle of Jordan's wide chest.

''I misjudged you. I know it's too late, but I wanted you to know I'm sorry.'' With difficulty she met the intense black eyes glittering down at her.

"I grew up in a little town outside Charlotte, but Joshua was born in Shreveport, yet he's never been on a boat or fishing, like I did when I was his age. If you ever have time when you're in the city, you have my permission to take him on a boat ride. Just the two of you. Good-bye." She started toward the play area.

A hand clamped on her forearm. "Don't I get a chance to say anything?"

Jordan's unyielding face wasn't reassuring, but he deserved to have his say. "Of course," she responded.

"What is it too late for?"

"Too late for us to be friends," she told him.

"I thought you just apologized for misjudging me, and you're already doing it again," he said mildly.

Her lips clamped together briefly. "You made it fairly obvious you don't want to be around me. Thank you for being kind to Joshua."

"If I wasn't a nice guy I'd let you stew in your own juices for a while."

"What?"

He smiled crookedly. "You're going to have to stop saying that if we're going to be friends."

Hope stirred within her. "You were so distant."

A long, lean finger stroked her cheek. "I was trying to be noble and do as you asked."

Lauren shivered at his touch, then took a deep breath and stepped out of the past into the future. "Joshua and I could both use a friend."

The intense satisfaction on Jordan's face cast aside the last of her doubts. "I promise—you have one." Taking her arm, he started toward the swings. "There's another empty seat. You ever been swung so high you thought you could reach the sky?"

"No, and I'm not sure I want to be, either."

"Chicken."

"Cluck Cluck."

Laughing, they went to join Joshua.

*   *   *

Jordan barely made it to the airport in time to board the last plane for New Orleans. Taking his seat, he buckled himself in and prepared for takeoff. He still wore a smile. He had forgotten how much fun simple things like walking, talking, and just being with someone you care about could be.

He hadn't been able to talk Lauren into trying to touch the sky, but it wasn't for lack of trying on his and Joshua's part. Lauren flatly refused.

Finally he had gotten in the swing himself, to show her how much fun it was. She protested just as loudly for him to stop. Her obvious concern had him grinning like a fool.

Joshua was like a whirlwind. He went from the swing to the jungle gym to the slide at full speed. All the time, Lauren watched him, cautioning him to be careful. Hunger was the only thing that finally slowed him down.

Despite Jordan's insistence that they go out to eat, Lauren had calmly held out her hand for his airline ticket. Seeing his flight was scheduled for later in the week, she had lifted sorrowful eyes to his. Not wanting her to blame herself, he had quickly told her something had come up and he had made reservations for a three fifteen flight to New Orleans.

Glancing at her watch, she had grabbed him by the arm and started toward his car. His plane had left an hour before.

With the cool efficiency he had admired even before he met her, she had used his car phone to book him on the last flight, arranged for the rental agency to pick up the car, and driven him to the airport.

At the boarding gate he had thanked her with a nonthreatening hug, and was pleased to feel her arms go around him, her body soften. Even more pleased to hear her give her phone number.

The closing door had him sprinting. He suddenly needed to go home and talk to his grandfather. Somehow he'd find another way of obtaining the information they needed to bring Strickland down. Using Lauren was no longer an option.

Her act of faith in revealing something about her past had

touched Jordan beyond measure. He couldn't repay her with deception.

She had made it sound simple, but he knew it had not been.

He knew with absolute certainty she had jealously guarded that information in the past. Lauren Bennett hadn't existed until six years ago.

Jordan pulled his Bronco into his detached garage an hour and a half after he left Shreveport. Considering that the flight was little over an hour, he had made good time.

Going through the open archway, he entered the house through the side door. As always, he felt a sense of pride. The graceful, three-story French Colonial had been meticulously restored, and some of the original antiques remained. He liked preserving a piece of the past while he helped shape the future.

Suitcase in hand, he started for the ornately carved staircase, somewhat surprised that no one had greeted him. He knew his grandfather was probably in his room at the back of the house, but Mattie usually stayed near the front.

His foot was on the second stair when he heard raised voices coming from the direction of his grandfather's room. Dropping the luggage, he ran in that direction. The door was open. Mattie was trying to keep his grandfather from hitting the TV set with his walking cane.

"What's going on?"

The housekeeper turned around, momentarily releasing her hold on his grandfather's arm. The elderly man took the opportunity to whack the set, and lost his balance.

Rushing across the room, Jordan caught his grandfather before he fell and eased him gently back into his chair. Eyes closed, Hollis Hamilton labored for breath.

"Easy, Grandad. Just relax."

Mattie cut the TV off, then handed Jordan a glass of water. "Drink this."

Opening his eyes, his grandfather glared at the blank screen of the TV set. He shook his head once in a negative gesture.

"You know I can be as stubborn as you." When that elicited no reaction, Jordan played dirty. "Do I have to call Angelica?"

The mention of his granddaughter caused his grandfather's attention to shift to him, as Jordan had known it would. His black eyes sparked with all of the intelligence of his grandson but only a fraction of the sparkling energy, calmed.

Slowly, his frail, trembling hand lifted and closed around the glass. Jordan watched the slow progress and clenched his hand to keep from helping. Pride was everything to a man like Hollis Hamilton. Enough had been taken from him—and Jordan was afraid he might have to take even more.

Only after his breathing had slowed to normal, and the glass was safely on the table, did Jordan ask, "What brought this on?"

The stubbornness came back. Hollis turned his head.

Hunkered down, Jordan wheeled on the balls of his feet and stared up at the agitated housekeeper. Except Mattie was more like a member of the family. She would have *been* if her niece hadn't run off and left Jordan's father shortly after he filed for bankruptcy.

"Why don't *you* tell me?"

Arms clenched around her stomach, the elderly woman glanced at Hollis. "You should tell Jordan yourself."

Jordan waited. Clearly, as he had always known and respected, Mattie owed her first allegiance and loyalty to his grandfather. Although he had known her since he came to live with his grandfather, she had only worked for Jordan since he bought the house.

After his grandfather's mild stroke two years ago, Jordan had insisted he move into the larger, more comfortable house. She had taken on the additional responsibility of caring for Hollis with gentleness and understanding. Beside Angelica, Mattie was usually the only one who could get him to do something without a fight.

Jordan didn't know if her loyalty was due to a friendship of over fifty years, something deeper, or misplaced guilt over her niece deserting his son. Whatever the reason, Jordan gratefully accepted her presence and made sure she hired additional help for the heavier housekeeping duties.

"Grandad, I'm waiting," Jordan gently prodded.

"He was on the TV."

Hollis spit out the words with such venom, Jordan didn't need a name. *Strickland.*

"As bold as anything," Hollis continued, his gaze on the television as if he could still see the hated image. "He was being interviewed on BET because of his success in the publishing industry. You should have seen him, all oozing with charm, telling how he rallied after he and his former business partner had filed for bankruptcy, to start his magazine."

"Grandad—"

"You wanted to hear it, so listen," Hollis interrupted. "The patronizing bastard had the gall to lie and say the newspaper was his idea, his dream, but poor management had caused the failure. An idiot could read between the lines and know since *he's* successful, it was Randolph's fault. Randolph's fault, when my son worked sixteen hours a day, seven days a week, while Strickland was 'in the field' and stealing him blind. But his time is coming."

The knot in Jordan's stomach clenched tighter. "Grandad, there may be some problems."

"Problems!" the older man cried, straightening in his chair. "You signed on that company she works for in Shreveport to get close to her, didn't you? You went back this weekend to get her on our side like we said, didn't you?"

"Yes, but things are complicated." Jordan wished he'd taken the drink the stewardess offered on the plane. "Lauren Bennett has been in hiding for six years. She's not going to willingly do anything to bring her near Strickland again."

"She doesn't have to see him, just turn over the books."

"We don't know if she has the ledgers," Jordan reasoned.

"We don't know that she *doesn't,* either," his grandfather said. "Strickland's son wouldn't have called me unless he was serious. He died before he could deliver the journals, and his family won't admit to knowing anything about a wife. If I didn't know how much that SOB doted on the boy, I'd be suspicious of his son's death."

"His wife is an innocent in this."

Hollis leaned wearily back in his chair. "I know that. This happened long before her. You'll see that she's taken care of.

You've made me proud. You and Angelica. The only thing that keeps me from being content is knowing Strickland destroyed your father's reputation and caused the woman he loved to run off with another man.''

If Mattie hadn't been standing silently behind him, Jordan would have told his grandfather that if Deborah had loved his father she wouldn't have cared that his company had failed.

"You've always made me proud, Son," Hollis repeated. "I'd still be living by myself if you hadn't hauled me over here to watch the house for you while you were out of town. Don't think I haven't figured out it was all a ruse, but it made me prouder of you just the same." He paused, then leaned up and stared Jordan in the eyes. "I've never asked you for anything, have I?"

The knot in Jordan's gut twisted painfully. His grandfather took great pride in having proved everyone wrong by keeping his teenage grandchildren. He was proud his grandson owned his own company, proud his granddaughter was a dentist, and prouder still that he didn't have to ask either of them for a red cent. If he ever found out Jordan and Angelica were behind some of the investments profits he had made over the years, there would be hell to pay. "No, Sir."

"I'm asking for this." His frail hand clamped on Jordan's arm. "Bring Strickland down. Will you do that for me like you promised?"

Jordan's muscles bunched beneath his grandfather's weak hold. He remembered another, more delicate hand on his shoulder that same day. He had made promises to both of them.

He touched his grandfather's well-read bible. Suddenly he recalled the passage about no one being able to serve two masters; for either he would love one and hate the other; or else hold to one and despise the other.

"Son?"

Jordan looked at the man who had always been there for him when his world tilted and bowed his head to the inevitable. Promises were hell.

Chapter Eleven

Lauren told herself she wasn't disappointed that Jordan didn't call Monday. After all, he was the CEO of a major company in the booming and highly competitive telecommunications industry. Timing was of the essence. A missed opportunity might mean losing millions of dollars. His first obligation was to his company—not to a woman and a little boy he barely knew.

She told herself the same thing Tuesday. However, by Wednesday afternoon all her rational reasoning couldn't keep the growing doubts from nagging her. Maybe she had read too much into Jordan's persistence in being her friend. Maybe he made a habit of befriending lonely, single mothers, then dumping them.

Whatever his motives, he had certainly put her life into a spin. Normally cool and unflappable, Lauren Bennett was rushing to answer the phone, asking people to repeat themselves, all thumbs when she was on the computer.

For a woman who had been perfectly content without a man in her life for the past six years, she was turning into a basket case. All because some man hadn't called. She had seen enough of her female co-workers' misery when the same thing had happened to them to not want to fall into the same trap herself, but that was just what was happening to her.

Perhaps she should have stuck to her original plan and not invited Jordan to be a part of her life. It wasn't like her to become dependent on anyone.

By the time Lauren got into her car to drive home from work on Wednesday, she had decided that Jordan's disappearing act had been for the best. She had learned early that he wasn't going to be a consistent, dependable part of her or Joshua's life. That she had secretly wished he would was her own problem.

Friendship meant different things to different people. She'd have to accept the time he was with her, if he bothered to show up again, and forget about him when he wasn't there.

Yeah, right, and I believe in the tooth fairy.

A frown on her face, she turned onto her street and came to an abrupt halt. She saw something she had almost given up hope of ever seeing on her block. A man in some type of lift was actually replacing the bulb in one of the streetlights. She pulled over behind the city vehicle and got out.

Shading her eyes against the glare of the sun with her hand, she called up to the worker. "Hello?"

The man gazed over the edge of the lift. "Evenin'."

"I'm glad you finally made it out here. The whole block has been out for months. I thought my calls and petitions were falling on deaf ears."

"You must have finally found the right person. The work order was stamped top priority," he told her, moving a wad of tobacco from one grizzly jaw to the other. "I wasn't supposed to be anywhere near this area today."

"I'm glad you are. The entire neighborhood will feel safer with the streetlights on."

"Yes, Ma'am." He started to spit, looked at her and paused.

"I'd better let you get back to work." Waving, she got back into her car and drove home. At least something good had happened today. The frown returned to her face. Her life must really be a nothing if the installation of streetlights was the highlight of her day.

Stop feeling sorry for yourself, she admonished. Her life was good. She had Joshua, and this week he had been happier than she had seen in a long time. There hadn't been one phone call from his teacher or the school nurse, which actually surprised her.

Lauren had thought not hearing from Jordan might upset her son. She had been wrong. Her son accepted Jordan's absence. His mother was the one having fits.

Turning into her driveway, she pulled the car into the garage and went into the house. Inside, she stopped only long enough to draw back the kitchen curtain to give the struggling ivy in the window some sunlight before heading for Sonja's house to get Joshua.

Crossing the street, she took the narrow walkway leading around the garage to the side entrance to Sonja's office. Since Sonja had a home/office typing service, she planned her schedule around Joshua's bus arrival. The almost two-year-old arrangement had worked out perfectly.

Lauren didn't have to worry if she worked late, and Joshua was crazy about Sonja. Most importantly, he had another consistency in his life, another person who loved him.

In the five years they had been neighbors, they had had their first and only major disagreement over Sonja's refusal to accept money for keeping Joshua. Her best friend initially accepted the money, then funneled it back to Lauren in gifts or clothes for Joshua. Lauren turned the table on her friend by doing the same thing.

Only recently had Sonja finally conceded defeat, when Lauren gave her a pair of expensive, handcarved, wooden earrings Sonja had wanted but said they weren't in her budget. On opening the gift, Sonja had blinked back tears, then laughed. "You win. We'd better stop before we both end up in the poorhouse."

They had stopped, but Lauren still planned to give Sonja the matching bracelet for her birthday in June. She deserved something special. She worked long hours and was a sucker for a sad story. People were forever "forgetting" to pay her. She tried just as hard to be a friend as Lauren tried to keep her distance.

"Bad day?"

Lauren looked up to see the object of her thoughts standing in the doorway. "I was thinking how unlike me you are."

Sonja grinned and glanced down at herself in a soft, muted, beige and blue tunic top, broomstick skirt, and sandals. "Yeah, I'd say about a hundred pounds."

Lauren's frown deepened into a scowl. "You say something stupid like that again, and I'll . . . I'll . . . I don't know what I'll do, but you won't like it, I promise."

Sonja sobered. "What's gotten into you?"

"I might ask you the same thing. Why do you say things like that?"

The other woman shrugged. "It's no big deal."

"I happen to think it's a very big deal. You're talking nonsense. If we start judging people by anything except their character we're all in trouble," Lauren said. "I'd be at the top of the list."

Sonja's eyes narrowed. "Did the heat get to you or something?"

Lauren realized she had gone from reprimanding Sonja to reprimanding herself. She wrinkled her nose. "When you start trying to correct someone, you'd better make sure your own house is in order."

"Girl, if you don't start making sense, we're going to the doctor."

"I'm all right, Sonja. I've just been doing some heavy thinking lately."

"Ah, huh." Sonja crossed her arms over her full breasts. "Now all this heavy thinking wouldn't happen to have anything to do with a brown-skinned, handsome man with a swagger in his walk and enough firepower in his body to back it up, would it?"

Lauren laughed in spite of herself. "You do have a way with words."

"Why do you think I have a secretarial service?"

"Because you wanted to be your own boss and got tired of the corporate rat race?" Lauren said.

"There was that. The fringe benefits are lousy, the pay isn't much better, but my ulcer is happy."

Lauren rolled her eyes. "You never had an ulcer."

"I know, and I'm going to keep it that way. Seeing my parents trying to climb that ladder was enough for me." The other woman smiled. "I think they've finally accepted that their only child doesn't have the drive or the inclination to be some high-powered executive."

"They love you. Parents just want the best for their children. Parents kind of pin all their hopes and expectations on an only child," Lauren said with feeling.

"I'm happy to see you aren't pushing Joshua to excell. A child should be a child for as long as possible." The other woman shook her head. "Heaven knows when you grow up the world can be a pretty cold and cruel place."

A memory flashed though Lauren's mind of Nathan Strickland ordering her out of his house and threatening to call the police, when all she wanted was to talk to someone who had known her husband and had loved him as much as she had. Her mistake was in thinking Strickland loved anyone except himself.

"Hey, Girl, are sure you're all right?" Sonja asked, waving her hand in front of Lauren's face.

Shaking off the memory, Lauren managed a smile. "Long day. I guess Joshua is in front of the television."

"Nothing wrong with a few cartoons. If I hadn't heard the fax machine, I'd be in there with him."

"I'll get him and be out of your way." Lauren headed for the den. As usual she always marveled that their houses looked so similar on the outside and were so different on the inside.

Sonja had a natural instinct for colors and decorating. There was a continuous flow of blues, pinks, and peaches. Brass gleamed everywhere. Greenery sprouted and cascaded. The brown panel walls had long since been painted a pristine white. Thanks to a carpenter friend of hers, she had a sunken tub, and a larger bedroom. She had laughingly said that the loss of one bedroom was well worth the price.

As Lauren expected, Joshua was stretched out in front of the

TV. "Hello, Sweetheart," she greeted. Immediately, her son rolled over onto his side. A wide grin on his face, he scrambled to his feet and ran to her. The Tasmanian Devil was forgotten.

"Hi, Mama."

Bending from the waist, she hugged him. "How was your day?"

"It was fun. We had a fire drill, and had to do it over again because some kids kept messing up." His chest stuck out proudly. "The principal announced the kindergarten class was the best. I was the last one in line. My teacher said that was just as important as being the leader. The leader can't see if everyone is following, but I could."

Silently, Lauren thanked Mrs. Bradford for her insight. She had probably made each child feel as important. "Your teacher was absolutely right."

"Next week we're having Show and Tell. Can I take my electronic organizer?"

"I don't see why not."

He grinned. "Mine will be the best one, I bet."

"Being the best isn't what it's all about. Learning from others is what's important," she said.

"Yes, Ma'am," he answered, but his expressive brown face said he disagreed.

"Come on, thank Sonja and say good-bye," Lauren said. Joshua had grown up calling her best friend by her first name because Sonja had wanted it that way. "We have to go."

"Do we have to?" he asked, drawing out each word.

"Yes, we do." Lauren had been dreading this confrontation all day . . . that is, when she wasn't trying to get Jordan out of her mind.

The little boy turned to Sonja. "I look all right, don't I?"

The other woman held up both hands. "You know I'm neutral."

"Joshua, we talked about this last night," Lauren reminded him.

His chin almost touched his chest. "I wish Mr. Hamilton were here."

I do, too, she thought, then chastised herself. She wouldn't get hung up on needing a man in her life. She had seen too many women settle for anything in order to say they had a man. That wasn't for her. "He's not. I'll have to do."

Joshua's head lifted. He looked at her a long time before his small hand slipped into hers. "I'm glad you're my mama, but I just wish he was here. Don't you miss him?"

"Yes, Joshua, I miss him, too." She had told enough lies to her son to protect him. She wasn't going to do the same to protect herself.

"He'll be back," he said with complete confidence.

She squeezed her son's hand. "We'd better get going."

He balked. "If I'm real, real good, do you think we might stop at McDonald's?"

His expression was so hopeful. She smiled. "A definite possibility."

Releasing her hand, Joshua rushed to pick up his black and purple backpack from the floor and put it on. "Good-bye, Sonja. Thanks. I'll see you tomorrow."

Sonja followed them to the door. "You still haven't heard from Jordan?"

Lauren's smile slipped a notch. "No."

Her friend looked at her meaningfully. "If I were you I'd be worried more about *when* he comes back, rather than if."

Lauren's frown deepened. "What are you talking about?"

"Jordan isn't a man easily deterred. He'll come after you with no holds barred."

"There's nothing between us," Lauren said, the words sounding more wistful than she would have liked. "He just wants to be our friend."

Sonja rolled her eyes. "You two can cloak it anyway you want, but before long things are going to get hot and heavy, and you'd better decide now if you're ready for that."

Lauren didn't know what she was feeling except it was wild and uncertain. She had never met a man as intense as Jordan. Admittedly, her feelings were a little deeper than they should be for a man she barely knew, a man who professed he only wanted to be her friend.

But his voice, his touch, the way he looked at her, sometimes made her skin tingle with anticipation, and caused her to think he wanted something wildly, hotly different.

That something was erotic and dangerous as hell.

"Mama, your face looks funny."

Lauren flushed. Joshua was in the middle of the sidewalk, waiting as usual for her to finish talking with Sonja. Lord, she'd had more sexual thoughts since meeting Jordan than she had in her lifetime. "I'm a little warm, that's all."

Sonja hooted.

Not daring to look at her best friend, Lauren went down the steps and across the street. After opening the front door, she got the mail. Sifting through the letters, she went into the kitchen. Except for the gas bill, the rest was junk mail. She hadn't expected much else.

She tended to pay cash or do without. She had no major credit cards. She wanted as little information as possible about her on some computer bank. Her decision had made her financial situation tight at first, but she'd made it.

If not for the sale of her mother's house and small bookstore's stock, Lauren's life would have been vastly different. The money had enabled her to put a down payment on the house she now lived in, and helped her take care of her medical expenses during her pregnancy. Spending the money had been difficult. The only thing that eased her conscience in doing so was knowing that without the funds she couldn't take care of herself or a baby.

When she was driven away from the life she had six years ago, she left with a great deal of pain and anger. She also had left a job in the field she loved, a job she couldn't possible apply for again. But she had also made it more difficult for her in-laws to find her if they ever tried.

During the two months she and David had dated, his wealthy parents had made it blatantly clear that a librarian from a middle-class working family wasn't good enough for their son. She'd never forget the evening she and her mother arrived for dinner at the Strickland's mansion, only to learn they had "unexpectedly" been called away.

Lauren had been hurt, but she had been more concerned

about David and her mother. David had been livid, her strong, no-nonsense mother spitting mad. They were both ready to wait for the Stricklands to return and give them a piece of their minds.

In the past David had always been apologetic for his parents 'no shows' and kept assuring her that they were going to love her almost as much as he did. She had believed him. She loved him too much not to. It wasn't just his boyish good looks and charm, he was also the kindest, the gentlest man she had ever known. He made her feel cherished and loved.

She didn't want to believe that once his parents knew she wasn't after his money, they wouldn't come to accept her. That night they proved them both wrong.

It had taken a lot of pleading by Lauren to get David and her mother to see that confronting the Stricklands would only make the situation worse.

They had gone to a restaurant for dinner, but the evening was ruined. The Strickland's snobbery hadn't hurt as much as their flagrant cruelty to David.

David had packed and moved out of his parent's mansion the next day and resigned from his father's publishing firm. Both his parents had called, threatening her with loss of her job, loss of her mother's lease for her bookstore. Not wanting David to be worried anymore than he already was, she and her mother hadn't told him about the phone calls. The estrangement had already changed him enough.

The laughing, easy to be with man had turned moody almost overnight. No amount of talking would get him to open up about what was bothering him. When he insisted they get married, she gladly consented, thinking that her love would help him.

Three days later they drove across the state to South Carolina and were married. Her mother had closed her bookstore and gone with them. David did seem happy after their marriage . . . then the accident occurred on their way home from their honeymoon. She had lost the two people she loved most in the world.

His parents blamed her for David's death, saying if she hadn't tricked David into marriage he would have been safe in Charlotte instead of at Myrtle Beach. His father refused to acknowledge the marriage, and threatened legal action if she pursued the matter.

Reeling from the death of her mother and David and the escalating threats, she had given in to her fears and left. The Stricklands hadn't known she had carried their only grandchild.

And they never would.

"Mama, I'm pretty hungry. Do you think we could stop by McDonald's on the way?" Joshua asked, bringing his mother back to the present.

Lauren smiled down at her son and touched the mail to his nose. He was a miniature of his father. "Nice try. I know Sonja gives you milk and a sandwich every day."

"She could have forgot."

"Did she?"

His sigh was long and telling. "I guess not."

"Come on." Tossing the letters on the counter, she picked up her purse.

She slowly backed the car out of the garage. Seeing another car coming down the street, she stopped and waited for it to pass. She frowned when a sports utility vehicle stopped in front of her house—a Bronco. The windows were tinted too dark for her to make out the driver.

She pressed the control to roll down her window. A car door slammed shut. Pensive, she waited for the person to come into view. When she saw who it was, her heart did a funny little flutter.

Jordan.

He strode toward her, as bold and as confident as any pirate. There was a definite swagger in his walk, a sense of purpose on his smiling, bearded face. His white shirt emphasized his broad shoulders and powerful build. Black jeans clung indecently to his long, muscular legs.

Just like in my dreams.

Her stomach felt just as fluttery as her heart. The man had a certain something that could cause women's bodies to go on impulse power at warp speed. Hers included.

White teeth flashed in Jordan's darkly handsome face as he

braced his arm on top of the car and leaned down. Spicy cologne tantalized her nostrils. "Hi, you two."

"Mr. Hamilton!" Joshua yelled and quickly unbuckled his seatbelt.

For someone who had been slouched in his seat a moment before, her son moved extremely fast. She just wished she could recover as quickly. She watched Jordan's bearded face break into a wide grin seconds before Joshua propelled himself into his arms.

"I'm glad you're back."

After a hearty hug, Jordan set the little boy on his feet, his gaze on Lauren. "I'm glad someone is."

What did he expect after her not hearing from him for three days? "Hello, Jordan."

The frown working its way across his forehead eased. "For a while I thought we were back to Mr. Hamilton."

"We were just on our way out," Lauren explained, feeling self-conscious and out of her element. Only Jordan made her feel insecure and unsure of herself.

"I'm glad I caught you," Jordan said.

"Me, too." Joshua said, smiling broadly. "I was wishing you could go with us, and here you are."

Jordan's gaze flicked to the excited little boy, then back to a strangely silent Lauren. "And where might that be?"

"To the barbershop," her son answered with none of his earlier reservations. "If you go, it will almost be just like in the book."

"What book?" Jordan hoped he wasn't getting into another minefield.

"The one about the man taking his son to the barbershop. I didn't forget what you told me, but I'd like to be the boy in the book just once. Mama takes me but she can't get in the chair, 'cause he'd shave her hair off," Joshua gladly explained. "Me and Mama wouldn't like her being baldheaded."

One of Jordan's lean brown fingers curled around a tendril of Lauren's hair. "I don't think I would, either," he murmured softly.

Lauren turned her head toward the sound of the deep, hypnotic voice and brushed her cheek against the back of his long finger. Her response was instant and electric. Unnerved, she jumped, jerking her head away. "Ouch!"

"You gonna make her baldheaded?" Joshua asked.

The question was so outlandish that Jordan and Lauren looked at each other and started laughing. By the time they finished the tension was gone.

"I think your mother's hair is beautiful. I like it just where it is," Jordan finally said.

Lauren tucked her head and rubbed the sore spot to hide her sudden spurt of joy. She had fought all her adult life to tame her unruly, curly hair. "You have a strange way of showing it."

"Maybe this will help." His big hand tunneled though her mass of curls, his fingers warm and firm as they massaged her scalp.

Lauren started to move away, then realized she was in danger of losing more than a few strands. While indecision kept her immobile, his fingers worked their magic on her head, soothing the ache in her head and starting one someplace else.

"Is that better?"

"Y—Yes," she said, her voice oddly husky. "Y—You can stop now."

"Pity." He slowly withdrew his hand.

Lauren glanced at her son staring up at Jordan worshipfully. "We need to get going, Joshua."

"Can't Mr. Hamilton go?"

"If I do, I'll sit in the chair, Joshua, but the barber is not touching one hair on my face or head," Jordan said firmly.

Lauren studied Jordan's full black beard, his head of equally black hair. He probably didn't go to a barbershop, but some exclusive, upscale salon where he was catered to. Somehow she couldn't see Jordan's large body in one of the scarred, orange tub chairs in the neighborhood barbershop.

"That really isn't necessary," she told him. "We may be gone a long time. The barber doesn't take appointments, and we plan to eat at a fast food place afterward."

WE HAVE 4 FREE BOOKS FOR YOU!

FREE BOOK CERTIFICATE

Yes! Please send me 4 Arabesque Contemporary Romances without cost or obligation, billing me just $1 to help cover postage and handling. I understand that each month, I will be able to preview 4 brand-new Arabesque Contemporary Romances FREE for 10 days. Then, if I decide to keep them, I will pay the money-saving preferred subscriber's price of just $16.00 for all 4...that's a savings of almost $4 off the publisher's price with no additional charge for shipping and handling. I may return any shipment within 10 days and owe nothing, and I may cancel this subscription at any time. My 4 FREE books will be mine to keep in any case.

Name _____

Address_____ Apt. _____

City_____ State_____ Zip_____

Telephone ( ) _____

Signature _____
(If under 18, parent or guardian must sign.)

AR0897

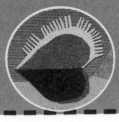

"Not a problem," Jordan said easily. "My calendar is free, and I have no plane to catch."

"Please, Mama."

She looked at her son leaning against Jordan's leg while Jordan's large hand rested easily on his shoulder. One of them should have a fantasy come true. "All right."

"Yeah!"

Jordan straightened. "Put your car back in and I'll get Joshua seated."

Lauren watched the two and hoped she wasn't making another mistake. It was becoming more difficult to put her feelings for Jordan into some rational perspective. One thing she knew, she was not going to get caught up in trying to create her own fantasy. Jordan wasn't for her.

The small barbershop in the neighborhood strip shopping center was filled to capacity. All six chairs were occupied. The barbers' clippers and shears were going fast and furious, but there was no way they were going to keep up with the demand—especially when some of the young men wanted everything shaved in their heads from football team trademarks to intricate designs.

Recalling his years of experience with barbers, the long wait wasn't bothering Jordan as much as Lauren's aloofness. Not once in the past hour and a half had she smiled or looked directly at him for more than a few seconds.

Although she was sitting next to him in one of the most uncomfortable chairs he had ever sat in, he might have been invisible. If he asked a question she responded, but otherwise she remained silent and stiff.

Dammit. He missed her smile, missed the way her brown eyes sparkled when she forgot to be afraid. "Are you sure I can't get you something to drink?"

"I'm fine, thank you."

She wasn't fine. And Jordan had a feeling that if not for her son she wouldn't be within a mile of him. He didn't know why they were back to being polite strangers, but he intended to find out when they were alone. For now, there were too many curious glances, especially from the men.

"You've been coming here a long time?"

"For about six months."

"Is it usually this crowded?" Jordan glared at one of the men openly leering at Lauren.

Lauren glanced around the crowded shop. "No. I heard someone say the prom is Friday night. Usually we can walk in and out."

That at least explained all the curious, speculative males. More than ever Jordan was glad he had accompanied them. To some men 'no' was a challenge to get a woman to say 'yes'. He'd turned a few 'nos' into 'yeses' himself ... Lauren's included. But he'd be damned if any other man got the opportunity where she was concerned. He might have to find Joshua a new barber. "Do you want to leave?"

She looked at Joshua playing with another little boy. "Not if I don't want a major confrontation with my son. I've never seen him this content to wait."

"He wants me to have my turn in the chair, huh?"

She nodded. "We could come back tomorrow, but we don't want to inconvenience you. Maybe I could ask someone else."

"Who?" The question sounded like an accusation, and there was nothing he could do about it.

"I don't know at the moment."

Jordan relaxed only marginally. She wanted to get rid of him. "Then it looks like I'm still the prime candidate. Let's get out of here."

Taking her arm, Jordan pretended he didn't notice her stiffen at his touch and walked to Joshua. "What do you say we take our turn in the barber chair tomorrow, and go get something to eat?"

Keeping one small fist in the air in front of him, Joshua took the other hand and wrapped it around the imaginary gearshift of a car, shot it forward, then jerked it back. "Varroom. Varroom. I'd rather wait."

Releasing Lauren's arm, Jordan hunkered down to eye level with the little boy. "It will be well past your bedtime before it's time for either of us to sit in the chair, and way past the closing of the restaurant.''

Both hands clamped around the invisible steering wheel, the child peered over Jordan's broad shoulder. ''You sure?''

''I'm sure. We can come back tomorrow.''

''You promise?''

''Joshua, Mr. Hamilton is a busy man.'' Lauren's hands clamped around her handbag. ''Maybe I can find someone else.''

''I want Mr. Hamilton!'' Joshua cried, his hands leaving the steering wheel.

''You've got me, Joshua.'' Standing, Jordan reached out to the little boy. ''I promise to take you tomorrow.'' At least this promise wouldn't churn his gut.

Smiling, Joshua placed his hands in Jordan's and got up from the chair.

Chapter Twelve

Jordan knew what was coming before he turned onto Lauren's street. The classic brush-off. The same brush-off he'd gotten the last time he had brought her home.

Lauren yawned for the second time in as many minutes. Delicately, her hand patted her mouth. "I am so tired."

"Not me," Joshua piped up from the backseat. "I wish we could have stayed at the playground."

Good for you, Son, Jordan thought. At least one person in the Bennett family wanted him around.

"You will be once your head hits the pillow." Lauren yawned again. "You're going straight to bed when we get inside."

"Ahhh, Mama."

"Thank Mr. Hamilton so we can go inside."

Jordan's grip on the steering wheel tightened. Once they arrived at the fast food restaurant, Lauren had tried to distance herself further from him by referring to him as Mr. Hamilton. Not once had she called him by his given name.

"Thank you, Mr. Hamilton."

"You're welcome." Jordan pulled into Lauren's driveway. The light from the streetlight shone around them. Absently he wondered if he might score points by letting her know he had called a friend who had called another friend and gotten the city works department moving. Probably not, he decided.

Lauren scrambled from the Bronco to get her child.

She rushed up the steps as if her feet were on fire. Opening the front door, she guided her son inside then blocked the entrance. "Good night, and thank you again."

At least she hadn't stuck her hand out for him to shake it. "What did I do, Lauren?"

Her eyes widened. She glanced away. "I don't know what you're talking about."

"Yes, you do, and I'm not going any place until you tell me," Jordan said, placing his hand on the open screen.

"If Mr. Hamilton is staying, can he read me the barber story?" asked a voice from behind her.

Lauren faced her son. "He is not staying. I want you to go to your room and get your homework ready for me to check."

"Bu—"

"Now, Joshua. No arguing."

Jordan heard a firmness in Lauren's strained voice he had never heard before. Apparently her son had, because he left without further argument.

Shoulders rigid, she gave her attention back to him. "Good night. I'm tired."

"So you've repeated every minute since we left the restaurant." Her chin came up indignantly. "What I want to know is, what happened between Sunday and today?"

"Nothing happened," she told him cooly, and tried to pull the screen shut. He easily kept it open. She tried glaring. "If you don't mind."

"As a matter of fact, I do." He took a step closer. "Why won't you smile at me?"

She gave him a smile rimmed with icicles.

He reached for her. She squeaked and jumped back. Jordan's hands fisted. "Stop that. You know I wouldn't hurt you."

"Then leave. Please." Her arms crossed over her chest. "Just leave."

The strain was back in her voice. The sound tore him up

inside, knowing he might have put it there, knowing he might not be able to take it away. "I'll call you tomorrow."

"Please don't. I'll be extremely busy," she told him.

"Lauren?" He extended his hand, only to shove it into his pocket before reaching her face. "I'll pick you and Joshua up at five."

Something sad flashed in her eyes, then it was gone. "Good night."

Slowly, Jordan went to his car, trying to analyze what had happened to the smiling woman who had hugged him good-bye at the airport and given him her phone number. There had been many times in the past three days he had picked up the phone to call her. He had resisted the temptation, and instead he'd concentrated on getting things in order for him to come back. Frankly, he hadn't known what to say.

Guilt rode him hard. He had asked to be her friend, and the way things looked he might have to betray that friendship. He loved his father and wanted to clear his name, but using an innocent woman and her child to do it was wrong.

As he sat in his office in Santa Clara, his objective had seemed simple . . . but that was before he looked into Lauren's sad, brown eyes, held her slender body in his arms. She was just as much a victim as his father. Taking advantage of her was as bad as what Strickland had done to his father. But unless Drake came up with something concrete against their common enemy, Jordan might not have a choice.

But only as a last resort. Because, no matter what his rationale or how he explained things to Lauren, she'd never want to see him again. He refused to think that might happen.

It looked as if it was happening, anyway, and he had no idea why. She wanted no part of him.

Maybe he should have called. The outcome wouldn't have been a tenth as hellish as the uncertainty he was going through now.

Stopping in the middle of the sidewalk, he stared back at her house. The porch light was still on. Despite everything, Lauren remained courteous. The light would stay on until he was inside the Bronco.

Remaining still, he tried to figure out what had gone wrong. Why didn't she want him to call, when once she had given him her numb—His thoughts stumbled to a halt. A frown puckered his brow. A part of their conversation clicked.

Rushing back up the steps, he knocked on the door. The doorbell might bring Joshua, and he wanted their conversation private. Nothing. He knocked harder.

The front door jerked open. An uncertain looking Lauren stared though the screen door at him. As he expected, she had stayed nearby to cut off the light. "You're upset because I didn't call, aren't you?"

Her startled expression gave her away.

"I thought about calling ten times a day, and you'll never know how sorry I am that I didn't."

Her chin lifted. "You don't owe me any explanation."

Stubborn, lonely woman. "Yes, I do. I messed up and I'm sorry. You probably thought I was handing you a line when you didn't hear from me."

She glanced away. "It's late."

"Let's go back to Sunday. Open the screen, Lauren," he said, his deep voice low and compelling. "I'd like another chance and another hug."

Her gaze jerked back to him. A tongue flicked over her bottom lip. "No."

He wanted to groan at the tempting sight of her tongue, but grinned instead. Lauren might be weary, but she wasn't indifferent. There was definitely something between them, and once Strickland was out of the way, Jordan fully intended to pursue the matter.

"I see you need convincing, and I'm just the man to do it. Good night, Honey. I won't let you down again. By the way, my phone number is five, five, five, six, seven, seven, seven.

Whistling, he walked to his Bronco and drove off.

Lauren had a terrible night, and her day wasn't getting much better. Joshua had been like a wet noodle, trying to get out of bed. A wreck had closed all but one lane of the freeway, causing her to be fifteen minutes late to work. Somehow she had gotten a run in her hose, and the copy machine in her office was out of toner.

And it wasn't nine-thirty yet. What else could happen?

Her office door opened and she groaned, thinking she shouldn't have asked. The sight of a man in a dark brown uniform caused some of her trepidation to ease.

"Yes, can I help you?" she asked, glad to put off the messy toner job a little longer.

"I've got a delivery for Lauren Bennett," he said, handing her his electronic pad with one hand and easing down a round crystal vase with the other.

Lauren glanced at the pad, the empty crystal vase, the name tag on the man's shirt—Flowers by Marie—then back to the sparkling vase. "I think you've made a mistake."

The gray-headed man frowned. "This is Lauren Bennett's office, isn't it?"

"Yes. I'm Ms. Bennett. But I wasn't expecting a delivery, and," she nodded toward the vase, "there are no flowers."

A relieved smile broke across the man's thin face. "That's the same thing I said."

"And what was the response?" she asked.

Once again, he frowned. "I'd rather not say. If you'll just sign, I have a lot of deliveries to make."

Signing her name, Lauren thanked the man and stared at the vase. Who would send an empty one? She had never received gifts or flowers at the office.

Except once.

Suspicion edged her closer. In the bottom of the deeply etched, diamond cut vase was a small white card. She stuck her hand inside, then drew it back.

It had to be Jordan. Why was the vase empty? Questions swirled around in her mind. She nibbled her lower lip.

Folding her arms, she watched the early morning sun turn the vase into an enchanting prism of light. Her fingers itched to run her fingers over the deep grooves and see if its beauty was as flawless as it appeared.

The sneaky devil. He had probably planned just such a reaction from her.

He had kept her awake most of the night, and now he was interfering with her day. She hadn't been able to forget the shimmer of promise in his voice or him calling her Honey.

More than anything she found herself wanting to believe his slight hadn't been intentional. Yet, the undeniable pain and disillusionment she'd experienced when he hadn't called had taught her she was too vulnerable and too inexperienced where Jordan was concerned.

Firmly, she turned from the vase and went back to putting the toner in the copy machine. Finished, she went to the bathroom, washed her hands, then ran the copies. Placing them beside the vase, she flipped on her computer. Jordan wasn't going to get the better of her, she told herself.

She was entering the second page of her report before curiosity and something else she didn't dare put a name to got the best of her. Her hands stilled. What harm could one peek do?

Picking up the envelope, she quickly opened it before she could change her mind. Only one word was written on the white card. *Beautiful.* A frown marred the smoothness of her brow. She laid the card aside.

She didn't know anymore than she had. If he thought she was going to be intrigued, he was sadly mistaken. She'd show him she wasn't interested. Whirling to the computer, she went back to typing.

By lunchtime, Lauren *was* intrigued, and fighting not to be overwhelmed. In her hand were a total of four cards, each with a single word she somehow knew Jordan had written in his own bold style. The crystal vase now held three inches of pale pink marbles, baby's breath, greenery, and five white lilies brushed with mauve.

She didn't know whether to go out to lunch as she had planned and chance missing the next delivery, or stay. She was sure there would be more. She glanced at the cards lined up on her desk, then called Sidney, one of her co-workers who usually went out to lunch, and asked her to bring back something. And waited.

Her turkey sandwich arrived at the same time as the fifth delivery—Birds of Paradise—and the florist, Emily. The talkative woman had initially filled the vase with baby's breath and greenery, but with each successive delivery, Emily had removed the fillers and added more flowers to create the most breathtaking floral arrangement Lauren had ever seen.

Watching the rapt attention and curiosity of her co-worker, Lauren knew two things: the staff would be watching for the next delivery, and they were going to hound her to tell them who had sent them.

She was right.

By four that afternoon there was so much *oohing* and *aahing* from the females crowded around in her office that Lauren was becoming embarrassed. More than one woman had speculated on the cost involved and intimated that if Lauren wasn't interested, she could hand over his phone number.

To her relief, Mr. Scott came out of his office. "Did someone declare a holiday I didn't know about?"

Women scattered. All except Cynthia Douglas. The office manager gazed at Lauren a long time. Lauren could almost hear wheels clicking in her head. Cynthia wasn't about to forget that Jordan had taken Lauren to dinner.

"Lauren, have you talked to Mr. Hamilton lately?" Cynthia asked. "I tried to reach him yesterday and had no luck."

"He hasn't called the office," Lauren answered truthfully.

"Cynthia, I'm sure Jordan will get back to you." Mr. Scott took her by the arm. "In the meantime, how about giving me a rundown on the plans you have for the Nelson project?"

Her gaze flicked to Lauren before she said, "Certainly."

Lauren relaxed. Mr. Scott on the prowl should keep people in their own offices. He wasn't a strict employer, but he didn't like people to loaf.

That suited Lauren just fine. There had to be another delivery, and for some reason she was more tense about it than any of the others. Unfolding the seven notes, she spread them out in front of her and read them.

Beautiful creations for some take longer. Please forgive

The last sentence was incomplete. She straightened on hearing the door open and glanced over her shoulder.

Jordan stood in the doorway, dark and imposing. A tailored, Italian gray striped suit fit his muscular body to perfection. He was the most magnificent human she had ever seen.

Lauren swallowed. She felt the familiar flutter in her stomach, accompanied by an ache in her heart. Faintly she heard the phone ring on her desk, but she was too aware of the man staring at her so intently to pick it up.

Crossing to her, he placed a deep red rose in the middle of the arrangement, handed her an envelope, then left.

Trembling, she opened the card. *Me.*

"Oh, Jordan, how could you do this to me?"

Jordan was waiting for her in front of her house. Legs crossed, arms folded, he leaned against the Bronco. The suit had been exchanged for a blue shirt and navy dress pants. The man looked gorgeous in whatever he wore. Lauren moistened her lips. Her hands flexed on the steering wheel. She had dreaded this moment since she left her office.

Jordan's gift and generosity were unlike anything she had ever experienced. So was his understanding. He sensed her fears and tried to alleviate them. The problem was, she feared him most of all.

Parking the car in the garage, she took a calming breath and walked to the Bronco. "Hello, Jordan. I'll go get Joshua."

"Hi, Lauren," he greeted easily. "No need. He saw your car and went to get his backpack."

"Oh." She glanced toward Sonja's house, feeling a ridiculous urge to seek the protection it offered from the unnerving gaze of the broad-shouldered man near her. She quickly squelched the idea. If he could apologize, the least she could do was acknowledge it. "The flowers were beautiful."

He chuckled, a deep, rich sound that did strange things to her body. "Then why do you look as if you were about to face a firing squad?"

"Because I'm more confused than ever," she blurted.

He straightened. His blunt-tipped fingers brushed across her cheek. "Then I'll have to work harder," he whispered softly.

She swallowed. "Don't, please."

One of his heavy brows arched. "I thought you liked the flowers."

"I do. The whole idea was like something from a fairy tale. But . . ." her voice trailed off.

"But," he coaxed.

"It's too extravagant, and the women in my office won't rest until they find out who you are," she murmured. "Cynthia Douglas already suspects it's you. She said she tried to call you yesterday."

"My secretary knows how to reach me if it's important. In the meantime . . ." He leaned closer, a dangerous smile hovering on his bearded face. "I don't care who knows we're friends, but if it bothers you we'll keep things just between the two of us."

His words caused a warm shiver to race down her spine. Grateful, she heard Joshua slam out of Sonja's house. She turned to greet her son, wondering in spite of herself what else Jordan had in mind.

The crowded parking lot in the strip shopping center was their first bad sign. The second was the several teenagers congregating outside the barbershop. Jordan and Lauren exchanged worried looks.

"Stay here. I'll go inside and see how bad it is," Jordan said, double parking.

"Aren't we going in?" Joshua unbuckled his seatbelt and scooted forward on the backseat.

Lauren turned to her son. "We'd planned to, Sweetheart, but it looks like it's more crowded than it was yesterday."

"But you and Mr. Hamilton promised," he wailed.

Technically, *Jordan* had promised, but it wasn't time to point that out to an unhappy five-year-old. "We didn't think . . ." Her voice trailed off as Joshua sat back in his seat with folded arms and bowed head.

"Joshua, I'm sorry. Maybe . . ." She stopped before she dug herself in deeper. She wasn't going to promise anything else she couldn't guarantee.

Unbuckling her seatbelt, she faced Jordan. "We'll wait. I hate to inconvenience you, but can I call you when we're next?"

"You do know barbershops have been known to stay open until two in the morning, don't you?" Jordan asked.

"I've never broken a promise to him," she said simply.

"If you think I'm going to allow you to to stay in there that long by yourselves, you're crazy. Besides, you didn't promise—I did." He faced Joshua. "Is this the only barbershop where we can get in the chair, or will another one do just as well?"

The little boy's head came up. "You know another one, Mr. Hamilton?"

Jordan smiled at the hopefulness in the small face. "As a matter of fact, I do. As soon as you and your mother buckle up, I'll take you there."

Jordan scrambled into his seatbelt. "Hurry up, Mama."

The parking lot in the upscale shopping complex was equally crowded, but no young men were congregating outside Pierre, only two cone shaped boxwood shrubs. Bold gold lettering scrawled the owner's name across the glass on either side of the recessed, ornate, teal door. A striped teal and white canvas awning fluttered in the evening breeze.

"We can't go in there," Lauren breathed, clutching her son's hand.

"Why?" Jordan asked.

"Why?" she repeated incredulously. "A haircut probably costs more than a week of my salary."

Jordan increased the pressure of his hand in the small of her back. "It was my idea to come here, so it's on me."

Lauren shook her head. "No."

"The way I see it, you can either give in gracefully or we

look in the phone book and find another barber who is willing to go along with Joshua's plan,'' Jordan told her.

Knowing he was right didn't mean she was willing to give in. ''You probably need an appointment to get in there.''

''I took care of that this morning.''

Her eyes widened. ''This morning?''

''Obviously you don't remember the hassle you had getting a beauty or barbershop appointment around prom time.'' He grimaced. ''Only Easter is worse.''

''I didn't go to my prom,'' she admitted without thinking.

This time he looked stunned. ''What was the matter with the guys in your high school?''

The expression of disbelief on Jordan's face went a long way to soothing the memory of being dateless on prom night and trying to convince her mother she really didn't mind.

''We're going in?'' asked Joshua, glancing from one adult to the other.

''We are as soon as your mother stops dragging her feet,'' Jordan told the little boy.

Lauren glanced at the two expectant males. So what if she had to take her lunch to work for the next two months? ''Lead the way.''

''Yeah!'' her son yelled, and reached for the door.

''Relax, Lauren. It won't be bad.'' Jordan ushered her inside.

Jordan was right. In fact, Lauren thoroughly enjoyed watching Jordan watch the barber as he snipped and snipped the air over his head. He looked enormously relieved to vacate the chair for Joshua, who was more than happy to take his turn. To her surprise, Jordan stayed nearby, instructing the barber on how to cut her son's hair.

Unlike the previous ones, Joshua grinned all through this haircut. Finished, the barber pulled the cloth from around her son's neck with a flourish, then turned to her, his gaze boldly running over her hair.

''I'd love to get my hands in that hair of yours.'' Reaching out, he plucked experimentally at the curls. ''Just as I thought.

Soft as cotton, A deep conditioner and a cut to layer around your face, and you'd stop traffic.''

Jordan pulled Lauren away. ''Joshua and I like her hair just the way it is.''

Pierre folded his arms across his chest. Once again his assessing gaze flicked over Lauren. ''I see.''

Lauren flushed. Her hand made what she knew was an effortless attempt to smooth her flyaway hair. She had taken it down just before she left the office. She had been trying to look good for Jordan, and had been embarrassed for her efforts. ''Perhaps another time.''

The man offered his card. ''In case you change your mind. No charge for the first visit.''

''Come on. Let's go.'' Jordan steered Lauren and Joshua from the private room. He stopped only long enough to plump some bills down at the front counter before continuing out the front door. ''I couldn't decide if the guy was trying to come on to you or drumming up business.''

''I doubt if he was trying to do either in this locale. Maybe he was right.'' Lauren resisted the urge to touch her hair again.

''Joshua and I are lucky we got you out of there intact.'' Jordan opened the back door of the vehicle. ''Your hair is fantastic. It's one of the first things I noticed about you.''

Lauren was so startled and pleased by the compliment that she simply stood until he faced her again.

''What?'' he asked when he opened her door and she remained unmoved.

''You like my hair?''

''Of course I do.'' He continued, seeing the doubt in her expression. ''Who're you gonna believe? Me, or some scissor happy guy who wears tight purple pants and probably moussed his scanty chest hair?''

He looked so fierce that Lauren smiled. ''You.''

''At last I'm making progress.''

She sobered. ''It isn't easy trusting sometimes.''

His hand brushed across her cheek. ''I know. Just don't shut me out.''

''Jor—''

"Hey, this was fun," Joshua said, his arms propped over the front seat.

"It might have been," Jordan murmured. Lauren tucked her head and got inside.

"I wanted to ask you something else," Joshua said when they were driving away. "Could you be my Show and Tell tomorrow at school?"

"Joshua, no. Jordan has already done enough for you."

"I'd be delighted," Jordan said. Lauren hadn't referred to him as Mr. Hamilton. Progress.

"Yippee! Mine will be the best ever!" cried Joshua.

Chapter Thirteen

Joshua would be right at home with The Wild Bunch, Jordan thought. The little boy had some pretty inventive ideas about how to prolong the evening once he arrived home that night.

Arms folded, Jordan watched Lauren read to her son. According to Joshua, it was the only way to get the monsters who lived under his bed to go to sleep. He had asked Jordan to come along, in case they became 'unruly'. Jordan could almost hear the little boy's teacher using the same word to describe her students who misbehaved.

Jordan's lips twitched on remembering Lauren's shocked expression. Apparently that was the first time she had heard of the little rascals. He had to give it to her, though—she had regrouped nicely and wanted to confront her unwanted houseguests.

Before they made it to his room, Joshua warned her that the monsters could become invisible any time they wanted to, just like the cartoon character Space Ghost.

Now, tucked securely under the bed covers after saying his prayers, Joshua was struggling to keep his eyes open. If he was anything like Jordan's seven year old nieces, the little boy had

less than five minutes before immobility lulled him to sleep—
if all the water he drank didn't send him to the bathroom first.

"Mr. Hamilton, you wanna sit beside Mama?" he asked
sleepily.

Lauren's hands jerked on the book, and her gaze remained
downcast. Jordan eyed the small place on the twin bed next to
where she sat, and opted against the temptation. "Thank you,
but I'm fine."

Joshua yawned and rolled over onto his side, toward Jordan.
"You won't forget tomorrow, will you?"

"I won't," Jordan said. "Now close your eyes. The sooner
you get to sleep, the sooner tomorrow will be here."

"Yes, Sir." He yawned again and closed his eyes, only
to open them. "You gonna be here when I wake up in the
morning?"

Lauren gasped. The book fell to the floor. "No," she cried.

Jordan crossed the room, picked up the book, and calmly
handed it to her. Obviously flustered, she took it without looking
at him. "I'll see you tomorrow at ten thirty."

"Okay." Joshua closed his eyes again. "Night, Mama.
Night, Mr. Hamilton."

"Good night, Joshua," Jordan said, and noted that although
Lauren bid her son good night, she didn't get up. Instead, she
fussed with his covers, ran her hand over his head.

Jordan thought about moving back and giving her some
space, then decided against it. Lauren had to accept their
attraction to each other, and know he wasn't going to use it
against her. He wanted her until his body ached, but acting on
his desire would lose Lauren forever. Believing that was the
only way he was able to maintain control.

"I think he's asleep," Jordan whispered after two minutes
has passed and the little boy hadn't moved.

With one last touch of her son's face, Lauren stood and
turned. The front of her body brushed against Jordan's. Her
breath caught. A jolt of awareness swept through her. Clutching
the book to her chest, she stepped to one side, her eyes wide,
her teeth clamped on her lower lip.

"Lauren?"

She heard the concern in Jordan's voice, saw it in his dark gaze, but there was also something much deeper there. It had been so much easier dealing with Jordan and her mercurial feelings when her son had been a constant buffer . . . until he had asked the question about Jordan being there when he woke up.

She didn't sleep around. She didn't even date. The problem was, she wasn't sure if she was more mortified by the question or aroused by the possibility. Swallowing, she glanced away.

"I'll go put on some tea."

Lauren didn't look up until she was sure Jordan had left the room. She wasn't good at this. She had never dated very much in high school or college. In whatever free time she had, she'd helped her mother in her bookstore. Soon the few boys who had asked her out stopped asking. She hadn't minded. Her mother had been her best friend.

By the time she had met David, she was a new graduate from college and her mother had hired someone to help her. David had been easy to talk to, and fun. There was nothing about him that caused the least bit of uneasiness.

With Jordan she was seldom aware of anything else. She wasn't sure how she was supposed to react to him, because her body reacted so unpredictably. There was an intense awareness between them that she was unable to ignore. Sighing, she took one last look at Joshua and started from the room.

Her reflection in the mirror of his dresser caught her attention. Not a trace of her lipstick color remained. The humidity and the wind had done a number on her hair. Maybe she should give Pierre a call. At least she could fix one thing. She reached for her purse on the dresser. In less than three seconds, plumb-colored lipstick glistened on her lips.

She paused. She had done it again.

She wasn't the type to stand in the mirror repairing her makeup and recombing her hair. Once she left work, she usually chose a colorless lip gloss, and seldom did anything to enhance the way she looked. In fact, she did everything she could to fade into the background.

Replacing the lipstick, she switched off the light and left the room. Jordan was not going to turn her into one of those anxious women who worried about how they looked all the time.

Standing at the kitchen counter, Jordan glanced over his shoulder the moment she came into view. Her hand went to her hair, in spite of herself. His gaze went to her lips and stayed there. Air became harder for her to draw in.

Finally, his gaze lifted to hers. The dark, compelling look in his black eyes caused her knees to wobble.

"I have a question to ask."

"What?" Somehow her brain and mouth cooperated enough to form that one word.

Slow steps brought him closer, until their bodies were almost touching. "About being your friend."

In spite of everything she had told herself, disappointment stabbed her. Her hand clutched her stomach at the physical pain. "I understand. We're demanding more of your time than you have to give."

Black eyes blazed. His handsome features harshened. "You certainly don't have very much faith in me, do you?"

She was unprepared for the hurt in his voice. How much she wanted to soothe it away. "It's not your fault. You're just too busy."

"I asked you once. I'm asking it again. Is it me, or all men, that you distrust?"

She gave him the only answer she could. "If I didn't trust you, you wouldn't be in my house."

He smiled, a slow easy smile like the sun breaking over the horizon. "You just redeemed yourself." His hands settled gently on her waist. "The question I wanted to ask is, how am I doing redeeming *myself?*"

"Oohhh."

"Caught you off guard, didn't I?" he said, his smile growing.

The tip of her tongue moistened her upper lip. Unsuccessfully she tried to steady her breathing, the thudding of her heart. "Joshua likes you."

"How about his mother?" His thumb lightly stroked her skin through her suit jacket.

She wasn't going to be able to remember her name if he

didn't stop touching her. Her hands clamped over his wrists, but instead of moving him away, she just held on. She became aware of the strength in his hands and the gentleness with which he held her. She liked both.

Too much. Finally she had met someone who awakened all the desires she thought she had buried with her husband. Jordan had also gotten closer faster than anyone in the past six years. A dangerous situation. Her hands flexed to push him away.

As if aware of her decision, his hands tightened. "There's no need for you to give me an answer now. You can tell me after your tea and foot massage."

She blinked. "Foot massage?"

He studied her closely. "You've never had anyone take care of you and pamper you, have you?"

"My mother was too busy making a living. Joshua's father would have, if he had lived." The memory of their tragic deaths saddened her. Withdrawing her hands, she stepped back. "I'm rather tired. I don't think I want any tea or the massage."

"All right, Lauren. I won't rush you." Taking her hand, he went to the front door. "I want to show you and Joshua something tomorrow."

"What?"

"It's a surprise."

"We can't stay for long. I promised Sonja I'd help her stuff envelopes."

"I'll pick you up around six. Dress casually."

"We'll be ready."

"Make sure you lock up."

She smiled indulgently. He certainly liked giving orders, but it was rather nice having someone worry about them. Just that little bit wouldn't hurt. "I will. Good night, Jordan."

"Good night, Lauren." After a quick kiss on her cheek, he went to his Bronco, which was parked in the driveway.

Locking the screen, then the door, Lauren slowly went to her room, her hand on her cheek, wondering how it would have felt to have his lips on hers. A part of her knew she was going to find out.

* * *

"Wow."

Lauren had to agree with her son. The French Mediterranean stucco-designed home with its red, barrel tile roof and black wrought iron railings was fabulous. What she didn't understand was why Jordan had parked in the circular driveway and was opening the back door for Joshua.

But then, she'd come to expect the unusual from the man who had charmed twenty-two kindergarten students, their teacher, the principal, half the staff, and several of the volunteer mothers on duty. Jordan had been an unqualified hit, according to the phone calls Lauren received at home and at work.

During those phone conversations more than one female caller had asked boldly if he was taken. She told each one to ask him. Three said they would if they saw him again. One had requested his number. When she told Jordan about the woman wanting his number, he had only expressed gratitude that she hadn't given it out, and hurried her and Joshua out of her house.

Now, looking at the mansion, Lauren was intrigued by the prospect of seeing inside. Unbuckling her seatbelt, she got out. Joshua was already investigating a painted green concrete frog spouting water in the small fountain near the front door.

"Who lives here?" she asked, her gaze flickering appreciatively over the well-tended yard.

"I do," Jordan said.

Lauren's head whipped around. "You! But your two main offices are in New Orleans and Santa Clara."

"And now I have business concerns in Shreveport. Besides, you don't like crowded hotels or elevators."

Shock swept across her face. "But . . . but—"

"Lauren, I don't like hotels anymore than you do. Besides, you can't tell me you'd feel comfortable coming to my hotel room, even if you didn't have to get there by elevator."

She looked wildly around the grounds of the two-story dwelling. "I don't know about this."

Jordan stared down into Lauren's worried face and wanted

nothing more than to pull her into his arms and promise everything was going to be all right. He knew he was laying a lot on her, but the quickest way out of the mess they were in was for her to stop hiding her feelings for him and from Strickland.

His hands cupped her face. "If I flew into Shreveport on business I'd have to stay someplace. The way I see things, it might as well be in a place where the friends and business associates I invite over and I can relax." He nodded toward her son. "He likes the place."

Joshua, squatted on the side of the frog, was stopping and unstopping the mammal's mouth, laughing as water spouted around his small fingers. The front of his shirt was wet, and so were his shoes.

Jordan knew Lauren was feeling a bit overwhelmed when she didn't order her son to stop playing in the water. "The backyard has a sunken garden with an arbor covered with wisteria and roses. The pool water looks so blue you think you're in the Mediterranean. You said you haven't gone swimming much lately. Even when I'm not here you and Joshua can come over whenever you want."

"I've never seen the Mediterranean," she said.

Jordan promised himself that she would one day. "Then let me show you a replica." His hand firmly on her arm, he opened the door and called for Joshua.

He watched Lauren's eyes widen as she stepped onto the hardwood floor of the two-story foyer. Directly in front was a spiral staircase and the spacious living room with multi-paned windows and French doors. To the right was a marble fireplace, the uniquely finished, red oak mantle highlighting the dining room. To the left were textured walls, a beamed ceiling, and stained, red oak bookcases in the private study and office.

He had asked his secretary to find a place similar to his home in New Orleans with a feel of the tropics and a Mediterranean flair—a place a man took a woman he cared about. He signed the lease the day he arrived back in Shreveport.

"It's beautiful," Lauren breathed.

"Come on, I'll show you the garden." He looked back at a

wet Joshua making squishing noises with his tennis shoes. "We better get you dried out first. Casper."

Lauren glanced around at her son. There wasn't one dry spot on the front of him. Water dripped from his chin. "Joshua, you'll mess up the place."

"No, he won't," Jordan said. "The floor is hardwood. I told you I wanted a place where we could relax."

"Good evening, Mr. Hamilton. You called?"

Jordan turned to see the rather asture, middle-aged butler/ housekeeper who came with the lease. He suspected the servant was there to keep an eye on whoever leased the place, but after he ate Casper's quiche the evening he arrived, that was fine with Jordan.

"Casper, this is Mrs. Bennett and her son, Joshua. As you can see, Joshua had a close encounter with the fountain. Could you find him a towel, then bring him outside to the arbor?" Jordan asked.

Casper inclined his head to Jordan, then Lauren. "Certainly, Sir. Madam. If you'll come with me, young man."

Joshua took a cautionary step closer. "You're name's Casper?"

The formally dressed man peered down at the little boy. "Yes it is, and no, I'm not any relation to the friendly ghost."

"You're sure?"

"Quite."

"Then you can't fly and go through walls?" the child continued, obviously disappointed.

"Only if I take an airplane and open a door," the servant said deadpan.

Joshua laughed. "That was funny."

The man looked with new interest at the boy. Apparently he hadn't expected the child to make the connection so quickly. "Shall we go?"

Jordan crossed the floor and grabbed the man's hand. "Okay . . . I like you."

The butler appeared startled. Then his hand closed around Joshua's. "You're proving to be of some interest to me, as well."

"I'll be," Jordan said as he watched the two disappear toward the kitchen. "I haven't been able to get Casper to say more than four words at a time."

"He does appear rather stiff," Lauren commented. "But can you imagine being stuck with a name like Casper all your life? I wonder if it's his first name or his last?"

Jordan shrugged. "Beats me. He introduced himself to me as Casper, and I didn't ask."

Lauren smiled up at him. "Don't tell me he intimidated you?"

"No, but after tasting his cooking, I decided he had a perfect right to be a little stuffy."

"Oh. So you can be bought?"

"Depends on the offer," he said and watched her tuck her head. "Come on, I want to show you the back." Taking her hand, he went through the living room, out the French door, and onto the stone patio flooring of the sunken garden.

"Oh, Jordan, it's beautiful," she breathed. The sun was still shining, but the dense shrubbery, mature trees, and the arbor gave the illusion of intimacy and coolness.

"Come on. I wanted to show you something special." Holding her hand, he walked past the vine covered columns and beneath aged wooden beams. "Now." He stepped behind her and turned her to face the wall.

"Ohhh," a musical sound of delight, of wonder, slipped past her lips. Their reflections stared back at her—the muscular, well-built man and the small woman standing in front of him. Total contrasts, yet somehow right.

Seeing Jordan with his hands resting lightly on her shoulders no longer frightened her—perhaps because the place seemed so out of touch with reality, perhaps because, no matter what his explanation, the man holding her so tenderly had gone to such trouble to create a place for her and her son. No one had done that before.

She leaned back against him and folded her arms across her waist. "It's lovely. I don't blame you for wanting to be here."

His chin rested on top of her head. "I admit the place has merit, but you're what makes it special."

A tiny thrill of pleasure raced down her spine. Suddenly she wanted to believe for a little while that this was real. She wanted to forget that anything more than friendship between them was impossible. All she wanted to do was remember that she was a woman and Jordan was a man she was wildly attracted to, a man she wanted to kiss. Half turning in his arms, she heard a familiar voice.

"Mama. Mr. Hamilton. Where are you?" Joshua called. "Mama?" The call grew closer and louder.

Startled, Lauren took the opportunity to distance herself. By the time Joshua came around the corner with Casper holding his hand, they were a foot apart.

"Anything else, Sir?" asked the servant.

"No, I think you've done about enough," Jordan said tightly. Casper's interruption had been for the best, but Jordan didn't have to like it.

"I do my best." Turning on his heels, the butler went back inside.

"Mama, you should see the room where Mr. Casper dried my clothes. It has a TV in the wall," Joshua said. Then he saw the pool. "Wow."

Jordan caught the collar of his shirt as he was about to take off. "No you don't. If you go near that pool without your mother or some adult being with you, I promise you won't even see it again, let alone get in it. Clear?"

Joshua's thin shoulders slumped. "Yes, Sir."

"Good. Don't look so gloomy. You have the entire summer to go swimming," Jordan said.

Excitement radiated in the child's face. "You mean I can come over?"

"Any time your mother can fit it into her schedule," Jordan told him. "So I advise you to be on your best behavior."

"I will."

Lauren smiled down at her son. "Come on, let's go home and put some of that best behavior into helping Sonja stuff envelopes."

"I can't talk you into staying a little longer?"

"I wish I could, but Sonja is counting on me." Disappointment tinged her words.

"Then how about tomorrow night? I'd like to show you the entire house. Afterwards we could go swimming."

She glanced at Joshua making faces in the mirrored wall. "He's been out a lot at night lately, more than I like."

"Then how about just his mother?"

Excitement vied with caution. "I don't know." It would be dangerous to spend any time alone with Jordan. She didn't know how to handle a man like him.

"Please. I'm not sure how much longer I'll be in town."

Her resistance crumbled. "Yes."

Chapter Fourteen

Lauren couldn't decide what to wear. Everything in her closet seemed too casual or too dressy. The wrong style, the wrong color. Wrong. Hands on her hips, she stared at the clothes strewn on her bed. Nothing caught her eye.

Her wardrobe was serviceable and versatile, planned for optimum use and efficiency to mix and match for an office setting. Black, blue, brown, and an occasional green or mauve. Nothing to turn a person's head or pique anyone's interest.

Least of all a sophisticated man like Jordan Hamilton.

Sighing, she sat on the bed and admitted what she had been fighting all day—if she weren't going out with Jordan, the selection would have been made hours ago, with very little fuss. Instead, she had been at this for more than two hours.

She wanted to look nice for him, for herself.

For once, she wanted to forget that the secrets of her past made any kind of future with a man impossible. Tonight she wanted to recapture the feeling of rightness she had experienced in Jordan's arms in the sunken garden. She wanted to capture the attention of a pirate.

She wasn't likely to do it wearing anything in her closet.

Sighing again, Lauren reached for the tan, long, empire-waisted dress that was perfect for running errands on weekends, but all wrong for enticing a man.

The doorbell chimed. She glanced at the clock radio in her room. Two fourteen. Joshua's coach had said he wouldn't drop her son off until around five.

Tossing the dress over her arm, she went to open the door. Seeing her best friend looking pretty and fresh in a white floral print against a ground of red, Lauren quickly seized the opportunity for salvation.

Opening the door, she pulled the other woman inside. "Thank goodness. With your sense of style, you can help me decide what to wear."

Sonja allowed herself to be dragged inside, then wrinkled her nose at the dress draped over Lauren's arm. "I've seen what's in your closet."

"That bad, huh?"

"There's only one solution." She pulled a shopping bag from behind her back. "Go get him, Girlfriend."

Lauren stared at the gold and beige shopping bag from one of the leading department stores and felt tears sting her eyes. It was a fantastically wonderful thing for Sonja to do. Squealing, she hugged the other woman.

Sonja smiled indulgently. "Don't you dare cry. You won't get Jordan's attention with red, puffy eyes."

"How did you know?" Lauren brushed the lingering moisture from her eyes. "I only figured it out myself this morning."

"Little things like the way your face lights up and becomes softer when his name is mentioned, the way you try so hard to convince me he means nothing to you." Sonja shook her head of short curls. "But the final clue was, after telling me about your date last night, you stuffed all the envelopes wrong."

Horror swept across Lauren's face. "Oh, no."

Her friend smiled. "Don't worry. It was a simple matter of flipping them over. Now, let's go to work. I only hate I won't be able to see Jordan's face when the butterfly emerges from the cocoon in this."

Grinning, Sonja pulled a dress from the bag. Lauren gasped, then laughed with delight.

* * *

Jordan was in trouble.

One look at Lauren in the halter-styled, hot pink sundress and he knew his plans for the evening were going to take a great deal more self-control than he had anticipated. If his body reacted so strongly to her smooth, bare shoulders, seeing her in a swimsuit was going to be pure hell.

The welcoming smile on Lauren's face faded. "Is something wrong?"

"No." He couldn't seem to take his eyes from her. "I've never seen you in anything like that."

Immediately her hand flew up to the honeyed swell of her breasts. "Is this too casual?"

The hurt embarrassment in her eyes made Jordan want to kick himself. "No. You're fine. It's me. I may be your friend, but I'm still a man and you're a beautiful woman."

As she removed her hand, her smile returned. "I think there's a compliment in there someplace. Come on in. I'll get my things."

Entering the house, Jordan groaned. The flared hem of the perky little dress barely skimmed the back of her knees. His first unimpeded look at Lauren's shapely legs only added to the stirring of his body. No wonder she usually wore long skirts. It was going to be a long night.

He cleared his throat. "Where's Joshua?"

She glanced over her shoulder. "Asleep. He had a game today, and afterward the coach took them out for pizza. He wanted to see you, but he's been down since seven."

No help there, Jordan thought, and wandered into the den. Sonja sat on the sofa reading a magazine. His eyes narrowed. Her breathing was erratic as if she had been running. "Good evening, Sonja, is anything the matter?"

"Hi, Jordan," she answered breathlessly, then smiled as she tucked her head to one side. "Everything's great, but maybe I should be asking you that. You look a little dazed."

"I'm ready."

Jordan turned. Once again he was struck by the beautiful

woman in front of him. Somewhere between last night and now she had lost her wariness of him. She radiated sensuality. He swallowed again. "Where's your swimsuit?"

"In here." Lauren held up a bag no bigger than five inches across and five inches deep.

"That's it?" he asked loudly.

From behind him he heard a strangled noise that sounded suspiciously like stifled laughter. Fearing what he'd see, he took Lauren by the arms and headed for the front door. "Good night, Sonja. I'm sure you know where to reach us."

"Good night, you two. Have fun, and don't rush home on my account." Going down the steps, he heard Sonja's laughter just before she locked the front door.

Maybe her dress was too much.

Trying not to chew on her lips and ruin her lipstick, Lauren sat quietly in the Bronco. Jordan hadn't said more than five words since they left her house. Trying to be unobtrusive, she attempted again to pulled the hem of her dress further down over her thighs.

"Are you cold?"

Lauren jumped, swallowed, and jerked her hands away from her dress. "I—I'm fine."

Silence descended again. Lauren felt a knot building in her throat. She might want Jordan, but that didn't mean he wanted her. What she knew about men could be put in one word—nothing.

She had assumed that his attentiveness, the way he looked at her sometimes, mean more than they did. She had read her own desires into his behavior. Her hand touched the tendrils of curls framing her face. All for him. All for nothing.

No wonder he was silent. She had gone from a potential friend to another unwanted woman on the make, creating an awkward and uncomfortable situation for both of them.

Pulling into his driveway, he cut the motor. Lauren wondered if it would be impossibly rude to plead a headache and ask him to take her home.

The moment passed into another. Her door opened. She slipped from the seat, her gaze somewhere in the middle of his wide chest. His blunt-tipped fingers lightly grasped her bare arm.

Inside, the brightly lit, two-story foyer that once fascinated her now provided Jordan with another opportunity to witness her clumsy attempt to attract him. She might not have to fake a headache.

"What would you like to do first, see the house or eat?"

She noticed that he didn't mention swimming. Her spirits plummeted further. Just as she preached to her son, you can't always have what you want. Somehow she'd get through the evening with her dignity intact. "Whatever is convenient."

He frowned down at her. "Is something the matter?"

Everything. She offered him a smile. "Long day."

Something flashed briefly in his eyes, then it was gone. "Let's start at the top and work down."

Jordan watched Lauren pick at her cold poached salmon and knew the special evening he had planned for them was a total disaster. The silent Lauren sitting across from him wasn't the same laughing woman who had answered her door over an hour ago. Neither was he.

Before then he had been certain he could control his desire for Lauren. Now he wasn't sure. He had never wanted a woman so intensely. It was one thing to desire a woman and control that desire, quite another to control the desire if the woman was willing. Lauren wasn't fighting the attraction between them, and although he thought it was what he wanted, it was testing his control to the limits.

Resisting Lauren was more difficult than anything he had ever done. Watching her retreat from him was even worse.

"Would you like something else?" he asked.

Her gaze bounced off his chest. "No thank you. I guess I'm not hungry."

"I messed things up, didn't I?" He laid his fork aside.

Stricken eyes met his. "What do you mean?"

"My reaction to your dress made you nervous. All my talk about being friends, and then my response was just short of leering," he told her apologetically. "Please forgive me, and let's start the evening over."

Her hand fluttered over the bodice of her dress. "Maybe I should have worn something different."

"I'm glad you didn't. You look beautiful." At least he could give her that much. "I think Sonja was laughing at me. No wonder. My tongue was probably hanging out."

She blinked those big brown eyes at him. "I've embarrassed you again," he said.

"No." She moistened her lips. "It's not your fault. I haven't dated much."

"Since Joshua's father died?" he asked, leaning forward over a small, candlelit table on the patio.

"At all," she said. Her finger nervously traced the rim of her wine glass.

He peered at her closely. "That's the third time you've mentioned not dating much. Any particular reason?"

For once, Lauren didn't feel her insides tensing at the mention of her past. Anything was preferable to discussing the fiasco of the evening. "My mother owned a small bookstore and she couldn't afford to hire someone, so I helped out after school and with the housework."

Jordan tried not to show his elation. "That must have been tough. Both Angelica and I were in a lot of extracurricular activities."

"Is Angelica the sister you mentioned?"

He smiled. "Yeah. I never thought the bratty, tomboy who followed me around would grow up to be a lady."

"Life often doesn't turn out the way we plan," she offered sadly.

"It must have been tough losing Joshua's father."

Her eyes closed briefly, then opened. "Yes."

His gaze narrowed, but all he said was, "Have you been back to North Carolina?"

Her hand stilled. "No."

"Is it because of memories of Joshua's father?"

Her hand jumped, spilling the wine. "Oh." Standing, she righted her empty glass and tried to sponge up the white wine seeping into the tablecloth with her linen napkin.

Jordan rounded the table and caught her hand. "It's only wine, Honey."

"Don't call me that!"

He tensed, staring down at her.

She lifted humiliated eyes to him. She had overreacted. Worse, feeling sorry for herself, she had let her guard down— the wrong thing to do around a perceptive man like Jordan. "I'm not feeling well. Could you take me home?"

"What's the matter? You're trembling."

She pulled her hands from his and backed up a step. "I want to go home."

"Lauren, of course I'll take you home." He matched her movement.

"Now, please?" she asked, hating the desperation in her voice.

"Come on." He reached for her. She whirled away and headed for the front door. Jordan's outstretched hand fisted. He started after her.

"You two are back ear—" Sonja's cheerful voice trailed off as she saw Lauren's pinched features, then moved on to Jordan's tense expression. Without another word, she unlatched the screen door.

Lauren, her little bag clutched in her hands, rushed inside and turned, effectively blocking the doorway. All she wanted to do was get rid of Jordan before she made a complete fool of herself and began bawling. "Thank you, Jordan. Good night."

"You sure you're going to be all right?" he asked.

"Yes. Sonja is here if I need anything." She glanced at her friend.

Sonja took the cue. "I can take care of things. Good night, Jordan."

He never took his gaze from Lauren. "I decided to stay in

town for the weekend. We can take Joshua on a boat ride tomorrow.''

Her grip on the bag tightened. "We have plans."

"I didn't say when."

Lauren flushed. "I assumed it was during the day."

His mouth tightened. "I'll call you."

"I'll probably be tied up."

"I'll call." Jordan gazed at the lines of strain bracketing her mouth. "Good night, Lauren. Sonja."

Lauren shut the door and leaned her forehead against it. "Please don't ask. Please."

A gentle hand touched her tense shoulder. "Do you want me to stay, or put a contract out on Jordan?"

Brushing away a tear, Lauren lifted her head. The anger in Sonja's face caused the knot in Lauren's throat to thicken. "Neither."

"If you change your mind about talking, call." Briefly giving Lauren a hug, Sonja opened the door, paused, glanced back at Lauren, then went down the steps toward the silent man standing by the Bronco. "What the hell did you do to her?"

Jordan accepted the condemnation he knew he deserved. "Why aren't you with her?"

"If you can't figure that out for yourself, you're not as smart as I thought."

He shoved his hand over his head. "I didn't want her hurt."

"Well, she is, and if you don't want to make it worse you'll leave." Her accusing gaze swept him from head to toe. "I think you've done enough for one night."

He flinched and looked at Sonja for a long time. Lauren had done well in choosing her friends. "Take care of her." He opened the door to the Bronco. "Go on home. I'll wait down the street until I know you're inside."

"That's not necessary."

"It is to me. I'm not quite the bastard you think I am." He drove away.

* * *

Jordan sat in his study Monday afternoon staring at the screen of his computer. He saw none of the data. His entire mind was on one person. Lauren. And she wanted nothing to do with him.

All weekend he had tried unsuccessfully to contact her. Hell, he had even sent her a telegram. Nothing worked. He must have left twenty messages on her answering machine, and he hadn't heard one word from her.

This morning he had called her job and learned she hadn't gone in to work. Benjamin Scott had been quick to tell Jordan that it was the first time she had used a sick day for herself. Sonja had come by the office to pick up the floral arrangement, and from the expression on her angry face, Benjamin didn't think she had been taking it home to Lauren.

The older man hadn't minced words on reminding Jordan of his promise not to add to his secretary's problems. Benjamin frankly stated that if it came down to Lauren or Crescent Communications, Lauren would win. Jordan had immediately given him the name of his marketing manager for all further contacts. Lauren needed her job, and a friend who put her above anything else.

Jordan wished he could have done the same.

"Damn."

"I knew you were in trouble."

Jordan spun in the chair and saw his cousin, Drake Lansing, filling the doorway. "I hope you're bringing me something that will get me out of trouble."

Advancing further into the room, Drake unbuttoned the jacket of his gray, tailored single-breasted suit and sat his huge frame in a leather chair facing Jordan. His hard-edged expression wasn't reassuring. "You've never postponed a board meeting before."

"There are a lot of things I haven't done before," Jordan said tightly.

"She got to you, didn't she?"

There was no accusation in the soft voice, and Jordan didn't try to deny the truth. "I'd give anything if we'd met under different circumstances, or if Grandaddy wasn't so adamant."

Leather creaked as Drake settled his weight deeper into the chair. "So what are you going to do?"

Jordan laughed without humor. "I wish the hell I knew. She won't even talk to me."

"What happened?"

"What else? Her past got in the way." He pushed from the chair and prowled in front of the oversized, designer window which looked out on the garden. "I asked her if the reason she hadn't gone back to North Carolina was because of Joshua's father. She panicked."

"Understandable, considering the situation."

Jordan whirled, his eyes intent. "What situation? What the hell did you find out, and why haven't you told me?"

Drake looked up through narrowed eyes. "It's a good thing I love you, or you'd be flat on your back by now."

"It's a good thing I love *you,* or I would have asked you *after* you were flat on your back," Jordan shot back.

Drake grunted. "I hope I never get it as bad as you have it."

"You have three seconds," Jordan said tightly.

Drake sobered. "I haven't even told you and already you're upset. I figured as much. That's why I didn't want to give you this over the phone."

"Dammit, what happened?"

"Strickland did more than refuse to acknowledge her marriage to his son. The bastard ran her out of town."

Sunglasses firmly on her nose, Lauren waited on the steps for Joshua's school bus. The shades kept the glare of the sun away, but every time she blinked her eyes hurt. Her own fault. She had cried herself to sleep for the past two nights.

Today she had cried only once, and that was when she had asked Sonja to take care of the flowers in her office. She couldn't face looking at them tomorrow. If her eyes didn't get any better, she might not have to worry. There was no way she would go into the office and face all the speculations.

One look at her red, puffy eyes and everyone would know

something had happened between her and the man they were speculating over so heavily last Thursday and Friday. Mr. Scott's message on her answering machine that Jordan would no longer be directly involved with Scott Resources hadn't helped. It only meant her boss knew what was going on. Then, there were the sharp eyes of Cynthia Douglas to consider. No way. No, sir.

Since she came home Saturday night she had taken the coward's way out and wallowed in her own misery, not even telling Sonja what had happened. The most trying times had been with her son.

His every other word had been about Jordan. In self-defense, she had taken him and his best friend to Water Town Sunday afternoon. Yet, as soon as he got home, he'd started in all over again.

Lauren glanced at her watch again. Four-fifteen. The school secretary had called and said the bus was having mechanical problems and would be running late. Lauren had offered to pick Joshua up, but was told that according to school policy a child couldn't be taken from the bus by a parent/guardian except at the regular drop off site. So, Lauren had waited and waited.

The sight of the yellow school bus turning onto her street eased some of the tension in her. The secretary had assured her that all the students were safe, but that hadn't kept Lauren from worrying.

Standing up, she watched the bus stop a couple of houses down on the other side of the street in front of Joshua's classmate's house. Usually Joshua got off at the same time and went next door to Sonja's.

The bus door opened. Travis emerged, waving to his mother, who had come out to meet him. The bus door closed and the vehicle pulled into the middle of the street, picking up speed as it passed Lauren.

"Wait!" Bewildered, Lauren lunged forward and banged both hands on the side of the bus. Immediately the vehicle stopped. "You forgot to let Joshua off the bus."

"No she didn't, Mrs. Bennett. Joshua didn't ride the bus home today," a small voice said.

Lauren whirled around, her heart pounding frantically in her chest and stared down at Travis. "What do you mean? Of course he rode the bus home."

"No, he didn't," confirmed the bus driver, now standing in the doorway.

Lauren spun. "He must have." Her terror growing, she climbed onto the bus, her eyes searching the faces of the children. Then she faced the bus driver again. "Where is Joshua? Where is my son?" she wailed.

Gently, the slender female driver touched Lauren's arm. "I don't know, Mrs. Bennett. All I know is that he didn't get on the bus after school."

Lauren shook her head wildly in denial, fighting the scream building in the back of her throat. "No. No, Please, God, no."

Chapter Fifteen

She was having a nightmare. She'd waken soon and everything would be as it was this morning. Joshua would be resisting getting out of bed. She'd be trying to entice him with waffles. In a minute she'd awaken. *Please, let me wake up in a minute.*

"He probably missed the bus and got confused," Sonja offered.

Hands clasped tightly in her lap, Lauren stared out of the window, hoping against everything to see Joshua with his backpack, walking home. With each passing minute, hope seemed harder to maintain. She'd already alerted the school, and their initial search had turned up nothing.

Lauren glanced at her watch. Four-nineteen. Joshua had been dismissed since three. *Please, God, let him be safe.*

When Sonja pulled up in front of the school, Principal King and a policeman were waiting on the steps of the one-story building. The sight of the policeman escalated her fear. With fumbling fingers she opened the door. She ran to them. "What happened? Have you heard anything?"

"Officer Powell is also the school crossing guard," Mrs. King quickly explained. "I called and asked that he come back to lend some assistance."

The tears Lauren had tried so hard to control started falling again. "I want my baby—where is he?" Dimly she was aware of Sonja's arm going around her shoulder.

"We're as anxious as you are to find Joshua," the policeman said. "We've already checked with his teacher and the teacher's aide who takes the children to the bus."

"Why didn't she make sure Joshua got on the bus?" Lauren asked. "Where is she? I want to talk to her myself." Without waiting, she started inside the building.

"Mrs. Bennett, wait. I know how you must fee—"

Lauren whirled, anger and fear pulsing through her. "Don't you dare say that, Mrs. King. My son has been missing for almost an hour and a half. Have you ever had a child missing?"

"No, I haven't, and I'm sorry," the middle-aged woman admitted softly. "But I have had school children missing in the past, and all of them have turned up safely. Perhaps he went home with a friend."

"I just left his best friend home safe with his mother," Lauren told her.

"Maybe there are some friends you don't know about," Officer Powell offered.

"He's five years old, for goodness sake. Of course I know his friends. I come to all the PTA meetings, his plays, his—" Tears fell, and this time she couldn't stop them. "Please, just find him."

"We will, Mrs. Bennett." The officer took her arm. "Come on inside. We need to talk."

"Talk?"

"As much as I can determine, no one saw anything suspicious at school. There's always the possibility he left on his own."

Lauren jerked away. "On his own? Joshua wouldn't run away."

"I'm not saying he did," the policeman said calmly. "Sometimes children see things differently than adults. Did you punish him for something you forbade him to do? Was he unhappy about anything? Was there something he wanted you wouldn't let him have? Can you think of any place he might want to go that you wouldn't take him?"

Lauren shook her head with the first question, but with each succeeding one her heart started beating faster. "No. Joshua wouldn't do anything like that."

"Principal King said he was having some minor problems until several days ago," the officer continued as they entered the building. "What changed, Mrs. Bennett?"

"Jordan Hamilton."

Lauren whirled toward her friend, who had spoken the name that had been drumming in her heart, her mind. She turned to Principal King. "Please, can I use the phone?"

Following the older woman into her office, Lauren could think of only one thing—*Joshua, please be safe with Jordan.* If he wasn't—she refused to think of the alternative.

"There is a phone call for you, Mr. Hamilton?" Casper said.

"I told you I don't want to be disturbed," Jordan said, his mood as foul and dark as it had ever been.

"Don't mind him, Casper." Drake pushed to his feet. "I'll take it."

"Mr. Hamilton will take this call," Casper said with supreme confidence. "It's Mrs. Bennett. I can't understand her clearly because she's crying. Something about—"

Fear slicing through him, Jordan grabbed the phone and punched in the blinking red button. If that bastard Strickland was bothering her again—"Honey, what's the matter?

"Lauren, please, slow down and stop crying. I can't understand you," Jordan said. Seconds later, he wished he hadn't. He plopped down in his chair. "I haven't seen him. Don't cry—" He heard a thump and a bang as if the receiver had been dropped.

"Lauren! Lauren!" he shouted, his entire body trembling.

The voice that came back on the line wasn't the one he wanted to hear. "Jordan, this is Sonja. She . . . she can't talk now."

"Son—" Jordan started, and found he couldn't push the words out past the knot in his throat.

"What's the matter?" Drake demanded, towering over his best friend and boss.

"Joshua's missing," Jordan finally managed.

Drake muttered one explicit word.

If he was barely coping, Lauren must be in sheer hell. "Sonja, where are you? What's going on?"

Listening, Jordan tried not to think of the children who disappeared and were never found again. *Lord, please,* he prayed, *let Joshua be safe.*

"You have a visitor, Mr. Hamilton," Casper said.

"Can't you see—" his voice stopped abruptly as he whirled. Casper stood with his usual self-possession. What created the tears in Jordan's eyes was the smiling boy by his side.

"Hi, Mr. Hamilton," Joshua said. "I came to visit."

Fighting tears, Lauren stood on the sidewalk waiting for the first glimpse of Jordan's Bronco. She'd spoken to Joshua on the phone, but she wouldn't be satisfied until she saw him with her own eyes, held him in her arms.

Seeing the vehicle, she started toward it. Knowing the Bronco was faster never entered her mind. The door opened, and out stepped Jordan with Joshua wrapped around his neck. Setting the little boy on his feet, he urged him forward with one hand on his shoulder.

Lauren paused, half afraid Joshua didn't want to come home.

"He's scared he won't sit down until he's grown," explained Jordan.

Her gaze briefly flickered to the large man standing behind her son, then centered on the child. Smiling through her tears, she went down on her knees and opened her arms.

"Mama, I'm sorry!" Joshua cried, and he ran to her as fast as his legs would carry him.

Neither seemed aware of the people milling around, the smiles, the tears. Parents hugged their children a little harder than usual. Joshua was safe, and so were their children. Sometimes life wasn't so kind.

"Come on, Lauren," Jordan coaxed, "let's go inside."

If she heard him, she didn't say anything, just kept holding her son, alternating between reprimanding him for scaring her, telling him how much she loved him, and thanking God for his safe return.

Gently pulling her upright, Jordan circled his arm around her trembling shoulder and led her into the house. The door had barely closed behind them before he picked mother and son up and went to sit in the den.

Lauren wasn't ready to release her son, and Jordan wasn't ready to release either of them.

"I need to get some information from Mrs. Bennett for my report." Officer Powell frowned at the closed door.

"You aren't getting it now." Sonja folded her arms across her ample breasts and positioned herself in front of the walkway.

"I'm sor—"

"Excuse me," Drake cut in smoothly, reading the man's name at the same time he extended his hand, "Officer Powell. I'm Drake Lansing, an associate of Mr. Hamilton. Since I was there when Joshua arrived, and I believe Ms. Adams has been with Mrs. Bennett, perhaps we can help with your report."

Sonja eyed the huge, brown-skinned man standing by her. My, he did look good, and she didn't feel like the Goodyear Blimp next to him—a rarity in her thirty-one years.

Of course she recognized the deep voice from their brief conversation, when Jordan had dropped the receiver to pick up Joshua and Drake had told her Joshua was safe. She didn't for a moment believe he remembered hers. Men found her painfully easy to ignore or forget. "How did you know who I was?"

Drake smiled. A dimple winked in his left cheek. Sonja thought she would melt like butter in a hot skillet. "With a voice like yours, how could I forget?" he answered, his voice as dark as his gaze.

In spite of the sudden warmth streaking its way through her, in spite of the rapt attention of her neighbors and the nearby policeman, she managed to ask cooly, "And what kind of voice is that?"

He chuckled, a rich, deep sound. Sonja braced her trembling legs. Trouble had just walked into her life. "Why don't I tell you when we don't have an audience?"

She might be in trouble, but she wasn't letting this gorgeous hulk know. Mustering up as much disinterest as she could manage with her body shivering, she asked, "Who says that's going to happen?"

He simply smiled and turned to the policeman. "Where would you like to conduct the interview? I don't think we should disturb Mrs. Bennett. Any suggestions, Ms. Adams?"

"I live across the street," she said, fully aware she was walking into a trap.

"Would that be agreeable to you, Officer Powell?" Drake asked.

The policeman smiled. "I got a feeling if I said otherwise, you'd find a way to get around it. I ran a check on Jordan Hamilton. Pretty high profile. What is it you do for him?"

For the first time the teasing light faded from Drake's dark eyes. "I try to make his life smoother."

"Yeah," Officer Powell said. "From what I found out that must be tough sometimes."

Drake glanced back toward Lauren's house. "Try impossible."

"You look like a man who could do the impossible," Sonja blurted and then clamped her mouth shut.

"I hope you're right, Ms. Adams," Drake said. "I certainly hope you're right."

Long after Joshua had been fed, bathed, and cautioned repeatedly against doing anything so dangerous again, Lauren couldn't bring herself to let him out of her sight for more than a few minutes. He could have gotten hurt because she was afraid of the emotions Jordan evoked in her, afraid to face the past.

She thanked God her son was safe. The phone had rung almost constantly, with people calling to say they were glad he was all right. Sonja and Drake Lansing, Jordan's friend, had fielded the calls. They had also been thoughtful enough to bring Italian take-out for dinner. Lauren flushed with embarrassment as she remembered Sonja using her key to let herself in and finding Lauren and Joshua in Jordan's arms.

She had scrambled out of his lap and almost fallen with Joshua. Only Jordan's strength and coordination kept them upright. As soon as they were steady, he had released her arm.

Seeing the hurt and longing in Jordan's face caught her completely off guard. So did the guilt, and her own longing to crawl back in his arms and just hold on.

Stunned by her need, afraid she might give in, she had backed away.

Drake had covered the ensuing silence by introducing himself and offering dinner. Lauren had grabbed at the opportunity to get her emotions under control. It wasn't until the meal was finished and the kitchen tidied that she realized Sonja had been unusually silent. However, before Lauren could talk privately with her friend, she and Drake were gone.

"He's asleep, Lauren."

She tensed at the deep voice in spite of herself. Despite her ignoring him, Jordan had never been far from her, watching her with those all-seeing eyes of his, making sure she ate, helping Joshua with his homework.

"I know, so there's no need for you to stay any longer. Drake is waiting for you at Sonja's," she reminded him. "Please thank him again for bringing the food over, and talking to the policeman."

"You told him yourself a number of times, but I'll tell him again."

"I appreciate everything you've done, but I'd like to get some rest."

"Come on, then, and lock up."

Hands folded around her waist, she followed him down the hall. She frowned on seeing him going to the stove.

"Drink this tea I made you, and I'm outta here." Cup in hand, he turned to her.

For some reason tears pricked her eyes.

Setting the cup aside, he pulled her into his arms. "He's safe, Honey. Joshua's coming to my house wasn't your fault."

She knew she should pull away, but the reassuring comfort of his arms felt too good. "He had to change buses two times and take a taxi. What if the bus drivers hadn't helped him? Anything could have happened to him."

"It didn't. He was so proud of himself—until I told him how worried you were because you couldn't find him." Jordan's hand swept up and down her back. "He looked up at me and said, 'But I left her a note on the 'frigerator.' "

Lifting her head slightly, she stared at the front of the refrigerator covered with Jordan's schoolwork and drawings. Positioned exactly at Joshua's eye level was a crayon drawing with a boy inside a bus and a house with Jordan's name on it.

"If he ever does anything so dangerous again I won't let him out of my sight until he's eighteen!" she cried fervently.

Jordan smiled. "I think he got the message. He went to bed the first time you told him without any coaxing."

"Why shouldn't he? You were at his beck and call. He idolizes you."

Jordan straightened and stared down into her eyes. "How about his mother?"

Lauren stiffened and tried to push out of his arms. "Please."

"Not until I've said a few things. I care about you. The last days have been agony for me, not being able to see you, to touch you."

"Please, there's no reason to lie. You find me about as attractive as an anthill," she said.

His hands anchored her waist, bringing her against his hard arousal. She gasped. Her eyes widened. "I've seen a lot of anthills in my day, but none of them have ever elicited a response like that."

She swallowed.

"I want you so much my teeth ache. I've wanted you, it seems, forever." His lips lightly brushed the trembling curve of her mouth.

Bewilderment clouded her featured. "But I thought . . . you were so distant."

"I was trying to keep from dragging you down and making love to you," he growled.

She shivered. "Oh."

Jordan looked pensive. "Honey, there are some things that I have to work out, but I want you to know I care about you and Joshua. Neither of you have anything to fear from me."

"Sometimes things happen without people meaning them to," she said sadly.

His finger and thumb brought her face around, and up. "Then I'll have to do everything in my power to see that only good things happen."

"I told you once, trusting isn't easy for me."

"Just take one step, Honey, and I'll be there," he vowed.

She gazed up into his dark eyes. She wanted so much, but she wasn't sure if she could go through another weekend of tears and doubts.

Correctly reading the doubt in her mind, he said, "You've had a trying day. We'll talk about it later," his voice deep and patient.

Visibly relaxing, her hands stilled. "Thank you."

"Don't thank me too quickly. I go after what I want, and I want you. Just so there'll be no misunderstanding." His mouth fastened on hers, demanding admission. After a moment's hesitation, she opened for him.

His tongue dipped in, sweeping, swirling with a wanton thoroughness. Lauren was powerless to do anything but hold on. She was swept along by the powerful emotions of the kiss. A kiss as hungry as it was gentle.

His large hands cupped her hips, fitting her intimately against him, letting her feel his desire. Air hissed over her teeth.

She expected shock at the blatant contact, not the exhilaration that pumped though her. Nagging doubts slipped away as the intensity of his kiss stripped everything from her mind but the need to get closer. Her arms tightened.

Jordan whispered Lauren's name, his hold a mixture of restraint and passion. Lauren gloried in the sound, then his mouth was on hers again, igniting a growing need within her, and once again she was swept into a place where there was only the taste and the feel of the man holding her.

His large hands swept under her knit top, skimming up her sides before closing possessively over her breasts. Her lace demi-bra offered little protection against Jordan. Her nipples puckered. His thumb swept inside. Lauren moaned, arching her back to increase the delicious contact.

She cried out when his teeth closed over one nipple, then the other. Shivers rippled though her. Then, he blew on one of the turgid peaks. Her knees buckled.

His mouth possessed hers again. She moved helplessly against him, caught up in sensations she had no way of controlling. Wanting, needing, to feel his naked chest, she awkwardly tugged his shirt from his pants. Heat and muscled hardness greeted her searching fingertips.

Abruptly his head lifted. A shudder tore through him. His breathing was ragged, his eyes dark.

Lauren shivered at the fierceness in his face. He'd take what he wanted and leave her to pick up the pieces. Even as the thought formed in her mind, she knew it wasn't true.

Her body was screaming for release. She would not have protested if he had taken her on the floor. Trembling fingers pulled down her top. His gaze followed her every movement.

Closing his eyes, he leaned his forehead against hers. The telling motion chased away the last of her fears. Jordan scared her, pushed her, but he had never taken more than she willingly gave.

His hands moved to her waist. ''I didn't mean to grab you, among other things.''

''I did mean to grab *you*, among other things,'' she confessed.

His head jerked up. He stared down into her smiling face, then he drew her tenderly into his arms again. ''Oh, Honey.'' The kiss was tender and full of promise.

His hands pulled her closer to him, fitting her slim body against his muscular one, fitting softness to hardness. Lauren moaned from deep within her throat. The drugging passion of the kiss beckoned her to take more, to give more.

The tenuous hold of his control threatened to slip free again with each heavy beat of his heart, each whimper of desire from the woman in his arms. A simple kiss had turned into something deeper, hotter.

Drawing on the last of his reserve, Jordan straightened. His breathing erratic, his heart pounding wildly, he gathered Lauren to him. "I think I grabbed again."

She laughed, but her voice was unsteady. "I know I did."

Wanting to see her smile again, he set her away. Her lips were swollen and moist from their kiss, her eyes dazed. "I wish we were back in the sunken garden again."

"There's always tomorrow," she said softly.

His thumb stroked across her lip. "I'm not sure I can wait that long."

She accepted the inevitable and refused to shy away from the hunger in his face, a hunger she shared. She just wasn't sure about here with her son. "I . . . I . . . don't—"

"Shhh." He kissed her nose, then smiled. "Maybe Sonja will sit for us."

"I'll ask."

"Could you do me a favor?"

"What?"

"Wear that pink sundress, and bring the swimsuit in the little bag."

Nodding, she smiled.

He leaned down to kiss her on the lips, paused, and brushed his lips against her cheek instead. They walked to the front door together. "Good night, Honey. I'd better go and take Drake off Sonja's hands. I'll call when I get home." Jordan turned and came to an abrupt halt. The one existing light in the front room in Sonja's house went out. His questioning gaze went from his Bronco to the dark structure.

"Oh, my," Lauren whispered.

"You can say that again," Jordan muttered.

Chapter Sixteen

"I don't think this will work," whispered an irritated female voice.

"I do," answered a supremely confident male one.

"Humph. Of course you do," Sonja grumbled, walking farther into the semi-darkness of the living room. "It was your idea."

Repressing a smile, Drake maintained his post in front of the window. The lady certainly wasn't shy about voicing her opinion. He didn't mind. In fact, he had already decided he could listen to her sultry voice all night and first thing in the morning.

"What are they doing now?"

Dragging his thoughts back to the situation at hand, Drake carefully lifted the light blue mini-blind. The streetlight one house over illuminated Lauren's front yard and did a fair job on Sonja's living room.

"Well? Don't tell me I almost broke my neck rushing to cut off the light in my bedroom for nothing?" Sonja muttered.

Impatience crackled in every word. "They're still on the front porch."

Sonja peered over Drake's broad shoulder. "If Jordan gives her any more misery, I'll shave him with a dull knife."

"He won't," Drake said easily. "Jordan is a man who knows how to seize an opportunity. All he needs is a crack. We've simply presented him an opportunity, in case Lauren has been less than receptive."

"He hurt her."

Drake straightened and looked over his shoulder. His arms brushed against something soft and giving. Eyes wide, Sonja jumped back and crossed both arms over her breasts.

He let her retreat. For now. "And he'll regret it for the rest of his life."

"He was awfully attentive this afternoon. He could hardly keep his eyes off her," Sonja admitted reluctantly.

"Are you sure you're down with this?" he asked, watching her closely in the half shadows.

"Sure." Her shoulders lifted beneath a coral-colored silk blouse. "Why wouldn't I be?"

Drake folded his arms over his wide chest. "You know what they and the neighbors are going to think is going on over here. Your reputation is at stake."

Incensed, Sonja planted both hands on her ample hips. "It's barely nine. You act as if it's a cataclysmic event for a man to be in my house with the lights out. Just because I have some substance doesn't mean I can't get a man."

"The thought never entered my mind." His hand gently stroked the magnolia petal smoothness of her jaw. "I just don't think this is your style."

She jumped. Eyes wide, she backed up another step. "Don't get carried away, Buster. You're not my type," she said, but the shakiness of her voice negated the effect.

"Good." Drake stared at the wariness on Sonja's attractive face a long time, then turned to lift the mini-blind. "I like making my own rules."

"Drake has the keys," Jordan said.

Lauren bit her lower lip, her glance shifting from the Bronco parked in front of Sonja's house to the dark interior beyond. "Sonja is a good woman."

"Drake's the best."

Lauren glanced at Jordan with both hands stuffed in his pocket. She was at a loss to explain the situation, as he seemingly was.

In today's society it wasn't unusual for a couple first meeting to end up in bed, but although Sonja talked a lot of trash Lauren knew her best friend had too much common sense and self-respect for that kind of irresponsible behavior.

"This isn't like her," Lauren mumbled.

"It's not like Drake, either." Finally, Jordan turned to face her. "So it's either a case of overpowering sexual attraction that sent them running to the nearest bed or—"

"Or what?"

"We're being set up," Jordan said lightly.

Lauren was trying to recover from the first part of his statement when he hit her with the second. Her eyes rounded. Unconsciously, she stepped onto the porch, letting the squeaky screen door close behind her. "Why would they do that?"

"They're our best friends, and they might have thought we needed some help getting back together." With deliberate slowness, he moved toward her. "The second that light went out, whether true or not, our minds immediately conjured up an evocative picture of them straining to get closer to the other, heard the sounds being drawn from her willing body, heard the answering response he couldn't deny from his," Jordan finished, his voice deep and raspy.

Lauren gulped, unable to look away from the intensity in Jordan's face. Images formed in her mind, but the two people locked together in a passionate embrace on the wide bed were her and Jordan. Her body, which had started calming, zipped to full alert.

A restless ache stirred within her. Her breasts throbbed. Nipples puckered. Her skin felt sensitized.

She opened her mouth to speak, but nothing came out. Swallowing, she tried again. "H—How do we decide which?"

"Give them a demonstration. I kiss you as if my life depends on it.'' Jordan's gaze locked on her lips, then lifted to her wide eyes. ''The only problem is that I'm not sure I can seperate fact from fantasy.''

The next step brought him closer until their bodies were separated by mere inches. ''If I'm wrong and I do kiss you, there's a good possibility of us ending up where they wanted us to think they were.''

Her throat dried. Heat and desire swept through her. Her legs quivered. She couldn't have spoken or moved if her life depended on it.

''The other choice is to call or go over there, or wait here,'' he continued, watching her closely. ''Your call.''

She didn't want to make the decision, because the one she so desperately wanted was the one she didn't have the courage to make. Instead of looking at the mouth she desperately wanted on hers, Lauren peered around Jordan's shoulder at the darkened house.

If Sonja had found someone she wanted, Lauren wasn't going to mess things up for her because of her own insecurities. Her best friend deserved some happiness.

She opened the screen door. ''Come back inside.''

''You're sure?'' he questioned, unmoved.

''Sonja is my friend, I don't want to embarrass her. I'll go check on Joshua.'' She disappeared inside the house.

With one last look over his shoulder, Jordan followed and closed the doors behind him. Deciding not to tempt his control any further than necessary, he perched on the edge of the sofa in the semi-darkness of the living room.

When he saw Drake again Jordan was either going to strangle him or shake his hand. He hadn't wanted to leave Lauren, but keeping his hands off her was going to be difficult at best, especially when she kept looking at him as if he were the cherry on top of an ice cream sundae.

''He's fine.''

Jordan glanced up to see Lauren in the living room again. Although casually dressed in a white, sleeveless T-shirt and faded jeans, her hair mussed from running her fingers through the curls countless times, she still took his breath away. He finally realized she always would.

When a woman possessed beauty and an unconscious sensuality in a svelte body like Lauren's, it was hard to resist. Add strength, determination, a capacity to love, and a hint of vulnerability, it was impossible. He wanted to be there for her in all the ways that counted between a man and a woman.

His fingers flexed with the need to touch her, to reassure her, to reassure himself that they had a future together.

"Why don't you turn in?" he suggested, sitting back on the sofa. "I'll go out the back door, let the garage door down, and sprint for the opening."

Outrage marred her features. "I can't leave you alone."

He smiled in remembrance. "You've done it before."

"I'm sorry." Embarrassment touched her face. "I didn't know what to think of you. You don't follow any rules but your own."

"That scared you." It was a statement, not a question.

"Terrified me," she confessed.

He wanted to take her in his arms and promise she'd never have to be afraid again, but he wasn't going to lie. He cared too much about her. Eventually he'd have to tell her everything—but not tonight, not today when she had gone through so much.

"I don't want you afraid of me. It tears me up thinking I might never be able to gain your trust completely," he told her.

"You've gotten closer to me faster than anyone has in six years," she said softly, holding his gaze.

Jordan felt a surge of joy at her revelation. "The same goes for me."

They stared at each other a long time, then Lauren said, "I'd better clean up the kitchen."

Jordan came to his feet. "I'll do it. You get to bed."

"Jordan, you really should do something about that bossy attitude of yours," she said and went into the kitchen.

He followed. "I dirtied the pot and cup. I should clean it up."

The teapot in her hand, Lauren looked up at Jordan. "Can you believe we're arguing over washing dishes?"

"Beats the alternative."

"What?"

"Thinking about how much we want each other," he said, his voice gritty with need.

"Jordan." Her voice quivered with the same need and longing. Swallowing, she turned away and placed the dishes in the sink. "I—I think I'll leave this until morning." Edging around a taut Jordan, she hurried away.

Out of sight in the hallway, she stopped and leaned against the wall, berating herself for running. Once again, she had run away instead of facing up to the truth. A six year pattern repeated itself. She wanted Jordan so much she ached, but she was letting the past and her insecurities get in the way.

Pushing away from the wall, she peeked in on a sleeping Joshua, then went to her room and sat on the bed. She glanced around the room.

Where Joshua's room had color, hers was muted, in a lush looking, beige, tone-on-tone woven jacquard print. She had saved for months to buy the comforter set, the blouson valance and curtains, the wallpaper border. It was a beautiful room she shared with no one.

Her gaze settled on her wedding picture in its heavy gold frame on the night table. David had given it to her the last day of their honeymoon in Myrtle Beach. She had expected him to tease her for crying. Instead, the troubled expression she had come to dread had saddened his boyish face.

"Remember I love you, and no matter what, I want you to be happy even if that means being without me."

She had teased him about wanting to get rid of her. He had silenced her with a kiss. It was the last time they had made love. Fighting the stinging moisture in her eyes, her trembling fingers lightly touched the smiling faces in the photograph, so in love, so hopeful for the future.

She shivered on hearing the squeal of brakes, the terrified screams of David, her mother, herself. One moment she had everything; the next, nothing. It hurt, it hurt so much. But time and Joshua had dulled the pain, helped her gain acceptance. Or they would have, if not for Nathan Strickland.

And she had let it happen. Her life had become so wrapped up in hiding that she had forgotten how to live. Worse, she had condemned Joshua to bearing the burden of the same fear, the same fate.

David wouldn't have wanted that for her or his son.

By giving into Strickland demands and threats, she had turned her back on the twin legacies David had given her: his son, and his hope for her happiness.

Picking up the photograph, she kissed David's lips. "Thank you, my love. I won't forget again."

Opening the drawer on the nightstand, she placed the picture inside. Standing, she went to Joshua's room. He hadn't moved from the sprawled position on his stomach of an hour ago.

"Is he okay?" whispered a familiar male voice.

Unsurprised, she turned and went to Jordan standing in the doorway. He backed up when she kept walking. She smiled. "Yes."

His back hit the wall. He eyed her strangely. "I was coming to check on him when I saw you."

The brilliance of her smile increased as she circled her arms around his neck. "We're both fine, thanks to you."

Jordan was torn between sizzling excitement and trying to remember that Joshua was less than ten feet away. His hands settled on her waist to keep her from coming closer. "Lauren?"

She kissed the corner of his mouth. "Yes?"

He closed his eyes as hot, rampant need raked through him. Need won. His hands flexed, drawing her closer.

"Yes, Jordan, closer, much closer," she whispered, her tongue tracing the outline of his lips.

His head twisted, capturing her mouth and deepening the kiss. Lauren melted against him, holding back nothing. With a control he hadn't known he possessed, Jordan lifted his head.

He stared down into Lauren's face until her eyes opened. In their depths he saw a passion equal to his own. Without another word, he picked her up in his arms and started down the short hallway. He entered the room with the door opened. Inside, he set Lauren on her feet and closed the door with a shaking hand, his gaze still on Lauren.

"Are you sure, Honey?" He brushed her hair away from her face. "I have to be sure."

"I've never been surer of anything in my life. I'm not afraid anymore. I trust you, Jordan."

Jordan felt a fist clamp in his gut. The wild elation he had felt moments ago was tempered by his own fear. He couldn't come this close and lose her. He couldn't. "Whatever happens, promise me you'll always remember that."

Arms looped around his neck, she smiled up at him with complete confidence. "On one condition."

"Name it," he said without hesitation.

"That you stop talking and kiss me."

He took his time, kissing the corner of her soft mouth, the bow of her upper lip, before he settled firmly against her. Desire rushed through him. His tongue searched out the warm, dark recess of her mouth with a greedy thoroughness.

He felt her shudder. Her hips moved instinctively against his hardness. Jordan groaned. His hands caught the hem of the T-shirt, stripping it away. Her bra followed.

His mouth closed over her nipple, sucking deeply, then stroking the point with his tongue. Breath hissed through Lauren's teeth as she struggled to keep from crying out. The sound rippled across his skin.

His eyes blazing with savage intensity, he locked one arm around her waist and strode to the bed. With his free hand, he swept the bedspread away. Immediately, they tumbled onto the waiting softness.

Lauren's hands were defter this time, and faster, as they disposed of Jordan's shirt. Impatient, hungry, she moved her hands over the hard, hot contours of his chest, his shoulders, his back.

Side by side, their legs sandwiched between each other's, they reached for each other's pants at the same time. Their gazes locked.

Lauren's hands stilled, and her lip caught between her teeth.

She looked as if she were going to cry. Jordan waited, praying that if she said no he could keep it together.

"What's the matter, Honey?" he asked.

Her hands moved away. "I'm not on the pill."

Relief rushed through him. Pulling her closer, he kissed her hard, possessively. "I'll take care of things."

Thick lashes veiled her eyes. "You knew I'd give in."

Jordan was in another of those minefields. "I'd hoped." Silence. "All right, I hoped and prayed."

"I guess it's all right to tell you something?" Her head lifted, her smile was off center. "Even when I was denying it to myself, deep down I was kind of hoping, too."

In that moment Jordan knew he had gone past just caring and was looking at the woman he loved. A woman with secrets and pain who trusted him with her body, but not with her past. He vowed one day she would.

With infinite tenderness his lips touched hers, letting the heat build slowly, inexplicably, between them. Their clothes were removed more speedily.

Jordan's hand caressed the slope of her back, the curve of her shoulder, then lowered to her breasts, their softness drawing his hand, his lips, again and again. His other hand went lower, past the dip in her navel, over her stomach, to the soft, black curls.

Anticipation and need had her twisting in his arms. His fingers stroked the softness of her inner thigh, then swept upward to thoroughly explore the liquid heat hidden within the most vulnerable part of her body.

Sensations swamped her. Her hands left his shoulder to grip the sheet.

Jordan moved over her, easing himself into her, stretching her, filling her, driving her out of her mind. She whimpered, her head flaying from side to side. She arched upward, her hands reaching for him, her thighs tightening around his hips, bringing him closer, deeper.

His mouth captured hers, taking her cries as he took her body—with equal parts of gentleness and possessiveness. With each powerful thrust, Jordan took them closer.

When release came it rocked them both. Lauren clung to Jordan as the only solid thing in a world gone careening off its axis.

Long minutes later, Lauren lay curled in Jordan's arms. "You're incredible," he breathed.

She angled her head up. "That was incredible."

He kissed her lips. "Because *you're* incredible. I've never known a woman with your strength, your capacity for giving, for loving."

A shadow crossed her face. She bowed her head again.

His arms tightened around her, pulling her closer, hoping he could get her to open up. For her own sake. Only for her. "You may not see it, but others see it in you. Those people who called about Joshua. Benjamin. Sonja."

"You think you should call Sonja?" Lauren asked.

"Nope." Jordan snapped off the light and snuggled down in bed, letting her change the subject. "I'm going to hold you until you go to sleep, then I'm calling a taxi. Drake and Sonja are on their own."

"Now what do we do?" Sonja asked. It had been over thirty minutes since Lauren and Jordan had gone back inside the house.

Drake peered though the mini-blind. "I don't know. I can't tell a thing from here."

Unlike Sonja's, Lauren's bedroom was in the back, but Sonja wasn't about to point that out. "Well, I know. You can take yourself home." She snapped on the light.

Grinning, Drake faced her, his brown eyes twinkling. "You wound me, Sonja. I thought we were becoming friends."

"What made you think something so idiotic?"

"Maybe because of this." He moved before she had a chance to escape. Once his lips touched hers she didn't want to. A delicious shudder racked her body. She clung to him, kissing him back with all the desperate urgency with which he was kissing her.

They were both breathing hard when he reluctantly lifted his head. "You want to go to dinner tomorrow night?"

"Yes."

He frowned. something in her heart lurched before he said, "I was hoping you'd be your usual stubborn self. I was looking forward to kissing you into submission."

Sonja always prided herself on her fast thinking. "I can always change my mind."

He grinned. The dimple winked in his dark face. His mouth took hers.

Chapter Seventeen

Jordan surfaced to consciousness slowly. Scents and sensations surrounded him. The floral fragrance that was so much a part of the soft woman in his arms, the sudden hardening of his body, the sun on his face—

Jordan sprang up in bed taking Lauren, who was sprawled half on top of him, with him. He heard her surprised cry and reflexively tightened his hold.

Sleepy eyes cleared instantly. "Jordan, what's the matter?"

"What time does Joshua's school bus pick him up?"

"Sev—" Lauren broke off as she noticed for the first time the room was bathed in a natural light. Inelegantly, she scrambled over Jordan, saw the clock and groaned. Seven twenty-five.

Her face told the story. "Five minutes."

"I'll take him to school in your car, then come back. Then you can drive to work." Doing some scrambling of his own, Jordan put on his pants and shirt. He couldn't remember the last time he had overslept, but then he had never slept with Lauren before. "You get Joshua. I'll get his breakfast."

Lauren didn't argue. Pulling on her robe, she went to get her son. He was his usual slippery self. Lauren wasn't having any of it. Several minutes later, with her help, he was dressed and entering the kitchen.

"Mr. Hamilton!" the little boy cried. All sleepiness vanished. He launched himself into Jordan's open arms. "I was hoping you'd be here when I woke up."

Lauren blushed. "Eat up, Joshua. Jordan is going to drop you off at school while I get ready for work."

"Oh, boy," he squealed and quickly sat at the table. "Hoping sure paid off."

Lauren and Jordan smiled at each other.

Jordan let himself into his house whistling. Joshua had made it to school on time, and Lauren had only been ten minutes late for work. Benjamin Scott had been so happy to see her return that he hadn't minded.

However, the killing glare he sent Jordan said her boss very much minded the puffiness beneath her eyes. Intercepting that glare, Lauren had quickly explained about Joshua.

If Jordan expected an apology from her employer, he was doomed to wait. All Scott had said before returning to his office was, "I'll be watching."

Jordan, more concerned with Lauren than threats, had reminded her of their date that night, then kissed her good-bye before she could tell him not to. To his delight, she came to him sweetly and without a moment's hesitation.

As he headed toward the master suite, his smile broadened. This morning had been one he'd always remember. Starting the day off with Lauren in his arms had seemed natural. Rushing to get Joshua to school and her to work had felt good and right.

Jordan took full blame for them oversleeping. Last night he had fully intended to only kiss Lauren good-bye after she fell asleep. But she had rolled toward him, murmuring his name, and he had pulled her under him and wrung even more cries from her lips, just like she had rung from his.

Need raked delicately along his nerve endings as he crossed the living room. He was getting as randy as an old goat.

"Morning, Jordan."

Jordan turned to see Drake leaning casually against the door frame of the study. As always, he was impeccably dressed. This morning, he wore a Valentino double-breasted, mocha-colored suit. With Drake's eye for detail, Jordan knew it wasn't lost on the other man that Jordan wore the same clothes he'd had on the day before.

"Good morning, Drake," Jordan greeted. He had taken a taxi from Lauren's office. The Bronco had been gone this morning.

"You read the paper yet?" Drake asked casually.

Jordan's black eyebrows arched. Drake knew the first thing Jordan did on awakening was read the paper. His cousin could have been delicately inquiring if the same thing that had kept Jordan out all night had kept him occupied this morning as well, or Drake could have a more practical reason.

Since he had Drake had long since given up the adolescent boasting of sexual encounters, Jordan reasoned it was the latter. "No."

Pushing away from the door, Drake crossed the room. Jordan met him halfway. "It's circled."

Quickly scanning the small article carrying an AP byline, Jordan bit back a curse. "How?"

"I'm still working on it." Drake nodded toward the paper in Jordan's hand. "But any number of people knew about Joshua being missing. When your name came up, it added a whole new ball game. At least the report is brief, and only says you helped find him."

Jordan's face harshened. "But it gives Joshua's name. If some reporter tries to dig for a deeper story, it's going to upset Lauren."

"And ruin your plans." There was no censorship in the deep voice.

"Not the way you think." He crushed the paper in his fist.

"Any scenario that doesn't leave you and Lauren together is not what you planned," Drake said calmly. "Or did I miss something?"

Jordan sighed. "You didn't miss anything."

"Thought not."

Jordan chuckled in spite of himself. "You were always full of yourself."

"Look who's talking."

Sobering, Jordan came to a decision. "I want you to start today on the plan we discussed yesterday."

A frown crossed Drake's dark face. "Jordan, you could leave yourself open for a takeover if we aren't careful. Maybe there's another way."

"I haven't thought of one. I want this over with," he stated firmly. "I want that bastard's fangs pulled so he's no threat to Lauren ever again."

"Grandaddy Hamilton wants more," Drake reminded him bluntly.

"Don't you think I know that?" Jordan scowled. "Don't you think I wouldn't give anything to give them both what they want?"

A large hand gripped Jordan's tense shoulder. "You're riding on a double-edged sword, but my money is on you. Always has been." Removing his hand, Drake walked toward the study.

"Drake." The big man turned. "Thanks. For everything."

"Any time," he said, and disappeared into the study.

"Breakfast, Sir?"

Jordan spun to see Casper, as composed and dignified as ever. The man's thin, expressionless face gave nothing away, but Jordan knew he must have heard his conversation with Drake.

"Eavesdropping doesn't become you, Casper."

"Neither do unfounded accusations by you, Sir. If you don't want your conversations overheard, may I suggest any number of rooms that have doors? This room does not."

Jordan watched an unflinching Casper through narrowed eyes. The butler had finally strung more than a few words together. Jordan didn't like the words or the tone. He had little patience with insubordination.

"How is Joshua this morning?" Casper asked.

The unexpected query completely threw Jordan off balance. His gaze narrowed further. "Fine. I took him to school." There was pride in that announcement.

"Have you eaten?

"No."

"Will grits and ham and biscuits be sufficient?" Casper
asked.

Jordan gave up trying to be indignant. It simply wasn't possible when the other person jumped from topic to topic. "Don't
think I don't know what you're doing, Casper," Jordan warned.

"Working for the less intelligent has never been a goal of
mine. Breakfast will be served in fifteen minutes in the dining
room." Bowing slightly, he walked away.

"Make it the kitchen," Jordan yelled, trying to get in the
last word. When nothing came to the contrary, he nodded his
satisfaction and started for the bedroom again.

Jordan was under the blast of the shower before he realized
his mood had lightened. He didn't feel helpless. The reason
had him laughing—Casper, the less than friendly butler.

Lauren was as nervous as a turkey the day before Thanksgiv-
ing. The reason for this was now reading a bedtime story to
her son. According to Sonja, Jordan had met Joshua when he
got off the bus and stayed at her place until almost time for
Lauren to come home. Then they had gone to her house. Going
home she had followed the sound of laughter and found them
in her backyard playing pirates. The two were sailing the sea
on a cardboard box, "The Shark", looking for treasure and
damsels in distress.

Seeing her, Jordan had yelled, "At last." Grinning, he had
raced across the yard, picked her up, then raced back to "The
Shark" and told Joshua, "Full speed ahead."

Giggling, her son began making steering motions with his
hands. The moment he turned away, Jordan had kissed her. By
the time they had reached the 'pirate cove', she was tingling
from head to foot.

Telling them she had dinner to prepare, she had escaped with
Jordan's word 'Tonight' ringing in her ear. It was a miracle
she didn't burn the smothered steak and rice.

Now the meal was over. With Jordan's help Joshua had

entered more information into his electronic organizer, done his homework, gotten ready for bed, and said his prayers.

Now she had to do something she had been dreading all day—face Sonja and ask her to sit with Joshua. Seeing her son's eyelids drooping, she knew she couldn't put it off any longer and slipped from the room.

Today at work she had been so busy catching up from yesterday and fielding phone calls regarding the newspaper article on Joshua that she hadn't had a chance to call and test the waters, so to speak. The piece hadn't alarmed her as much as it foretold her what a fishbowl her life might become if it were known she and Jordan were romantically involved. A disquieting thought.

However, the thought of never seeing him was far more terrifying. Closing the front door behind her, she crossed the street. She noticed a luxury sedan parked in front of the house and breathed a sigh of relief. If Sonja had a client, neither one of them would feel awkward.

From the office, she knew women liked to talk about their sexual encounters, but there had never been a reason for such a conversation between them before. Until Jordan. Maybe until Drake.

Lauren rang the doorbell. No response. She waited, then rang again. No response. A frown drew her brows together. She glanced at the strange car. Uneasiness swept through her. Sonja never took this long to answer the door.

Her fist pounded on the door. ''Sonja! Open up. Sonja!''

The door yielded under her fist. At least, she thought it had, until she saw Sonja holding the knob. The sight wasn't reassuring. Lauren's heart rate increased.

Sonja, even at home, was always meticulously neat and well-groomed. The woman before her had mussed hair, and her lipstick was smudged. The pale blue, silk buttons of her blouse weren't matched to loops, and it was half out of her skirt.

''Sonja, are you all right?'' Lauren asked frantically. ''What happened to you?''

Sonja flinched. She glanced away.

Lauren concern escalated to outrage. "Where is the no good jerk that did this to you? I'll—"

Tall and imposing, an equally disheveled Drake stepped up beside Sonja. "You wanted something, Lauren?"

The situation hit Lauren. She stumbled backward. "I'm . . . I'm sorry." Turning, she ran back across the street and into the house.

"Can she si—Honey, what's the matter?" Jordan asked, hurrying across the living room to take Lauren into his arms.

She looked up at him with horror in her eyes. "Oh, Jordan. I didn't think."

The question he was about to ask was interrupted by the doorbell. Lauren jumped. Her eyes widened. "It's them."

Jordan didn't know who 'them' was, but no one was going to frighten his woman. Pushing her behind him, he opened the door. Surprise drew his brows together as he saw Drake and Sonja. Jordan glanced back at Lauren. She was studying her sandals as if she'd never seen her feet before.

"May we come in?" Sonja asked.

"Sure." Jordan stepped aside. The instant he saw the disheveled couple in the light, he understood.

His lips twitched, but one look at the fierce protectiveness on his cousin's face and Jordan knew he was courting disaster.

The never-at-a-loss-for-a-saucy-word Sonja looked uncertain. "Lauren, did you need something?"

Finally, Lauren lifted her head. Her gaze skirted away. "We, er, needed a babysitter."

"Sure," Sonja said.

"Sorry," Drake said.

Sonja's glare at the brawny man beside her did little good. Drake glared back. Jordan laughed. Drake swung toward him. Jordan held up his hands. "If you hit me, you're liable to break my jaw, and you'll end up with me in the hospital, instead of with Sonja."

Sonja tucked her head. "I don't mind sitting."

"We have dinner reservations," Drake pointed out.

"She's my best friend," Sonja said softly, and turned to Lauren. "That is, if you still want me to."

Lauren gasped at the implication. "Oh, Sonja, I acted like a nut. Please forgive me."

"You don't think bad of me?" Sonja looked uncertain.

"How can I think bad of you when I wanted a sitter so I could do the same thing?" Lauren asked with disarming frankness.

Jordan choked.

Drake laughed and hit Jordan on the back.

Neither woman noticed the reactions of the men. They were too busy hugging and asking for forgiveness, fighting tears and talking at once.

Jordan and Drake stood by helplessly for all of fifteen seconds, then exchanged nervous looks and pulled the women apart and into their arms.

"Go have fun," Lauren said, sniffing and smiling.

"No wonder you wanted to rent your own car," Jordan teased. "I always knew you had to watch the quiet ones. Now get out of here, like Lauren said."

"You're sure?" Sonja asked.

"They're sure. Thanks." Drake ushered her out of the house.

The door closed and Lauren sighed in Jordan's arms. "I like Drake."

He kissed the top of her head. "Sonja will give him a run for his money."

She leaned her head back. "I guess we can't go out."

"Who says?"

"We need a sitter."

Jordan grinned. "I know just the person."

"Who?"

"Casper."

Arm in arm, Jordan and Lauren strolled in the sunken garden. The fragrant scent of hundreds of blossoms permeated the air. Jordan snapped the stem of a red hibiscus and placed the flower behind Lauren's ear.

"Glad you came?"

"Yes." She hadn't been sure about Casper until she had

seen him looking down on her sleeping son. Almost imperceptibly, his stoic face had softened. They were out the door ten minutes later.

"At least this time I know you saw the house," Jordan commented.

She smiled. "Had my mouth hanging open, huh?"

"I hope you noticed I took advantage of it, too," he said.

Lauren's body warmed at the memory of their heated kisses.

"You look sensational in that dress." Jordan eyed the pink sundress appreciatively, then pulled her body against his.

"You're not so bad yourself." Dressed casually in a banded collar white shirt and black slacks, he looked rakish and handsome, an irresistible combination.

Instinctively, she did something she had wanted to do all evening. Her trembling fingers stroked his full, black beard, marveling at its silky texture. "Your beard is softer than my hair."

He slanted his head, kissing her palm. "Good. I'd shave the thing off if it marred your skin."

"You would?" she questioned. "But you like your beard."

"I like you more, a lot more." His gaze heated.

"Jordan," she whispered, pleased and a little scared. Standing in his arms she felt safe and protected, but for how long would she be a part of his life?

His arms drew her closer. His chin nuzzled the top of her head. "Relax, Honey. All I'm going to do is hold you. Facing Sonja and Drake is one thing, Casper another."

Her head came up. "You're afraid of what Casper will think?" she asked in disbelief, momentarily distracted from her own problems.

The pad of his thumb grazed across her lush lower lip. "This is new to you, and you're sensitive about people knowing we're intimate. With Casper's sharp eyes, he'd spot the signs the moment he saw you."

"He couldn't tell by looking at you?" she questioned with growing curiosity.

"The odds are against it," he said. "Women wear that look of boneless satisfaction longer than men."

Something about the way Jordan casually made that state-ment bothered and challenged her. "You mean I couldn't put that look on your face and make it stay?"

Something about the way Lauren had tilted her head bothered Jordan. "Lauren, you're going to be sensible about this, aren't you?"

"Let's go for a swim." Stepping back, she undid the tie at the back of her sundress neck and shimmied out of it. "Since we got a late start, I thought it would save time if I wore my suit."

Jordan's mouth dried. The white strapless bikini top molded to her high, firm breasts; the high-waisted bottom revealed shapely legs, and the whimsical, see-through swim skirt drew his eyes like a magnet. His hands itched to touch the soft places of her body, to make her his again.

His body did the rest. He was hard, and getting harder. With difficulty, he tore his gaze away. "You aren't going to be sensible, are you?"

Slender arms curved around his neck. "I'm tired of being sensible. Is that so bad?"

He gazed down into her dreamy eyes. All he had to do was say yes and step away. He was unable to do either. Lauren in a seductive mood was proving irresistible. She was testing her newfound sensuality, and he had to admit it was a heady feeling knowing she had enough trust in him to do so.

He moved closer, his hands spanning her narrow waist and drawing her against his blunt arousal. "What do you think?"

"In your arms I don't seem able to think very well, just feel," she admitted, kissing his bearded chin.

He angled his head downward, taking her mouth in a kiss of tenderness and passion. In Jordan's arms, she never had to worry. Lauren gave herself up to the feelings only Jordan cre-ated within her. The kiss seemed to go on and on. She heard a whimper and recognized it as her own cry of longing.

Somehow, they were on their knees facing each other, their mouths still hungry. Then, faintly, she became aware of the smooth blades of the grass against her back. The coolness beneath her and the heat of Jordan's large body over her sent delicious shivers coursing through her body. Then a different kind of sensation took its place as his large hand traced a path from her shoulder down her side to her hip and back in a relentless sweep.

The yearning in her deepened. Arching her body into his, she tried to appease the ache building within her.

"Easy, Honey," he murmured, kissing the curve of her jaw. "Or we won't make it into the house."

She nipped his ear. She wanted him here. Now.

Jordan groaned and insinuated himself deeper in the notch of her thighs. The heat of her desire burned through his restraint. He needed Lauren. Here. Now.

He lifted from her just enough to discard his shirt and her bikini top. She moaned slightly at the contact of naked flesh to naked flesh. Her hands traced the corded muscles of his back; her tongue teased his taut nipple.

Air hissed through Jordan's teeth. His pants and briefs were hastily discarded.

Lauren had a brief glimpse of the blatant proof of his desire, then opened her arms for him. He came, covering her. Her nipples hardened, pushing insolently against his hairy chest, begging attention. Jordan's hand closed over one soft mound, molding it to fit his hard palm, then plucking the nipple to a rigid peak.

"Jordan," she whimpered, need making her voice hoarse and strained.

His hand swept down one side of her thigh, then the other, and took away the patch of cloth. His fingers slipped inside her, stroking, testing. Readying himself, he joined them in one long, slow thrust, then rolled.

Lauren's eyes widened to find herself staring down at Jordan. Her initial reaction was wariness, then he moved. Sensations spiraled though her.

"Put your hands on my shoulder, Honey, and do what comes naturally," Jordan instructed, his voice tight and strained.

"I don't kn—"

He moved again. The glorious, undeniable sensation came again, this time stronger, a siren's call her hips and body were powerless to keep from reaching for again and again.

She braced her hands on his shoulders and moved toward the elusive satisfaction just out of reach. Her body jerked when Jordan's mouth closed hotly over her nipple and sucked greedily. She would faint if he didn't stop; she would die if he did.

She arched her back and gave herself over to the overwhelming pleasures spiraling through her body. Faster, faster, her knees locked against Jordan's hips. His body locked with hers.

"Give me your mouth."

Lauren heard the hoarsely muttered command. She just wasn't able to comply. A strong arm clamped around her hips, keeping her in place as Jordan raised upward, taking what he wanted. The hot, dark taste of him had her wanting more. Her arms slid around his neck, bringing him closer.

Something began to tighten within her. She started to pull back. Jordan wouldn't let her. He surged into her again and again, taking her with him, letting her take him to a shattering, glorious finale.

It was a long time before Lauren felt she could move, and then it was only enough to edge her head toward Jordan's face. She saw the determined thrust of his strong chin.

She needed to see his expression. To do that she'd have to summon enough strength to sit up.

She smiled. Jordan was apt in his terminology—*bonelessness*—yet she was acutely aware of the sound of the water spewing from a stone fish's mouth into the fountain a few yards away, of the smell of the honeysuckle in the arbor, could feel the night breeze brush across every inch of her naked flesh.

Boneless, but alive in every pore and nerve ending. And she wanted to see if she had made Jordan feel anything as beautiful.

She worked her way up from her chin, inadvertently brushing her nipples against his hair-roughened chest. Jordan's hand, which had been resting lightly on her hip, clenched.

A good sign, she thought, lifting herself up higher until she saw his face. Her breath caught. Raw power and possessiveness stared back at her. She should have known a pirate would be different.

For the time being, he was her pirate. He had given her so much. Perhaps it was time to give back and lay the past to rest.

"Six years ago I woke up in hell," she said.

Chapter Eighteen

Shock tautened Jordan's body and widened his eyes. From the faint illumination of the accent lights he saw the pain in Lauren's eyes. Torn between not wanting her to relive the horror and wanting her to face her past and move on, he laid his palm against her cheek. Not once did he think of his grandfather.

She shivered beneath his touch. Averting her eyes, she lay down on his chest.

Jordan grabbed the tail of his shirt and pulled it over her. "You want to go inside?"

He felt her shake her head in a negative gesture. He tried to see her face but saw only the top of her head. Tension emitted from her. His hand began a slow glide down her back, letting her know it was her call to continue or stop.

The breath that shuddered across her lips wafted across his bare chest. "When I was eight my parents divorced, and my mother moved us from San Francisco to Concord, North Carolina. She had driven through there with some friends on vacation and liked the friendliness of the small town."

Her hand idly traced a circle on his shoulder. "She had always wanted to open a bookstore, so that's what she did."

Lauren lifted her head. "She was a strong woman, and my

best friend. I never minded not going out much, because she was such fun to be with. I would have done anything for her.''

Jordan heard the pride and the love in Lauren's words. ''You're lucky to have had her.''

Lines bracketed Lauren's mouth. She lay her head down again. ''Yes, I was. My father was a sax player with a small jazz band, and we never heard from him much. He died the year I graduated from college. My mother never mentioned any other relatives.''

A pain clutched Jordan's heart. At least when his mother, then his father, died, he'd had Angelica, his grandfather, and a host of cousins, aunts, and uncles. ''So it's just you and Joshua?''

She tensed. ''Joshua is all I have, but he has relatives in Charlotte.''

''I got the feeling Joshua would love having cousins to play with,'' Jordan said carefully, trying to walk a thin line between encouragement and probing.

''These relatives wouldn't want Joshua any more than they wanted me in their family. My mother and I weren't good enough for them.'' Bitterness tinged her words. ''I met Joshua's father when he got lost and came inside the store to ask for directions. We were attracted to each other. The next day he was back. He asked me out, and I accepted.

''It was easy to fall in love with David. He was kind, sensitive, and gentle. I didn't know he was wealthy until his parents started calling and demanding that I leave David alone. We thought they'd come around once they knew I really cared for him so my mother and I accepted his invitation for dinner at his house.'' Her voice took on a sharp edge. ''His parents were noticeably absent.''

Jordan's strong hand continued to glide up and down her back and shoulders, trying to ease the tightness beneath his fingertips, trying to ease his own growing anger.

''I didn't know until later that evening that David had planned to ask me to marry him with both our parents as witnesses. He hurt for me. I hurt for him. I accepted his proposal. The next day he moved out of his parents' mansion.''

"Good for him," Jordan said.

"It wasn't. He loved his parents, and whatever happened affected him." She paused, then continued, "Afterward, he wasn't so quick to smile. He seldom laughed. When he insisted we get married, I said yes. Since we weren't having a traditional wedding, David insisted my mother accompany us. The two had always gotten along. So the three of us set out across the state line to Dillon, South Carolina."

Her body grew taut, and Jordan braced himself for what he knew was coming. The report Drake gave the day he arrived in Shreveport had been very detailed.

"Four days later we were driving back from our honeymoon in Myrtle Beach and ran into a thunderstorm. My mother was asleep in the backseat. It was raining so hard David could hardly see." She burrowed close. "He was trying to find a place to pull over when we saw the glare of headlights. The next thing I remember is the impact and the screams."

Jordan shut his eyes against the image and held on to the woman in his arms.

Her breathing changed, and her voice thickened. "When the rescue squad was trying to cut me out of David's car, they kept assuring me my mother and David were all right. I kept drifting in and out of consciousness. When I was awake the pain was unbearable. All I wanted to do was escape. A man wouldn't let me. He kept telling me to fight, to hold on. I couldn't." She swallowed and took a deep breath.

"D—drifting off again, I heard him mutter something about not losing another one. I thought he meant the passengers in the other vehicle. The next time I came to, he had the wedding photograph David had given me. He stuck the picture in my face and told me to fight to live for my husband. He shouted at me to focus on the picture. Despite the pain, I did just that, and stayed awake until I reached the hospital."

"Oh, Honey," Jordan cried, holding her closer.

"The next few days are still a blur. I had emergency surgery for a ruptured spleen, and internal bleeding. My collarbone was fractured. The first time I was awake for more than a few minutes, I had a visit from my in-laws' lawyer.

"He told me quite bluntly that my husband was dead and if I wished to spare his family any embarrassment, I would not say anything about the marriage. The only thing I understood was that David was dead. I told him to get out and rang for the nurse. I wanted my mother." Her fingernails dug into his shoulder. "That's when I learned my mother had died before she reached the hospital. I was left with nothing. At that moment I hated the man at the accident site at much as I hated the Stricklands."

"Honey, I'm sorry." Jordan didn't want to hear anymore, but he knew he didn't have a choice.

"The chaplain came and helped me make arrangements for my mother to be sent home. I couldn't even go with her. I didn't know where David was buried. I called his house and his mother called me a murderer and hung up on me." Anger propelled her out of his arms. She sat up, drawing the shirt around her bare shoulders.

"The lawyer was back within the hour. He was very explicit in his warning not to worry his client's family any further. I told him to get out. I rang for the nurse and asked to have my personal effects. There was nothing there to connect me to David—not my wedding ring, the license, the camera, or the several rolls of film. Somehow the lawyer had taken everything."

If Jordan could have gotten his hands on Strickland at the moment, he would have been a dead man.

"The nurse came in, saw me near hysteria. Opening the bedside drawer, she handed me the photograph. The man I had cursed minutes before had brought it to the hospital. He didn't want it to get lost or damaged. If he hadn't been so thoughtful, the lawyer would have taken that, too." She ran her hand through her hair. "I didn't think I could feel worse. I learned I could.

"Later that day I received a call from my immediate supervisor at the library where I worked as a librarian. They found a pornographic magazine in my desk. I could resign or have a public hearing. She pointed out that people would recall that I never dated much."

Jordan saw the devious hand of Nathan Strickland. "The bastard."

"I just wanted to pull the covers over my head and sleep forever. I stopped eating, and had to be fed intravenously for a week. The only reason I started eating again was to be able to go home and be left alone."

His hand swept her hair. He felt her shiver, and eased her back into his lap. When she leaned against him, he breathed easier.

"But first I went to David's parents, to at least learn where he was buried. His father, Nathan Strickland, threatened to call the police if I didn't leave." She leaned against Jordan's hard chest. "I was numb. I went home and discovered the house had been burglarized. The TV was gone. I knew it was Strickland."

"How?"

"The few letters and pictures I had of David were missing also. A thief wouldn't have taken those."

Tension coiled in Jordan. "Was there anything else David had given you that was missing?"

"No. The dried flowers and empty boxes of candy could have been from anyone. I got a phone call that night telling me to leave town or the burglar might come back when I was home."

Jordan muttered a savage expletive.

"The next morning I woke up nauseated. By the third morning I went to the store and bought a home pregnancy test. I saw blue, and knew I had to leave to protect my child. It was a miracle I didn't lose the baby in the accident.

"I knew I was right about leaving when I couldn't start my car the next day. Every hose had been slashed, and sugar was poured into the gas tank. The same day I put the house up for sale, moved to an apartment in the next town, and began using my mother's maiden name. Within two weeks I was gone, and I've never been back."

"He's going to pay for what he did," Jordan said with absolute conviction.

"One day, but not until Joshua is older. He wants a family too much to learn his father's family hates his mother."

"You can't let him get away with this," he told her forcibly.

"What do you suggest I do? Nathan Strickland is rich and powerful."

Jordan's face hardened. The bastard wouldn't be for long. "So am I."

"No."

"Lau—"

"No," she repeated, climbing out of his lap and pulling on her clothes. "Don't make me regret telling you."

Jordan came after her with no concern for his nakedness. "You can't go on living in fear."

"Don't you think I know that?" She pushed an impatient hand through her hair. "I'm trying, Jordan. You make me want to try. But I have to do this at my own pace."

He pulled her into his arms, her words 'You make me want to try' ringing in his ears. Only this woman could send him to the highest heights or lowest depths with just a few words or a look.

Her arms circled his waist. "Please, Jordan, try to understand."

"All right, Lauren. We'll do it your way."

"Thank you." She leaned away. "You don't know how difficult it is to carry secrets."

Jordan felt a familiar tightening in his gut.

Lauren noticed the turmoil in his expression and frowned. "You don't think very much of me now, do you?"

"Honey, no." He rushed to reassure her. "Strickland is the one who should be ashamed. You did the only thing you could. You took care of Joshua."

"I know, but there are days when I wish I could have stayed and told the world David and I were married. He was nothing like his father," she said softly. "The accident took so much from me. Strickland tried to take what was left, my self-respect and my dignity."

Jordan's large hand cupped her chin. "I'm glad he didn't succeed."

"Me, too. Otherwise I wouldn't be here with you," she said softly.

Jordan gazed down into Lauren's eyes and felt his gut tighten. If he told her he had manipulated events for them to be together, she'd never forgive him. Worse, she might never reach out to another person.

"What's the matter? You're frowning again," she said, a frown on her own face.

"Just thinking I don't want to lose you."

A tremulous smile on her face, she leaned against his broad, bare chest. "You won't."

Jordan pulled her closer to him, praying that she was right, praying that they had a future together. "I'd better get you home."

"You think Casper will be able to tell?" Lauren asked.

Jordan allowed her to change the subject. "Not a chance."

Not by one word or look did Casper indicate he knew what his employer had been doing with the mother of the child he was sitting with. In his usual efficient way, he gave Lauren a report on a soundly sleeping Joshua, snapped shut his briefcase, bade them good night, then drove off in his dark green Jaguar.

Lauren closed the door and turned to Jordan. "I expected him to drive something more conservative."

"Casper, as the saying goes, is deep." Jordan slung his arm around her shoulder and followed her out of the living room. "I caught a glimpse of some of those papers before he shoved them back in his case. Stock reports. I'd say Casper does all right for himself."

"I'm glad. I like him." She started down the hall to check on Joshua.

"Don't like him too much." Jordan advised.

Lauren's heart fluttered at the possessive note in Jordan's voice. "I won't," she whispered, then eased open Joshua's door and went to his bed.

He was sound asleep. Although he was tucked in snugly, she adjusted the covers, brushed his precious cheek, then kissed him good night. Discussing her past had brought home how much of a miracle he was. After one last touch, she tiptoed back out and went into the den.

"I had a wonderful ti—I mean . . ." She bit her lower lip.

Smiling, Jordan tugged her toward the sofa. "Then, I guess you'll miss me when I'm gone."

"Gone?" she repeated in dismay.

"I need to get back to work and take care of a few things," he explained. Strickland would be at the top of the list.

"Why didn't you say something earlier?"

"I didn't want to spoil our evening, and then other things came up."

Lauren flushed again, recalling her involvement in the 'other things'. She looked away. "Of course. I understand."

"Do you really?" he asked.

Glancing back around, she opened her mouth to say polite words, but the somber expression on his face wouldn't let her. She might be running from her past, but not from her deepening affection for Jordan.

"I understand the reason for your leaving, but I wish you didn't have to go," she admitted. "We'll miss you. I'll miss you."

One arm curved around her shoulder, the other around her waist. "No more than I'll miss you. I'll be back as soon as possible."

"What time does your plane leave?"

"Around noon."

"You'll call?"

He kissed her forehead. "Every night. I've learned my lesson."

She played with a button on his shirt. "Don't you need to pack?"

"Not really." He settled more comfortably in the cushion. "I'm going to New Orleans first."

"You need to get some rest," she persisted, pushing to the back of her mind that Shreveport was one of several business layovers for Jordan.

"I am resting."

She tried again. "Not properly. You should be in bed."

"You wouldn't be there, so I wouldn't get much sleep, anyway."

Neither would she. Funny how her body had grown accustomed to his so quickly. She could just imagine the grueling pace Jordan would set for himself. "Morning will be here before you know it."

She felt him smile. His warm breath fanned her forehead. "Nice try. Now, please stop fussing and let me enjoy you in my arms a few more minutes. Then I'll go and let you get some rest."

Realizing she wasn't getting anywhere, Lauren relaxed, her head seeking and finding a comfortable spot on his hard, muscular chest. He certainly liked having his way, but thus far his decisions had all been in the best interests of her and her son.

She had made the right choice in telling Jordan about her past. Strickland might have tried to ruin her life in the past, but she wouldn't let him ruin her future. With that thought, she closed her eyes and listened to the comforting sound of Jordan's heartbeat.

Lauren woke the next morning with a newfound peace. She hadn't conquered all of her demons, but she had a few on the run. Best of all, there were no more secrets between her and Jordan.

Hugging the pillow to her cheek, she stretched languidly on the bed. Her skin tingled. Jordan's doing. After awakening on the sofa, he hadn't left until a very satisfying hour later. She probably wouldn't be able to keep her eyes open today, but making love with Jordan had been definitely worth losing sleep.

Her smile growing, she climbed out of bed and headed for the shower. Forty-five minutes later, she hustled out the front door with Joshua to wait on the curb for the bus.

The first time the late model, black sedan passed by slowly, she didn't pay any attention. The second time she drew Joshua a little closer.

"What's the matter, Mama?" he asked.

"Nothing," she said with a smile. Talk of Strickland had

her looking for trouble where there was none. She and Joshua were safe. The person was probably trying to read the house numbers.

She told herself that, but she held on to Joshua until the bus arrived and instructed him again about not talking to strangers and getting on the bus.

"Yes, Ma'am," he said, and wriggled out of her arms to climb aboard the bus.

Walking back to the house, she wrapped her arms around her waist. Lauren's gaze searched the tree-lined street. *Please, dear Lord, let us be safe.*

Guilt and worry made poor bedmates, Jordan thought, sitting in his study. He hadn't slept worth a damn. He missed Lauren, and he couldn't help but think time was running out for them. Around six he had given up and come into his study to work.

He slid a glance at the files on his desk and rocked back in his chair. That, too, had been a wasted effort. His concentration was nil. The pumped excitement wasn't there.

He had been out of his office longer than he had anticipated, and he wasn't anxious to get back as usual. While he didn't mind delegating authority, he prided himself on being on top of things. A stack of untouched faxes spoke for themselves. The executive chair scooted backward as he lunged to his feet.

He'd remained in Shreveport because of Lauren and Joshua. They needed him. Just like he needed them. Need made a man re-examine his priorities. He just hoped Drake came through for him today at the stock exchange. If he did, the hardest part lay ahead—telling Lauren the real reason he had sought her out.

He glanced at his watch. Ten-five. He should get to the airport. He didn't look forward to telling his grandfather they couldn't involve Lauren, especially since he wasn't sure how they were going to be able to bring Strickland down.

A light knock sounded on the closed study door. "Yes."

Casper opened the door. "Your grandfather and a Mrs. Johnson to see you, Sir."

Unease went through Jordan. His grandfather hadn't traveled outside New Orleans since his stroke two years ago. Long strides carried Jordan out the door.

His uneasiness grew on seeing his grandfather leaning heavily on his walking stick and Mattie standing nervously by his side watching him.

"Hello, Grandad, Mattie. Why are you standing in the foyer? Don't tell me Casper put you off?"

"Hello, Jordan," Mattie greeted, her anxious gaze switching back to his grandfather.

"What's the matter?" Jordan questioned.

"I want to know about this."

Jordan eyed the newspaper clutched in his grandfather's frail fist. "I take it there's something in there about my helping to find Joshua Bennett."

"You're supposed to be working on the mother, not fooling around with her kid," the senior Hamilton accused.

"Sit down, grandfather, and we'll talk," Jordan said.

The older man shrugged aside the hand reaching for his arm. "Not until I have some answers. I ask you again, what's going on?" He looked around the luxurious home. "You never rented a house at any of the other sites. Why here?"

"I'll answer your questions as soon as you've sat down," Jordan said, noticing the pinched look around his grandfather's mouth.

"Come on, Hollis. I'd like to rest these bones after driving most of the night," Mattie said, gently easing the elderly man toward the living room.

Jordan thought of the two elderly people on the long, narrow roads from New Orleans and he wanted to shake both of them for doing something so dangerous. With difficulty he held his words until his grandfather eased into a chair.

"Have you had breakfast?" he asked.

Mattie shook her head of gray hair. "He wanted to come straight here."

No breakfast meant no medicine. Jordan's lips tightened. "Casper, please prepare some breakfast."

As he suspected, Casper was nearby. "I'll bring something out directly."

"I'm seated," his grandfather snapped. "You gonna answer me?"

"Lauren is afraid of elevators," Jordan answered simply.

Rage flushed his grandfather's pale skin. "I knew it. You're doing all this for her, and forgetting about your promise."

"Grand—"

"Aren't you?" the older man interrupted.

"Lauren received just as raw a deal as Daddy."

"But she's living. My son, your father, isn't."

"I know that," Jordan said, his voice strained. "I stood on that riverbank in the rain, hoping, praying, that he'd somehow made it to shore, or another boat had picked him up. I stayed on that bank five hours—until I watched them pull his body from the water."

"Jordan. Hollis, please," Mattie pleaded. "Don't let Strickland turn you against each other."

"It's him that's doing it," Grandfather Hamilton accused.

The slight tinkling of china had three heads turning. Casper wheeled a serving cart into the living room. With crisp efficiency, he spread a napkin on Jordan's grandfather's lap and paused over the silver-covered dishes. "Will grits and toast be sufficient, Sir?"

Jordan watched his grandfather struggle to say no, then lose. Grits were his favorite breakfast food. "I like lots of butter."

Mattie's lips pursed. "He's not supposed to have butter."

"It's my body." Hollis glared at his friend and housekeeper, and missed Casper adding a butter substitute. The older man accepted the bowl with a brisk nod and began eating.

"Mattie, please help yourself," Jordan said, his own appetite non-existent. With a nod, the woman prepared a plate and sat across from the men.

"Shall I cancel your flight reservations, Sir?" Casper asked.

"Please."

Hollis swallowed, his eyes becoming animated. "So you were coming to your senses."

"I was coming to see you. To tell you I'm going to break

Strickland just as I promised, but I'm not using Lauren Bennett to do it.''

Anger propelled the senior Hamilton to his feet. The bowl of grits clattered onto the hardwood floor. Only Mattie noticed or cared.

"You promised!" Hollis yelled, his face flushed.

"I'll keep my promise, but I'll do it in my own way," Jordan said. "Now, please sit down."

"I raised you, Boy. You can't tell me what to do," the elder man flared.

"Yes, you did," Jordan answered calmly. "But I'm a man now."

Hollis's burning gaze didn't waver. "Age don't make a man."

Jordan shrank from the words as if they were a physical blow, but he didn't back down. "I know. That's one of the things you taught me."

The older man wavered, then plopped down, his hand flexing on the curve of the walking cane. "You promised."

"I'll keep that promise, but in my own way." Bending, Jordan picked up the bowl and began wiping up the spilled food.

"Allow me, Sir."

Standing, Jordan moved aside and let Casper clean up the mess. As soon as he finished, Jordan knelt by his grandfather's side. Faintly, he noticed Mattie moving to stand by the French doors.

"Strickland abused her horribly. He ran her out of town, caused her to lose her job. He tried to ground her into the dirt. She survived. I can't, won't, let him near her again to hurt her."

"My son didn't."

"She's suffered enough," Jordan said.

"What about my suffering? Putting your child into the ground is hard. Knowing he didn't have to be there is a pain that will never end," Hollis spat, his expression as tired as his body.

Jordan tensed. The possibility of anything but an accidental drowning had never been discussed in the Hamilton family or by the police. Randolph Hamilton was an excellent boatsman and swimmer, but there had been an unexpected storm. Accidents happen.

Jordan gazed into his grandfather's sad, tired eyes and saw what Jordan had always suspected and never said. His father had gone to the lake intending to never return. "I loved him, too."

"I know." His grandfather's other hand patted the top of Jordan's. "Guess I'll have to wait a little longer for my threat to Strickland last week to come true."

The tension which had been easing out of Jordan doubled. "Grandfather, what are you talking about?"

"After you left New Orleans, I called him and told him his time was up," the elder Hamilton explained. "I wanted him to sweat."

Jordan was the one sweating. Tipping off Strickland was the worst possible thing his grandfather could have done. He had alerted their enemy, and an animal is at its most vicious when cornered.

Chapter Nineteen

Lauren let the garage door down and entered the house. She had been right about being sleepy at work—she had barely made it home. The one bright spot was Jordan's call telling her he wasn't leaving as planned.

She smiled and gave her ivy another sip of water. If he expected them to go out, she'd probably fall asleep on him. Considering the way Jordan woke her up, she wouldn't mind.

Setting the glass in the sink, she headed for Sonja's house. Her friend had called her at work to tell her about her date with Drake. Apparently, he rated off the scale, and had captured her heart when he had picked her up in his arms after she slipped in her heels.

The doorbell rang just as she reached for the door. Jordan. Smiling, she opened the door—and froze.

Nathan Strickland stood on the other side of the screen door. A number of emotions—fear, pain, hatred—swept through her. Fear was uppermost. She started to swing the door closed.

"I want to see my grandson."

The six words chilled her. Her grip tightened on the doorknob. "You have no grandson."

"These say differently." He held up several photographs of

Joshua. Fear congealed in her heart when saw Joshua wearing the striped blue shirt and jeans he had on the day before. "Stay away from my son."

"He's my grandson." He jerked the screen door and cursed when it didn't open. Cold, black eyes lanced up to Lauren. "Open the door."

"Leave."

"Open the door, or I'll send Tony across the street to get Joshua," he threatened. "I prefer not to frighten the boy, but it's your choice."

Lauren glanced at the wide-shouldered man behind her father-in-law and shuddered. His neck was almost as round as her waist, and his arms were just as massive. His hard black face held not a trace of kindness or weakness. "Leave us alone."

Strickland turned to the silent, black man behind him. "Go ge—"

"No," Lauren screamed, her fingers fumbling to open the screen door.

"Wise of you, My Dear." Strickland stepped inside. The hulking man followed—he had to twist sideways to get through the door.

Swallowing, Lauren backed up. "You're in. Say what you have to and get out."

Strickland's eyes narrowed in his thin face. "No manners. I'll never know what my son saw in you."

"Apparently more than he saw in you, since he walked out of your house and your life and married me," she said with spirit.

The dark shadow behind Strickland shifted. His employer held up his manicured hand. "You weren't so difficult to deal with six years ago."

"I was scared, grieving for the two people I loved most in the world, and you took advantage of that grief." Her chin lifted. "You won't get away with it this time."

"Won't I?" he said silkily, and glanced around the living room. "Surely the money I paid you let you buy a house with a little more style."

His lawyer had offered, but she had never accepted. "Your lawyer lied. I never took one cent of your money."

He smiled, showing serrated teeth. "My dear, naive Lauren. Do you really think your mother's house could have sold in less than two weeks? I believe you were handed a check for twelve thousand, five hundred for the loan assumption on the house, and another for five thousand on your mother's bookstore stock." Hitching up his black trousers, he sat in a chair. "You'll be pleased to know I turned a profit on both deals."

Her hand clutched against her queasy stomach as she struggled against the truth. Everything she had, she owed to a man she despised.

"I thought I handled things quite nicely. No payoff you could prove, just a nice, straightforward business transaction," he said, gloating.

"I'll pay you back. Every cent."

"No need. As it turns out, it was money well spent." Reaching over, he picked one of the several pictures of Joshua on the end table.

"Put that back." She started toward him. Tony stepped in front of her. Cold, merciless eyes stared down at her. Her fists clenched in silent fury and frustration.

"He looks like his father at this age," Strickland mused. "His grandmother is already anticipating his arrival. I haven't seen Maryann this happy in years."

"He's not David's child," Lauren said, fear making her voice tight. "I met someone after I left Concord."

Strickland's finger snapped and like a trained dog, Tony moved to his side. "Whatever breeding you lack, your morals were good. Joshua is a Strickland, and he deserves all the privileges that name entitles him to."

"Privileges," she spat. "A child needs love and understanding. Something you and your wife have no concept of. David turned his back on those 'privileges'. He said he had no family outside me and my mother."

"Lies. All lies. David loved us. He would have come back if you hadn't poisoned his mind." He shook the picture in his hand. "This is my grandson, and I want him."

Lauren surged forward again. This time she grabbed the picture before the bodyguard pushed her away. She stumbled, then righted herself. "Get out."

Standing, Strickland brushed his long-fingered hand across his expensive sports coat. "I'll go for now, but I'll be back. It won't be too difficult to prove you're an unfit mother."

"I'm a good mother."

He sneered. "Are you? Then why is he having problems in school? Why did he run off? Or were you too busy sleeping around with your latest lover to notice or care?"

Each damning word was like a knife in her heart. "Get out! Get out!" she screamed.

"I'll be back for my grandson. Don't bother packing any of his things. We'll only have to give them to charity. If you know what's good for you, you won't mention this conversation to anyone. My lawyers will be in touch."

Strickland paused by the door Tony had opened. "Oh, yes, thank Jordan Hamilton for leading me to you."

Her mind spun in confusion and bewilderment. "What are you talking about?"

His laugh was nasty. "You *are* naive. Do you really think a successful man like Jordan Hamilton would want you unless he had an ulterior motive? He used you, My Dear, for his own selfish reasons."

"I don't believe you," she managed. "You'd say anything to make me feel alone again."

Strickland took the three steps to bring him back to her. "You *are* alone. Ask Jordan why he picked a small PR firm like Scott Resources. Ask him why he picked you, of all the women in the world. Believe me, you won't like the answers. Get rid of Jordan, and I might let you see the boy at Christmas for a few hours. Otherwise, you'll never see him again." He whirled away. The door closed behind him.

Clutching Joshua's picture, Lauren sank to her knees, tears streaming down her cheeks. Dear Lord, that monster wanted to take her baby, and Jordan had led him to her.

* * *

Jordan pulled up to Lauren's house with a squeal of brakes. Lauren's call to him twenty minutes before had scared him. She wouldn't tell him why she was so upset or let him call Sonja. She just wanted to see him.

Sprinting from the Bronco, he ran up the walkway. Alternately, he pounded on the door and called her name. Finally, the door opened. Her wild eyes and tearstained face sent his heart racing.

"La—"

"Is what he said true?"

Jordan frowned. "Lauren, what's the mat—" He reached for her. She shrank away. The rage in her eyes almost seared him.

"Is what Strickland said true?

Dread pounded though him. "What did that bastard say to you?"

"The truth, apparently," she said, her voice thin and drawn. "He was right. You used me and Joshua, didn't you? I can see it in your face."

Jordan decided it was time for the truth. "Sixteen years ago Strickland embezzled funds from a monthly newspaper he and another man owned. Strickland took those funds and parlayed them into the publishing empire he has today. The other man died broken and disillusioned, leaving behind two children.

"There was no proof of Strickland's crime until his son contacted the partner's father six years ago. He said an incriminating second set of ledgers were in a safe place, but before he could return from his honeymoon and turn over the records, the son was killed in an automobile accident."

With a smothered cry, Lauren backed further away.

"Since that time, the father of Strickland's partner and his son have been looking for those ledgers. The man Strickland cheated was my father."

She stared at him in rising shock and fury. "All you ever wanted were the ledgers."

"It wasn't like that."

"Don't lie and make it worse. I couldn't understand why you kept after me." Her laughter was a hollow sound. "I was afraid, then flattered. I must have been so easy for you. Strickland told the truth, for once."

"Lauren, stop it. I care about you."

"You care about getting Strickland because of your father. You care about getting your hands on those ledgers," she accused. "Joshua and I were just a means of obtaining what you wanted. You wasted your time. Strickland probably has them."

"No, he doesn't. My guess is, he searched your house for more than just pictures of David. Those could be explained away," Jordan told her. "A second set of books would have sent him to jail. From what I've leaned about David, he would have gone to his father and asked for an explanation."

"So that's why he was so distracted," she said thoughtfully. "Poor David. Trying to love a man who had no love in him." She shook her head and mumbled, "Just like me."

With a muttered curse Jordan reached for her. She snatched her arm aside. "Don't touch me. Don't make me hate myself any more than I already do."

"You have nothing to be ashamed of."

"Yes, I do. Because I was gullible enough to listen to your lies, I may lose my son."

"No one is taking Joshua from you," he said fiercely.

"Get out."

"Lauren, please listen."

"You've said enough, done enough." She pulled her hand through her hair. "I was so proud of myself telling you about my past. You must have laughed yourself silly."

"I never laughed at you," he said. "I love you."

"I loathe you." Her eyes were as cold as her voice. "Leave before I call the police."

"I'm not letting you go, Lauren. You or Joshua." Spinning on his heels, he walked out the door.

Across the street, Sonja and Joshua stepped out onto the

porch. Seeing Jordan, the little boy started running. His mother's scream of "No!" stopped him.

Lauren raced across the street and picked up Joshua and went back inside her friend's house. A puzzled Sonja followed. Jordan heard the little boy call for him and fought the thickness in his throat. Getting in his Bronco, he drove away.

Jordan had been on the phone for the better part of the day. After leaving Lauren's house yesterday he had called a security agency his company used to get someone to guard Lauren and Joshua. Next, he had called Drake and informed him what had happened.

The calls today were to business acquaintances and friends. In the business world money was equated with power, and power ruled. To defang Strickland, Jordan had to get him where it hurt, in the pocketbook. Drake was digging into Strickland's business deals for misconduct and quietly buying up his stock. Jordan had instigated another plan.

Strickland's magazine owed a great deal of its success to corporation advertisers. Contracts had probably been signed, but it wouldn't hurt for the powers that be to know, confidentially of course, that Strickland was about to take a fall, that it would be in their firms' best interests to disassociate themselves from Strickland with all due haste. If Drake didn't come up with something, Jordan was looking at a very large libel suit.

Striking off another firm, Jordan reached for the phone just as it rang. Less than ten people had the number. Lauren was one of them.

"Hello."

"Mr. Hamilton? Is that you, Mr. Hamilton?" asked a teary voice.

"Joshua, what's the matter? Is your mother all right?"

"No, Sir. That's why I called. It's all right to call, isn't it?"

Jordan felt a familiar knot in his throat. "That's why I gave you the number."

"She's crying. Her door is closed, but I hear her crying."

The little boy started crying. "Do you think you can come over and get her to stop?"

Eyes closed, Jordan rocked back in his chair. "There's nothing I'd like better, but your mother doesn't want to see me."

"She said we couldn't trust you," the little boy admitted.

"I made a mistake, Joshua, but I love you and your mother," Jordan said.

"Then please come over and get her to stop. I don't know what to do. She wouldn't let me go to school today. I thought I would like that, but she keeps crying. She won't let me go outside. Please, Mr. Hamilton. I don't know what to do to help her."

Jordan swallowed several times to dislodge the lump in his throat. "I'll meet you on The Shark in twenty-five minutes. Six o'clock. Don't come out of the house until you see me."

"Yes, Sir."

The gate to Lauren's backyard was locked. Jordan easily scaled the obstacle. He had gone less than a dozen feet before Joshua appeared at the back door. Jordan stuck his finger to his lips.

The little boy nodded and eased the door closed. Turning, he ran across the yard and into Jordan's arms. The child clasped to him, Jordan sat on the pirate ship. "Is . . . is she still crying?"

"No, Sir. Sonja came over with dinner, and they're talking. I think she's been crying, too," he confided.

Another problem. Drake said Sonja didn't want to see him again because she considered it disloyal to Lauren. What a mess! "You mother has a right to be upset with me."

Sad brown eyes stared up at him. "Then you have to hug her and promise not to do it anymore."

"I tried. She wouldn't listen," Jordan said.

"You have to keep saying it, because sometimes mothers aren't listening," the little boy advised. "Don't you 'member when I went to your house and she was upset with me? I was trying to talk, and she wasn't listening. Mothers get mad because they love you."

Out of the mouths of babes. Despite everything, Jordan felt a spark of hope. The tightness in his chest eased. Lauren loved him. She wouldn't have given herself to him otherwise. He just had to make sure she didn't give up on them.

Hugging the little boy to him, he set him on his feet. "Take care of your mother. When I get back I'm going to hug her until she forgives me."

"Don't be long."

"I'll do my best to hurry." His hand touched the child's shoulder. "Go back inside and make sure your mother eats. Sonja, too. Tell her I'm having enough problems with Drake."

"I will, and I'll be extra good. I don't want Mama sad anymore," he said.

"None of this is your fault."

The little boy studied his bare feet. "I wish I was older so I could help."

"What about the remedy you just told me? I bet she could use a hug about now."

Joshua's head came up. His face brightened. "Mama says I give the best hugs in the world."

"Give her one for me, too." Jordan urged the child toward the back door, then started for his Bronco. He had a lot to do before he could get his hug.

Joshua slammed through the back door, his little legs going at top speed. He headed straight for his mother, who sat with Sonja at the kitchen table.

"Joshua, don't sla—"

His arms wrapped around her neck. "I love you, Mama."

The reprimand died on her lips. Shutting her eyes tightly, she held his warm body close to hers. She wouldn't lose him. She couldn't.

Opening her eyes, she blinked away tears and smiled down into her son's smiling face. "I love you, too."

"Mr. Hamilton was right."

Her hands clutched. "When did you talk to Mr. Hamilton?"

"A little while ago, then just now," he confessed, his smile disappearing.

Lauren strove to keep her voice even. "I thought I told you we weren't going to talk to him or see him again."

His lower lip trembled. "I know, Mama, but you were crying all the time and I didn't know what to do. I thought he could help. Don't be mad at me." His chin dropped to his chest. "I told Mr. Hamilton I'd be good and see that you eat and give you a hug, but I guess I can't do any of that stuff right."

Tears streamed down Lauren's cheeks again. "Oh, Joshua. No, Sweetheart. You did everything just right. It's Mama. Not you. Never you."

By slow degrees his head came up. "Then why are you still crying?"

Sniffing, Lauren reached for the tissue Sonja handed her and blotted away the moisture. With each dab, her resolve strengthened. Her pity party was over. The only thing crying and feeling sorry for herself was accomplishing was increasing Strickland's chances. And making her son unhappy. She refused to think about Jordan.

"See? All gone." She smiled.

He glanced at the pot on the stove. "You have to eat."

"I'll fix her plate," Sonja said.

"You too, Sonja," Joshua ordered. "Mr. Hamilton said I was to see that you ate, too. He said something else about Drake, but I can't remember."

Sonja stopped reaching for the flatware and glanced at Lauren, the indecision and need plain on her attractive, round face.

Lauren faced her son. She knew Sonja had refused to see Drake out of loyalty to her. She also knew how much it was killing her best friend inside to do so. One of them in that kind of pain was enough. "I bet you can remember if you try hard, Sweetheart."

Joshua glanced at the two women and screwed up his face in concentration, then grinned. Sonja moved closer, a plate clutched to her chest. "Mr. Hamilton said to tell you he was having enough problems with Drake. I guess Drake doesn't want you crying and not eating, either.''

"Ohhh," Sonja began, but a stern shake of Lauren's head had the other woman turning away. "T—thank you, Joshua. Like your mother said, you did everything right.''

"Good." He looked enormously pleased. "What's for dinner?''

Both women burst out laughing. Joshua's laughter was the loudest. He had made his mother smile.

Long after Joshua had gone to bed and Sonja had left, Lauren lay in bed staring at the ceiling. Her mind refused to shut down. No matter how she tried not to, thoughts of Jordan's silken betrayal kept sneaking up on her. So, she had simply ceased running and faced the facts: Jordan had used her to obtain some mysterious ledgers, ledgers that David had wanted to give to Jordan's father, ledgers that would send Strickland to jail.

And protect Joshua.

Resting her forearm on her forehead, Lauren tried to think of where those books could be. David had never mentioned them.

They were in a safe place.

She replayed Jordan's words over in her head. But where? David had moved out of his family's home and into an apartment in Charlotte. She had visited a couple of times, but when she called the apartment manager after his death, she was told his father had already cleared out the place.

So, if Jordan was right the ledgers were still hidden. No easy task if they were the size of her mother's ledg—She reared up in bed.

The day before she and David were married, she had walked into the back office of her mother's bookstore and seen the two of them with their heads together, whispering. Thinking they were planning a surprise for her, she had stood there trying to keep from laughing. When David finally noticed her, he had straightened abruptly, knocking her mother's ledger off the desk.

Lauren frowned. She had assumed it was her mother's ledger because it was the same size and color, and her mother had stuck it on the shelf with the rest of her records. *What if?*

Her gaze lifted toward the ceiling. Throwing back the covers, she put on a robe and rushed into the kitchen for a flashlight. She started for the garage, then reached for the phone and hit the radial button for Sonja's number.

As soon as her friend answered, Lauren said, "If you want to kiss Drake before the next century, you'll meet me in my garage ASAP," and hung up the phone.

Opening the back door, she let up the garage door. By the time it was up, Sonja was hurrying up Lauren's driveway, her silk robe flapping.

Chapter Twenty

Lauren hated creepy, crawling things and took great care to stay away from places they frequented. Tonight, she had no choice.

Her flashlight gripped firmly in her hand, she searched the attic for the corrugated boxes the movers had stored there almost five years ago. Head and shoulders stooped, she slowly worked her way farther to the back.

"You're still down there?" she yelled.

"Just like you ordered," Sonja shouted. "Be careful just the same."

Lauren nodded, then realized the other woman couldn't see her. "I am. I just feel better knowing I'm not alone."

"See anything yet?"

"No, but there are some boxes over in the corner. Keep talking," Lauren said, pushing a box of Christmas decorations aside and listening to Sonja's chatter.

Evelyn Bennett Morris had kept meticulous records for The African Bazaar. She had always maintained that if the IRS came calling within that ten year period, she'd be ready. When Lauren had left Concord, she had been in too much of a hurry and too upset to decide what to keep. She had packed the records with the rest of her mother's things. Her favorite books and her Hummingbird collection were in the house, but the ledgers should be. . . .

"I found them!" she yelled. "I found them!"

"Are you sure you want to do this?"

Jordan answered without breaking his long strides. "It ends today, Samuel."

Samuel Applegate, dressed in a conservative, blue pin-striped suit, shorter by several inches than Jordan, hurried to keep up. The balding man glanced over at Drake, on the other side of Jordan. Both looked grim and determined.

The grooves in Samuel's bronze forehead deepened. "Jordan, as your lawyer I must tell you that you've opened yourself up to libel already. Threatening Nathan Strickland in his own home will only compound your problems. What you're planning could put a serious dent in your bank balance or land you in jail."

Jordan took the steps to the imposing white mansion and jabbed the doorbell. "You let me worry about the money and concentrate on keeping me out of jail."

Samuel shook his head. "Just don't touch him."

Jordan's eyes were glacial. "It's his call."

"Now, Jo—"

"Yes?" Samuel's plea was interrupted by the housekeeper.

"Jordan Hamilton. We're expected."

"Yes, Sir. Please come in." The middle-aged woman opened the door wider. "He's in his study. I'll show you the way."

The trio followed the woman through the luxurious home. All Jordan saw was his father's downfall and a man's greed. One way or the other, Strickland was going down.

As soon as the study door opened, Strickland stood. A polite smile firmly in place, he rounded his massive desk and stuck out his hand. "Jordan, I hope this visit means we can put past misunderstandings behind us."

"Coming from a man who embezzled funds from my father, that's really asking a lot," Jordan said.

Strickland's face twisted. His hand slipped into his coat pocket. "Those unfounded allegations can cost you in more ways than you know."

From near the window, a man moved. His shadow fell across Jordan and the two men with him. Jordan barely glanced his way. "There's nothing I'd like better than to tear your worthless hide apart. Just give me a reason."

Without looking toward Tony, Strickland held up his hand. "Threats. Libelous remarks. I hope you can afford the check your mouth is writing."

Jordan took a step closer. "You can bank on it. But what about you, Strickland? My sources tell me you've overextended yourself."

The other man nervously fingered his blue and burgundy silk jacquard tie. "Your sources are wrong."

"Maybe, maybe not." Jordan crossed his arms. "Maybe your creditors haven't heard that you're about to lose half of your subscribers."

"What? What are you talking about?" Strickland yelled.

"I just thought the advertisers should know what kind of slime they're dealing with."

"I'll have you in court for this," he bristled.

"I don't think so. Because if you do, I'll have to produce the ledgers."

Strickland swallowed, then recovered. "I don't know what you're talking about."

"Yes you do." Jordan's smile was feral. "The way I see it, you have two choices—try to take me to court and land in jail for embezzlement, or leave Lauren Bennett and her son alone, and I'll leave you alone. Your company for Lauren and Joshua."

Jordan took a step closer. "You'd better make the right choice, you no good bastard, because this is the one and only chance I'm giving you."

"You—you'll leave me alone if I leave them alone?"

"Yes," Jordan answered without hesitation. Ruining Lauren and Joshua's lives wouldn't bring back his father.

"How do I know I can trust you?"

"That why I brought my lawyer. You can call yours and we'll get it in writing. Deal?"

"I—"

"No deal," shouted a female voice.

All the men in the room turned to see Lauren advancing across the room. Tony, who had been motionless, moved to stop her. Lauren saw the massive man moving toward her and stopped. Her hand lifted defensively before she snatched it down.

"If you touch me again, I'll press charges."

Jordan moved like a silent, deadly shifting of light. "Did he hurt you?"

Lauren was so rattled by the savagry in Jordan's face, that she could only shake her head. Jordan whirled toward the bodyguard.

"If you even look at her sideways again, you'll answer to me." The man's expression remained unchanged. Jordan continued, "I won't come after you when you expect, but I'll be there. And I won't fight clean. I'll be as brutal as you. Just so you'll remember—"

Jordan's hand flashed out, hitting the man in the wind-pipe. He dropped to his knees, gasping for breath. His hands clutched his throat. Jordan hunkered down and peered into the man's watery eyes. "Think about that the next time you try to frighten a defenseless woman, especially if that woman belongs to me."

"Er, Jordan," Samuel said. "Should we call the paramedics?"

"Nope." Drake walked over to the fallen man. "He'll be all right. Jordan pulled his punch."

Lauren tried to compose herself. She hadn't planned on ever seeing Jordan again. His defense of her completely threw her off balance, just as much as the almost irresistible desire to fling herself into his arms. Firmly, she turned away from him.

"Mr. Strickland, I believe Mr. Hamilton offered you a deal, a deal concerning me, and one I feel completely unacceptable."

"Let me handle this, Lauren," Jordan ordered.

Bracing herself, she faced him. "This is my life, and I'm

going to live the rest of it with my head up and my son unafraid.''

He looked at her a long time, then walked to stand by her side. Drake and Samuel moved behind them. "You have the floor, Honey.''

Gripping her purse, trying not to be swayed by Jordan's words or the glimpse of pride in his eyes, she turned back to Strickland. "David loved you. He was so proud of you. The night my mother and I thought we were coming to dinner, he wanted to show you off, I think, as much as he wanted to show me off. But you and your wife had other plans.''

"We wanted better for David," Strickland defended.

"Better than what? By whose standards? You lie, cheat, steal, intimidate, threaten . . . how can that be better?'' she questioned. "Do you know how hard it was for me, losing David and my mother, then not even knowing where he was buried? You won't even give me that.''

From behind her, she heard a woman gasp. Lauren turned to see a slender, dark-skinned woman. From a picture in David's apartment, Lauren recognized the woman as Maryann Strickland, his mother.

"You only wanted his money. You lured him away from us," the woman accused.

"Go to your room, Maryann. This is none of your affair," Strickland ordered.

"If you loved David the way I did, you wouldn't allow this woman into our home. You never understood him.''

"That's not true. I just wanted him to be stronger.''

"David *was* strong!'' Lauren cried, cutting across the two people arguing. "In all the ways that mattered. That's why he refused to stay here. Now, I have to finish what he started. I found your ledgers stored with my mother's records last night in my attic.

"If you hadn't been so anxious to run me out of town and given me time to sort her things, I probably would have kept only one as a memento and destroyed the rest. Now, they're going to destroy you. Before I came here, I dropped them off at the Charlotte Police Department.''

"What?" Strickland cried. "You stupid bi—"

Jordan's fist connected solidly to Strickland's jaw, sending the other man staggering backward.

Maryann cried out in alarm, Lauren in surprise.

Drake sighed. "You could let me get in a little action."

Samuel grunted and mumbled, "Defending one of you is quite enough."

Tony staggered from the room.

"I think you can continue, Lauren," Jordan said.

Lauren looked at the man standing by her side. He had put two men on the floor in less than five minutes, and he wasn't breathing hard. She swallowed and watched Strickland drag himself upright. Wringing her hands, his wife stayed where she was.

"Thanks to David, you'll be too busy trying to stay out of jail to worry about me and my son. Joshua is the light of my life. David could have been yours. He was a kind, wonderful man. You missed a great deal by trying to measure him by your own crooked standards. You're also going to miss your grandson. I'd feel sorry for you if you didn't deserve everything that's coming to you."

She stepped closer. "Think about that when you're old and there's no one to comfort you. Not even a memory. My son and I want nothing from you." Opening her purse she took out a check for seventeen thousand, five hundred dollars and laid it on his desk, then walked to Maryann. "If you truly loved David, you would have wanted his happiness over your own. You were willing to take his child, not so much because of love for David, but hatred of me."

Maryann dropped into a chair, her head bowed, her hands clasped.

Head high, Lauren walked from the room, closing the door softly behind her.

Jordan crossed the study to stand in front of a cowering Strickland. "I think we have some unfinished business."

* * *

She had done it. She had taken charge of her own life. Standing on the steps of the imposing mansion, she took a deep breath, then started for the waiting taxi.

"Lauren, wait."

Lauren increased her pace, but she wasted her time. Jordan easily caught up with her. The touch of his hand on her bare arm opened a floodgate of memories. With grim determination, she made herself look into his face.

"Yes?"

"I know this was hard for you. For what it's worth, I was proud of you. You didn't need me."

She needed him too much. Her gaze dropped to his chin. It would be so easy to succumb to the warmth in those devastating eyes of his. "Why did you change your mind about prosecuting Strickland?"

His other hand cupped her chin. "Love changes a man."

Her heart did a crazy leap. She refused to believe. She twisted her chin free. "Or a guilty conscience."

"You're going to be stubborn about this, aren't you?"

"If the situation were reversed, I'd have to leave the country."

"But I'd find you, sweet Lauren."

"And make my life hell."

"No. Hell is trying to get through the night without you."

Lauren couldn't have agreed more. "If you'll excuse me, I have a plane to catch."

"You could fly back with me."

That statement brought her gaze arching upward. Questions formed in her mind, but she refused to voice them. Where he stayed and for how long didn't concern her. He had only made her believe it did. "No, thank you."

"Stubborn, but I'm willing to work hard to get you to forgive me." His thumb stroked her bare skin of her upper forearm. "I didn't miss you calling me Mr. Hamilton."

She discreetly tried to free herself, to no avail. She should have worn a longsleeved jacket.

"Where's Joshua?"

"With Sonja."

"Did he go to school today?"

"Yes," Lauren answered, hoping the questions didn't become personal.

"He's quite a kid."

"Jordan, I'd appreciate it if you didn't try to see either of us again."

His lips tightened into a straight line. "I can't do that. I made a mistake, and I'm willing to do anything you want, but one—stop seeing you and Joshua."

"You can't just barge into our lives if I don't want you."

"Oh, but you do, Lauren. I can see it in your eyes, feel it in the slight trembling of your body." He leaned closer. "Shall I taste it on your lips?"

She staggered back. This time he let her go. "Stay out of our lives and leave us alone."

"For today we'll do things your way. I'd like to show you something."

"What?"

"David's grave."

She couldn't stop crying. As she knelt on the soft green grass by the big marble headstone, her tears flowed unceasingly.

"Lauren, you're going to make yourself sick."

She shook her head. She should have been there for him. His parents had taken that away from both of them.

"Lauren, please. I shouldn't have brought you here."

Brushing away another tear with the handkerchief Jordan had given her earlier, she glanced up at him through a sheen of tears. "Why did you?"

"Because enough has been taken from you. I wanted to give back what I can. His lawyer disposed of everything else. I'm sorry."

Lauren cringed at such cruelty, then pushed unsteadily to her feet. "This won't change how I feel about you."

"I didn't expect it to. The cab is waiting."

Stepping around Jordan, Lauren headed for the taxi. Guilt

weighed heavily on her shoulders. She had cried as much for David as she had for Jordan. Both were lost to her forever.

"Mama, why can't we see Mr. Hamilton again?"

"I've explained it to you over and over, Joshua. Mr. Hamilton can't be trusted."

"Yes, he can, Mama. 'Member, he didn't take anything the time I found him asleep on the sofa," Joshua reminded her, his gaze expectant.

Lauren continued setting the table for dinner. "I know he didn't steal anything tang—I mean anything you can see—but he did something far worse. He betrayed . . . didn't tell me the truth."

"He said he was sorry."

"That doesn't make up for what he did." *Or make me hurt any less.*

"You tell me to forgive people. Why can't you forgive Mr. Hamilton?"

"Because I just can't," she said, her voice trembling. "When you're older you'll understand. Now, I don't want to hear anything more about Jor—Mr. Hamilton. Please go to your room and do your homework."

"It's done. Drake helped me with it," he said.

Lauren tried not to let herself be jealous. Sonja deserved the love of a good man. If it hadn't been for Sonja's insistence and generosity, Lauren wouldn't have had enough money to pay Strickland back. It was just that Drake was a blatant reminder of what Lauren had thought *she* had. He had almost beaten Lauren back to Shreveport. His car hadn't moved from Sonja's driveway since last night.

"Then go wash your hands. Dinner will be ready shortly."

"I'm not very hungry."

Lauren turned from reaching to take the casserole out of the oven and peered closely at her son. Joshua not being hungry was rare. Stripping off her oven mitten, she pressed the back of her hand to his forehead. "Does anything bother you?"

"No, Ma'am. Can I go to my room?"

Her concern mounted. "You're sure you feel all right?"

"Yes, Ma'am. I just wish . . . but you wouldn't like it."

"Go on to your room and I'll come get you when dinner is on the table," she said, and watched her son, head bowed, start for his room.

Instead of getting the casserole, Lauren slumped into a chair. Elbows propped on the table, she leaned her forehead into her palms. Missing Jordan was going to be terrible for both of them for a while, but they'd survive, just as they had in the past.

Survive or live? a small voice whispered.

Jordan had been right about that. She had hidden away until he had helped her gain the courage to take a tiny step in reclaiming her life. What she couldn't face was the possibility that a guilty conscience, not any deep feeling for her, had motivated his actions.

No matter how things had turned out, Jordan wasn't a mean, heartless man to those he cared about. He had proven that by offering Strickland a deal to keep her and Joshua safe, then taking her to David's gravesite.

But what were his motives?

Love changes a man.

Wanting to believe and not sure she could, Lauren got up and took the casserole from the oven just as the doorbell rang.

Cautiously, she walked into the living room and peeked though the sheer white curtains. A man stood on the porch. From his build she easily saw it wasn't Jordan.

Telling herself she wasn't disappointed, she opened the door, "Yes?"

The man slowly faced her. Thin and leaning heavily on a walking cane, he was dressed in navy blue slacks and a crisp, white cotton shirt. He appeared to be in his mid-seventies. The black eyes studying her seemed much younger, and vaguely familiar. "Are you Lauren Bennett?"

Lauren studied the elderly man as intently as he studied her. "Yes. Do I know you?"

"I'm not sure, but I sure wanted to know you." He shifted. "Can I come in?"

Beads of perspiration dotted his brow. The frail hand clutching the cane began to tremble

She hesitated only a second before unlocking the screen door and letting the stranger inside. Her actions were uncharacteristic, but she couldn't stop thinking she had seen him before. After he eased into a chair, she asked, "Are you all right? Can I get you something to drink?"

"Yes, thank you. I don't suppose you have any bourbon in the house, do you?"

"Coffee, tea, juice, or water," she answered.

He made a face and settled back. "Not supposed to have any anyway. Guess I'll pass."

"You look familiar. Are you a grandparent of one of Joshua's friends?" she asked.

"Yes, I am." He chuckled, then pinned her with a stern look. "Only Joshua's friend hasn't been doing so well lately."

She sat in the sofa and leaned forward. "I'm sorry to hear that. Is there anything I can do?"

"You can forgive him."

She straightened. A frown danced across her forehead. "Forgive him? You must have made a mistake. What would I have against one of Joshua's friends? Mr. . . . . I didn't get your name."

"No you didn't, but that's not important. What's important is that my grandson is having a bad time of things since you refused to forgive him," he told her.

The thought briefly ran through Lauren's mind that the man must have mistaken her for someone else. If he had, how did he know her name?

The elderly man leaned forward. "Do you believe in a person keeping their promises and honoring their elders?"

"Yes, but—"

"Well, that's what my grandson was doing. He was doing it for me. He was trying to keep a promise to me." He shook his graying head. "I got what I wanted, but I may have lost more than I gained. He mopes, he won't eat, seldom sleeps."

"Jordan," she breathed, everything falling into place. He

could have just as well described her actions for the past few days. "You're Jordan's grandfather."

"Hollis Hamilton." He inclined his head. "Your husband called me after he found the books. I was madder than Hel— Hades. My son never got over the bankruptcy of the newspaper. He sunk his life savings and his dreams into making the paper solvent. It didn't help that the woman he was engaged to ran off with another man a month later. He changed, and then—I lost him."

Lauren placed her hand on Hollis's trembling one. "I'm sorry."

He nodded. "I wanted Strickland to pay, and I didn't care how. Jordan did. He didn't want you or the boy to get hurt. I was the one who called Strickland and caused him to start snooping around. If I had kept quiet and let Jordan handle things, you and him might be together now."

"Or we might not have. Jordan's betrayal hurt."

"But that's just it, he didn't. Except for the sin of omission, he did everything in his power, including risking his company, and a lawsuit." At her stunned expression, he quickly told her about Jordan contacting the advertisers in Strickland's magazine.

"The second time he came to New Orleans after meeting you, he told me he didn't want to involve you. I wouldn't listen. So, if you want to blame someone, blame me, not my grandson. I wanted vengeance. Jordan wanted justice."

Lauren stared at the man who loved his grandson, and put his happiness first. She couldn't find it in her heart to fault him. He had acted out of love. Would her actions have been any different if she had been in his place?

"We were just about to eat. Would you care to join us?"

"What're you having?"

"Chicken and broccoli casserole."

"You've got yourself a guest. Casper mentioned baked fish." He eased himself up from his chair with Lauren's help. Just as he was upright, the doorbell rang. Without looking, Hollis said, "That's probably my grandson. I left him a note where to find me."

Lauren looked uneasy. He patted her hand. "Let him in, Lauren. I can't stand to watch him pace in that garden one more night."

She opened the door. As impossible as it seemed, Jordan appeared as uneasy as she was. "Hello, Lauren. Is my grandfather here?"

"Yes, but before you come in I want to ask you a question." His shoulders braced. "Yes?"

"Can you forgive me for thinking of my pain, and not yours?"

A fierce light lit his face. He pulled her into his arms, his lips finding hers. After a long time Jordan lifted his head. "Only if you marry me."

"Yes." She smiled through her tears.

"You two have all your lives for that. I'm hungry," Hollis grumbled good-naturedly.

"Where's Joshua?" Jordan asked.

Automatically, she turned toward the hallway. The house was quiet. Too quiet.

Moving swiftly down the hallway, she entered Joshua's room. Empty. Her heart pounding, telling herself not to panic, she checked the bathroom, then the entire house, steadily calling his name. Jordan was close behind her.

There was no answer. Joshua was gone.

"How long ago did you see him?

"Not more than ten minutes, seven at the least." She stared wildly around her son's room again.

Jordan pulled her into the comfort of his arms. "He couldn't have gotten far. I'll find him. Try not to worry."

She clutched him to her. "If anything happens to him—"

"It won't. Joshua is smart." He kissed her on the cheek and whirled toward the door.

"Does that kiss mean you forgive Mr. Hamilton, Mama?" Joshua asked with a hopeful grin.

Lauren and Jordan pivoted to find Joshua peeking from beneath his bed. Jordan plucked the child up in his arms.

"You scare your mother like that again, and you won't be able to sit down for a week," Jordan said.

One arm around Jordan's neck, Joshua stared at him. "But I had to. I tried to tell you about the kissing and hugging, but just like a mommy you didn't listen. I waited and waited, then I 'membered the way you and Mama hugged when I was missing."

"Looks like you have a smart boy there," Hollis commented.

"Who's going to give me my first gray hairs," Lauren groaned.

"And I'll be there to watch every one of them change colors," Jordan said, pulling Lauren to him with his other arm.

"Come on, Joshua, let's go get acquainted over some of that casserole." Hollis held out one hand. "By the way, I'm going to be your great-grandfather."

Joshua's eyes widened as he took the elderly man's hand. "I never had one of those before."

"You do now, and I'm betting some sisters and brothers to go along with your aunts and uncles and cousins."

"Oh, boy. I'd like a hundred zillion sisters and brothers," Joshua told Hollis.

"It looks like we'd better start picking out some names," Jordan said, smiling down at Lauren.

"Your grandfather put the idea into his head." Lauren looped her arms around Jordan's neck. "He's quite a character."

Jordan's expression turned serious. "He's also my lifesaver. He got you to forgive me."

Lauren looked thoughtful. "It wasn't so much forgiving you as trying to figure out if your actions to keep me and Joshua safe were motivated by a guilty conscience. I loved you too much—"

His body tautened. "Wait—say that again."

"I love you."

"I thought I'd blown every chance of ever hearing you say that."

"It would be nice to hear it from *you* again."

"I love you, Lauren, and I'll do everything in my power to make you happy and keep your trust."

"You're doing a pretty good job already."

"Pretty good? Tell me what else I can do, and it's done."

She smiled up at him saucily. "When we're alone tonight I'll show you."

Jordan's grin was pure devilment. "I just hope I can wait that long."

Laughing, Lauren took his hand and started for the kitchen. "It will be worth it. I promise you."

"That, my love, is a promise a man can live by."

Epilogue

The lush green lawn was crowded with laughing, running children and equally happy adults. In the middle of all the activity sat a partially eaten, six-foot, lemon wedding cake, two swan ice sculptures, tables decorated with crisp white linen and flowers, and a string quartet.

"Honey, we have to go," Jordan whispered to Lauren.

"I know." Lauren looked around for Joshua and saw him playing chase with his new twin cousins. "I doubt if he'll miss me."

"We'll take care of my great-grandson," Hollis said.

Lauren smiled at her grandfather-in-law. He had gained weight, and his health was steadily improving. He and Mattie had married quietly the week before.

Putting Strickland behind them had been good for them all. He had been indicted, and his assets frozen. The case was set to go to court in a month.

"The Wild Bunch will keep him so occupied he won't know we're gone," Jordan commented.

"Stop referring to my angels that way," said Angelica, her laughter light and airy.

Lauren smiled at the exotically beautiful woman's quick

defense of her three children. Considering what she and the three had been through together, it was a miracle any of them could still smile. "Thank you for keeping him."

"My pleasure. One more won't matter. Besides, Casper has agreed to stay with us until you get back from your honeymoon."

Lauren turned to Casper. "I still can't believe you own that house."

"My employer willed the place to me two years ago. It had been my pleasure to keep the house as it was. Leasing proved the most financially advantageous," Casper explained, sipping his champagne. "Enjoy your time there."

"Thank you, we will." Lauren hugged a glowing Sonja, who had been her maid of honor and would walk down the aisle herself in another month. "I guess we did it."

Sonja sniffled. "That we did."

"Sonja, don't you dare start crying," Drake ordered. "You know I can't stand it when you cry."

Drake and Sonja's parents smiled indulgently at the couple.

Jordan took the opportunity to grab his wife. "We're aren't getting any closer to Shreveport."

"All right. Let me say good bye to Joshua," Lauren said.

Smiling, Jordan followed. His smile grew as he noticed that it took his wife a couple of trips to get their son's attention. His reluctance to leave his cousins was obvious. If the butterfly they were chasing hadn't flown over the ten foot wall in the backyard, it might have taken longer.

Three out of breath children ran up to them. Joshua was in the lead, but his cousins were a close second. "Yes, Ma'am?"

Ivory chiffon fluttered around Lauren as she bent down in front of her son. "We're leaving now. I want you to be good."

"I will, Mama." Joshua glanced between the two identical faces on either side of him. "The twins promis—" He broke off as a tiny elbow jabbed him in the side.

"Have fun, Uncle Jordan and Aunt Lauren," chorused the twins.

Jordan chuckled and pulled a frowning Lauren to her feet.

"Try not to initiate him into too much trouble, girls. His mother is used to a quiet life."

The girls smiled sweetly.

Lauren bit her lip. "Jordan?"

"He'll be fine." Jordan leaned down to Joshua and hugged him. "Bye, Joshua. You know where to reach us."

"I won't let him forget."

Jordan glanced up to see his fifteen year-old nephew sauntering over. There was a wicked grin on his youthful face. "You did say to call any time."

"He sure did," the twins chorused.

Joshua nodded solemnly. "Don't worry, Daddy. I won't lose my organizer with the phone number."

Jordan's throat tightened. Joshua calling him Daddy was worth all the calls they were going to receive. "I know, Son."

Pushing to his feet, his arm circled his wife's slender waist as he stared down into his son's beaming face, then into his wife's radiant one. "Welcome to the family."

Joshua's smile grew. "I knew he was the one," he announced proudly to his new cousins. "I just knew he was going to be my daddy."

Francis Ray, the bestselling author of FOREVER YOURS and UNDENIABLE, is a native Texan and lives with her husband and daughter in Dallas. After publishing sixteen short stories, she decided to follow her love and write longer works which would show the healing power of love. She launched the Arabesque line with FOREVER YOURS and was included in the Arabesque December anthology, SPIRIT OF THE SEASON. A school nurse who cares for over 1500 children, she is also a frequent speaker at writing workshops and is a member of Women Writers of Color and Romance Writers of America.

Look for these upcoming Arabesque titles:

September 1997

SECOND TIME AROUND by Anna Larence
SILKEN LOVE by Carmen Green
BLUSH by Courtni Wright
SUMMERWIND by Gail McFarland

October 1997

THE NICEST GUY IN AMERICA by Angela Benson
AFTER DARK by Bette Ford
PROMISE ME by Robyn Amos
MIDNIGHT BLUE by Monica Jackson

November 1997

ETERNALLY YOURS by Brenda Jackson
MOST OF ALL by Loure Bussey
DEFENSELESS by Adrienne Byrd
PLAYING WITH FIRE by Dianne Mayhew

SENSUAL AND HEARTWARMING
ARABESQUE ROMANCES FEATURE
AFRICAN-AMERICAN CHARACTERS!

BEGUILED   (0046, $4.99)
by Eboni Snoe
After Raquel agrees to impersonate a missing heiress for just one night,
a daring abduction makes her the captive of seductive Nate Bowman.
Across the exotic Caribbean seas to the perilous wilds of Central America . . . and into the savage heart of desire, Nate and Raquel play a
dangerous game. But soon the masquerade will be over. And will they
then lose the one thing that matters most . . . their love?

WHISPERS OF LOVE   (0055, $4.99)
by Shirley Hailstock
Robyn Richards had to fake her own death, change her identity, and
forever forsake her husband, Grant, after testifying against a crime syndicate. But, five years later, the daughter born after her disappearance
is in need of help only Grant can give. Can Robyn maintain her disguise
from the ever present threat of the syndicate—and can she keep herself
from falling in love all over again?

HAPPILY EVER AFTER   (0064, $4.99)
by Rochelle Alers
In a week's time, Lauren Taylor fell madly in love with famed author
Cal Samuels and impulsively agreed to be his wife. But when she
abruptly left him, it was for reasons she dared not express. Five years
later, Cal is back, and the flames of desire are as hot as ever, but, can
they start over again and make it work this time?

*Available wherever paperbacks are sold, or order direct from the
Publisher. Send cover price plus 50¢ per copy for mailing and
handling to Penguin USA, P.O. Box 999, c/o Dept. 17109, Ber-
genfield, NJ 07621. Residents of New York and Tennessee must
include sales tax. DO NOT SEND CASH.*